AF422157

NICCOLO WOULD LIKE A WORD

JAN GRAHAM

CANTANKEROUS BOOKS

Published by Cantankerous Books.

ISBN: 979-8-9942530-1-4

Cover Designer: Mark Mechan

Interior Designer: Daniel Morales

CHAPTER ONE

SHANNON

I live deep in the woods, like a witch in a fairy tale. Gnarled white pine and dense thickets of laurel guard the house; sharp-eyed birds patrol the perimeter. The drive home from work is scenic and twisty, a full forty-five minutes weaving through the Berkshires.

But somehow, I'm pulling into the driveway already. Too much churning in my head to even remember how I got home.

Grant Pritchard, the man who killed my sister: he's still out there.

I make myself unclench my hands from the steering wheel, resting my palms against my thighs. That's better. The fabric of my jeans feels familiar, undemanding. I take a long deep breath. Then let it out.

I have to act normal. Pretend nothing's wrong.

When I open the kitchen door, Niccolo jumps down off the counter and runs to greet me. He's a gorgeous Lilac Point Siamese with a frosty white coat, gentle dove gray accents, and vivid blue eyes.

I pick him up, cradle him.

"Did you miss me? Are you hungry?"

He meows back at me, twice. A "yes" to both questions.

Like many of his breed, he's chatty. But his face is rounder than most Siamese, not so angular and severe. And he doesn't have the typical aggrieved chesty bleat. His voice is soft and musical.

His paws rest against my chest, he nuzzles my chin with his cheek. I feel his whiskers and his warmth and it helps bring me back to myself.

I put my mouth close to his ear. "You wouldn't believe what happened at work today." Then I lower my voice even more. "I did something I'm not supposed to."

He answers me again, his meow a cheerful "good for you."

"Tell you all about it later, okay?"

I kiss the top of his head and set him down on the floor. Open him a can of cat food, refresh his water.

I adopted Niccolo, along with four of the others, almost a year before Brian moved in. As a single, middle-aged woman, having conversations with your cat—that's pretty much on brand, right? Not a big deal. But it made my boyfriend uneasy, so I stopped doing it when he's around.

And where is Brian? It's his one night a week to cook. There should be a pot of chicken soup already simmering on the stove.

"Bri, I'm home!"

I find him in the living room. A white headset covers most of his face, and he's clutching a game controller in each hand. I hear explosions, machine gun fire, grunts and screams and crashes.

"Brian?"

He's been talking for months about upgrading his video gaming to a virtual reality setup, and I guess he went for it. He moved in four years ago, but for reasons like this, we don't pool our money. He sells HVAC systems, makes decent money, spends every penny. I used to do that too. I'm way more careful now.

He's wildly swinging his arms around, so I don't get too close. He's a big burly guy, gym-obsessed, strong as a superhero.

"Brian!"

He finally takes off the headset, sees me standing there. He looks dazed, unhappily interrupted. But he tries to recover.

"Hey Shan, you're home already!" He checks his watch. "Shit. Let's see, the soup… that'll take too long. How about I nuke the leftover meatloaf? More protein too—you don't get nearly enough. Some broccoli, salad, maybe garlic bread?"

The last thing I feel like tonight is meatloaf. And Brian's garlic bread is so low-carb and dreary he might as well butter up bathroom tiles and sprinkle garlic salt on them.

"Sure, sounds great," I say.

I'm not that hungry anyway. Still agitated.

"So how was work?" Brian asks. "Was Cynthia in a good mood?"

What he's really asking: did you get there on time? Did you do anything careless? Did you get too mouthy with her?

"Yeah, she was good. It all went great today."

Cynthia is my boss. She owns The Wombat's Attic, a cross between an art gallery and a gift store. The job's just part-time and the pay isn't fantastic, but it's easy work, and Cynthia lets me sell some of my own clothing designs there.

"Not too busy or anything. I helped this sweet old guy; he was totally stressed out looking for a birthday present for his wife. He thought she might want a scarf but…"

Brian shifts his weight; I can see him trying to freeze his face into a patient expression.

"But I found him something else, something better."

"That's good, then."

The old guy beamed at me so brightly when I showed him the silver and amethyst necklace. Went on to tell me all about what a tough time his wife was having after her heart surgery.

But I can see from Brian's face that he's done; he remembered to ask about my day.

I'd ask him about his day too, but he always shrugs me off with "fine." Or, "okay, I guess."

It was so different, that first year. We were practically stapled together, no filters, sharing every insane thought that came into our heads. I miss that sometimes.

He shifts his weight, waiting to be dismissed.

"I'll just go take care of the outside cats," I say.

* * *

How did I end up with eight cats? It wasn't on purpose. Most are rescues from the local shelter—I just couldn't bear to see them euthanized. Such a dainty word for "killed because no one gives a shit about you." Then the ferals started arriving. But Niccolo is the only one who gets to stay indoors. He couldn't handle living alongside the others; they were too rough on him. Something about him just seemed to piss them off, and he had no clue how to defend himself.

Out in the garage, I put a few big scoops of kibble into a pail, fill the water jug from the sink next to the washing machine. I add my barn coat to my heavy sweater—the weak sunlight of early spring does little to soften the mountain briskness. With a pooper-scooper tucked under my arm, I stuff a couple of plastic bags in my pocket. But all the while my head is elsewhere.

So many other things I didn't tell Brian.

Like: when the nice man paid for the necklace, the name on his credit card was Graham Pritchett. Not Grant Pritchard. But so close.

These last few years I've been trying so hard to pretend he doesn't exist. Yet all it took was a similar name to break me into pieces.

Something else I didn't mention to Brian: Cynthia took the afternoon off to go to the dentist. So when my phone felt too puny, too trivial for what I suddenly, urgently needed to do, I used her PC in the back office. Incognito mode. Sitting at her desk, surrounded by neatly stacked boxes of inventory, carefully labeled supplies and seasonal decorations, I typed Grant Pritchard's name into the search bar.

Then I hesitated. Because what I was doing was completely off-limits.

I've been behaving myself. I've deferred to Brian and my therapist, taking their worries so seriously. I'd stopped searching Pritchard out, following him, even mentioning his name. They think I was "obsessed." That my interest in him wasn't healthy. Instead I should just keep going to therapy, meditating, maybe sign up for a few more yoga classes. Forget anything ever happened.

So when I finally decided to hit the enter key, I half-expected sirens to blare, or a squadron of men in uniforms to come bursting through the door.

But no, it was quiet. Just pages and pages of search results.

When I open the door to the cat shed, Buster, Betty Lou, and Mr. Potato Head are all waiting for me. The others will be here before long.

"And so how's everyone doing today?" I ask.

Often they like a little attention and petting, but this evening, they're intent on their food bowls. They leave me to my thoughts as I pour in kibble, change water, scoop their boxes, survey them for any injuries that might require a visit to the vet.

Pritchard was still just a high school English teacher when he got my older sister pregnant. She was fifteen years old. He didn't technically kill her—Maureen drove off the road, she did that herself—but he might as well have. I was crushed to find out that he still hasn't been sued or fired, let alone convicted of anything. Two more novels, even a movie deal. And he still lives in Massachusetts! He didn't move to L.A. after all, like he said he was going to in that Globe interview. Married to the same woman, a paralegal who supported him when he quit teaching high school to write his first novel. And he's still at the same expensive private college where I'd tracked him down before—though he's head of his department now.

It's been probably five years since the last time I followed him. Pritchard never noticed me. I'd slip into the back row of the lecture hall for his most popular classes; eat my fries at an inconspicuous table at his favorite Tuesday-afternoon burger joint; trail behind him as he'd meander through the campus, often stopping to chat with female students and staff. Touchy, teasing, always a little too close. Smug. Serpentine. And the grad student I'd chatted up at the pub near campus, she'd had plenty of stories. It was an open secret, what he'd put so many women through. Probably girls too. The rumor mill said he still liked them young.

I feel antsy, itchy. The old stirrings: they're back.

Pritchard stays busy. I found out he's got book signings, panel discussions, writing workshops. And one of them is in Provincetown this summer.

Provincetown. I haven't been able to stop thinking about it. I spent most of a summer there after my senior year of high school, hanging out with my best friend Allison.

I wonder if Allison still spends time in Ptown? After my sister died, I transferred into her high school for my last year. We bonded instantly, both of us misfits. But fucked-up in entirely different ways.

And then… off we went to college in different states. Life before internet: we wrote a few letters, then lost touch. I'd love to see her again.

Pritchard's writing workshop is just one of the offerings at the Provincetown Fine Arts Center. They've also got painting classes, drawing, sculpting. Could I sign up for one of them? It's been forever since I've let myself do something like that.

But it's probably a crazy idea. Brian would never go along with it.

I leave the cats to their dinner; close the shed door.

A deep breath: witch hazel, with a hint of pine. The sky is turning a dusky pinkish orange. I stand there for a moment, surrounded by grass and dirt and woods and sky and life and I just take it all in, the curious busy peacefulness of nature. Insects humming, birds trilling and squawking, leaves rustling in the breeze.

My sister would have loved it here. As kids we'd spend hours rambling in the woods; we lived near a big tract of conservation land. Being a year older, Maureen was the bolder of the two of us, but I'd doggedly follow her whenever I could, sloshing into ponds and creeks in the summer, through snow and over ice in the winter, climbing trees and scrambling over rocks and rolling down hills. She pointed out all the details I would have missed: enchanted butterflies that fluttered like fairy princesses; crazy neon yellow mushrooms straight from Mars. Downed trees that looked like dragons.

But she'd be so much older now. Would she still see the dragons?

When I get back to the kitchen, Brian has gotten busy, pulling out leftovers and chopping up veggies. He's pretty adorable right now. Maybe it's his look of intense concentration, or the way his big meaty hands dwarf the kitchen knife as he tries to be patient and precise. Sometimes when I look at him I see the old Brian, earnest and tender.

"You need any help?" I ask. I slip in behind him, wrap my arms around him. Feel the dense bulk of muscles he spends so many hours attending to.

He stiffens a bit, waiting for me to let go so he can return to his dicing.

"No, I got it—maybe another ten or fifteen minutes?"

"No problem, just holler."

What did I expect?

I grab a few cat treats, put them in my pocket. I need to ask Niccolo a favor.

I adore my funky house, but it has a hilariously random floor plan. I suspect Niccolo is in the sunporch, which means passing through three consecutive tiny rooms, railroad style. Energetic hippies bought this place in the seventies when it was just a two-room cabin, then proceeded to build up and out, clearly no architect involved, each new addition a creative afterthought. But I love the exposed beams and copper pipes. Like me, the previous owners were big on recycling and creating. So my paintings, my thrift store finds, my hand-crafted side tables and planters and vases, they fit in perfectly with all the reclaimed hardwood, the charmingly mismatched fixtures, and the circular stained-glass windows.

I find Niccolo on the daybed, where he likes to watch birds. But he's sleeping. I waft the treats in front of his nose to get his attention.

His nose wrinkles, his eyes open wide.

It's a silly game I play with him sometimes when I'm mulling things over. Like flipping a coin, or consulting a Ouija board. Though I'd like to think it's not quite as arbitrary.

I walk back about six feet, put three treats on the floor, equidistant from him.

"This one on the left, that means I just let it go. It's been so many years."

Niccolo looks at me, then the treats. Starts to roust himself.

"This one in the middle? It's the book fair in Boston. He's doing a reading in a couple weeks."

He's sitting up now.

"And this one on the right? That's the workshop in Provincetown in July. What do you think, would you like to come with me? Go on an adventure?"

Maybe it's the way my voice tilts upward when I say "adventure?" But I could swear that Niccolo just understands me, knows what I need to do. He jumps off the daybed, makes a beeline for the treat on the right and scarfs it up.

Then he looks at me, quizzical.

Does he sense that something's not quite right? Can he tell there's something I need to take care of?

I often wonder what he's thinking.

* * *

Before I'd even finished clearing the dinner dishes, Brian was back in the living room, mowing down enemies in his new virtual world. He told me not to wait up, so I went upstairs, got out my laptop. Niccolo is purring by my side.

Earlier at dinner, I said I was thinking about an oil painting workshop in July, and Brian said "mmm hmm" in a vague way. So he can't say I didn't run it by him! Meanwhile I've been scrolling through Vrbo and Airbnb, entering the dates. But prices are outrageously expensive.

And then I see it. So much cheaper than the others. As it should be, because it's such a dreary rental: ugly furniture, badly photographed, everything backlit so that the interiors look dark and murky. There's finally some sunlight in the last picture, showing the unit from the outside.

But it can't be, can it? The Marshall's cottage?

I look at the owner's profile. Allison Marshall. No picture, but it has to be her. She's renting it out for her parents?

The air feels suddenly charged; my skin tingles. I can't believe it. How is that even possible? It's as though just by thinking about Allison after all these years, I summoned her up. Complete with a crappy but cozy cottage hideaway, where I can plot and scheme and finally seek justice for Maureen.

Allison was such a sweet, odd kid. Conspicuously tall, brainy, awkward. She looked like a guy. Funny how diffcrent it was back then. No openly gay kids at school, no one had heard of "non-binary" or "gender-fluid." You could see from the way she slouched and cowered, tried to take up as little space as possible, how hard it had been for her. Level-headed and loyal, she was just the sort of friend I needed back then.

I could say and do the most outrageous things, and she never judged. She was the only one I told about Maureen. I didn't want people looking at me weird, pitying me over the "dead sister" thing.

I look at the photos again. I've never been inside the cottage; I stayed with Allison and her parents in the main house. It was nothing fancy, built back when land was cheap, then passed down through several generations. Allison's family wasn't even close to being rich, not like "having a summer home" sounds.

My parents were the rich ones. For all the good it did us.

I double check the dates and the price. It's totally doable.

And now I'm starting to wonder: is this all really just a coincidence? It feels too perfect. Like destiny. I can finally right this terrible wrong, with Allison by my side again. Brian won't have to know it's anything but an art class.

I close the laptop, finished for the night. After wash my face and brush my teeth, I retrieve all my prescription vials from the medicine cabinet.

I look at my reflection in the mirror. My strawberry blond hair has a sprinkling of gray, and I've got wrinkles now too. I'm forty-five, never great about wearing sunscreen, so whatever. I'm not gorgeous, but I look... well, normal. Not like someone who should have to take so many pills just to get through her days.

I took the antidepressant this morning. I don't mind those. But these others, the mood stabilizer, the antipsychotic, the tranquilizer—God I hate them. And not just because I've gained a bunch of weight since I started taking them. I just really miss life's bright colors, crisp edges, the twists and turns and bumps and spins. Now it all just blurs together. Life is mayonnaise: smooth and unremarkable. There's no crackle, no crunch.

I fill up a glass of water. Take out the capsules, line them up on the bathroom counter.

Because I don't really have a choice, do I?

I don't want to go back to how things were when I was younger. Arrests, hospitalizations, fights. I don't even remember a lot of my late teens and twenties. The car accident didn't help either. I hit my head pretty bad. So sometimes pieces of my past are just… gone.

Although I don't regret it all. I loved living large, taking big bites, having a blast. That three-day houseboat party in Sausalito, the last-minute trip to Budapest with the French fashion photographer I'd met on the subway. Festivals and raves, hitching rides from handsome strangers, hiking alone off into the mountains, forever counting on good weather and good luck. Sneaking in where I didn't belong, taking things that weren't mine, getting away with so much. The whole world seemed like a theme park—why not keep jumping on all the rides?

Life is a lot calmer now. It's been at least ten years since I've been hospitalized, and that was because I'd skipped the antidepressants. Definitely learned my lesson there.

The others though. I look down at the capsules lined up and what I see are bullets. I'm a big-game hunter in a pith helmet, taking aim at a colorful gathering of zebras and giraffes.

I'm standing there, my hands resting lightly on the countertop, just breathing, when I hear a soft noise behind me. Niccolo jumps up on the counter.

"Hi sweetheart. You thirsty?"

I turn the cold-water faucet on just the tiniest bit; he likes a very thin dribble. When he finishes drinking, I turn off the tap and he shakes his head and wipes his face dry with his paw.

He sees the pills too. Stares at them intently. Starts to approach. I know what's coming next: he's a cat, after all.

I should stop him.

But all I can do is watch as he puts out a paw, and slowly scooches one of the pills to the edge of the counter. Then pushes it off.

He starts maneuvering the second pill, and then the third. His eyes widen a bit in thrilled surprise each time a pill tips off the edge and tumbles to the floor.

Is he telling me to take a break? To stop trudging through life, meekly accepting the unacceptable?

Maybe he's right?

I watch him bat the last pill off the counter. When he's done, I bend down, pick them all up again. Put them back into their vials, and close the medicine cabinet.

CHAPTER TWO

ALLISON

It's dinner time and I'm about to pour myself a bowl of cereal when I hear someone knocking at the door. Bobby, my next-door neighbor, holds a big pan covered with aluminum foil.

"You haven't eaten yet, right?"

He doesn't wait for an answer, walks straight through to the kitchen, and I follow in the wake of the amazing smell: roasty, meaty, garlicky. Bobby has a catering business, and he's generous with leftovers.

"Allison. For God's sake!"

He's staring at the box of Lucky Charms. He shakes his head.

"You still have tequila?"

Bobby's also a bartender, and proud of his creations.

"Sure, there's plenty."

"Be right back with the rest. Just set the table, and I'll need the cocktail shaker and the citrus juicer. And how about the fancy glasses this time? Not those cheap purple plastic tumblers."

Bobby's bossy, but I like him. He invites himself over every week or so, even though he's got better places to be. He's friends with practically everyone in town, from the A-list celebrities who breeze in for festivals, to the summer workers who clean their toilets and bus their dishes. He's invited me to parties at his house, but I've made excuses. I can picture it all too easily: throngs of new people all at once who already know each other, noisy hilarity that makes it hard to hear anything, in-jokes and banter that zip by way too fast for me.

"So how's work?" he asks, once we're settled at the kitchen table, enjoying our feast. Chicken wings, pot stickers, hummus and veggies, a Thai chicken salad.

I'm a senior HR compliance analyst; we're battling over DEI issues and…

But no. I don't know how to make work chat interesting. I'll end up stranded on my own conversational island, useless words washing back at me as I get more and more self-conscious.

"Busy. You know."

"They're still letting you stay virtual? So many people have to go back now."

"Yeah, but they're saving so much money on office space, I think I'm safe."

I know I'm lucky to have remote work. But it's been almost three years, and I still haven't adjusted to year-round life in Ptown. We were just summer people; it was family time. When the summer crowds leave, the winters can be desolate, and I haven't made much progress on social outreach. Well, I do volunteer to drive seniors to their medical appointments in Hyannis. So occasionally one of them will wave to me at Stop and Shop. And there's Bobby, thank God.

Back when I lived in Boston, I'd take the T to work every morning. Walk across the gleaming marble floors in the lobby, say hi to Ricardo, the security guard. Familiar and predictable, but in a good way. We had a free Nespresso machine in the break room, and I had a few work buddies. Sometimes we'd all go out to lunch together. My parents lived close by, and I'd see them Thursday nights, when Courtney had book club. After dinner my dad would go off to watch TV while my mom and I would hang out in the kitchen and talk. About anything, everything. She had such a contagious laugh! My dad would sometimes have to poke his head back into the kitchen just to find out what was so damn funny.

I take a bite of a chicken wing, feel the spicy tingle in my mouth. I wash it down with a sip of my cocktail—sweet and sour like a margarita, but stronger, bitter, a little herbal. Bracing. That helps. It brings me back to the present, which is where I'm supposed to be.

But Bobby's eyes have slipped down to his phone.

He frowns and scrolls.

"Anything promising?" I ask him. "Or has Prince Charming not gotten around to posting his profile yet?"

"Oh sorry," he says, looking up. "No, so far, no princes. Just frogs."

He says he's on the lookout for a future husband, but in the meantime, he seems happy to hook up with any nearby hottie he can find. I didn't realize the "dick dock" was even still a thing until I met Bobby.

But he'll find the right guy when he's ready. Unlike me, he's confident, sociable, attractive. He's nearly my age, but whether it's due to good genes, hours at the gym, or Botox, he could pass for thirty. His dirty-blond hair is the same color as mine, but mine is limp and frumpy, while Bobby's looks straight out of a Gucci ad.

He puts his phone down on the table, then scooches it away a foot or so, as though now he's safe from its magical powers.

"And how about you? Seen any more of Cleo lately?"

"You mean Chloe?"

"Whatever. Your coffee-house crush. That sounded promising."

I made it sound promising? I probably shouldn't have said anything at all.

"That's not really a thing."

"I thought you guys were dating?"

"No. Not dates. We've just started sharing a table if we're there at the same time. Mostly just working on our laptops."

"So you haven't even tried to make a move?"

Make a move? What would that even look like? Bobby and I live in completely different universes.

It's been almost a year now. We've had a few good conversations, but that's all. Soft-spoken and thoughtful, Chloe asks such unexpected questions, she's so observant.

But I know Chloe is just a fantasy, a distraction when I start feeling sad, a little trapped. Moving here full-time—it was probably a terrible decision. But how do I undo it now?

I couldn't think what else to do. The house was right here waiting for me: lifeless by then, but at least familiar.

To build a *new* life? Not so lifeless, not so familiar? I'd have to be brave. Energetic. Proactive. Persistent.

In other words: a different person.

There's a sudden buzzing sound.

"That's your phone, not mine" says Bobby. "Hey, maybe it's Chloe?"

We haven't even traded phone numbers. Still, I feel a little twist in my stomach just imagining it.

Of course it's not her. But it's good news.

"Airbnb notification," I say. "Someone finally wants to rent the cottage. In July."

"I still think if you did *anything* to fix that place up, you'd never have any vacancies at all. Plus, you could charge five times as much. Rustic is one thing, but…"

I'm looking at the potential renter. "Oh my God."

"What?"

"I can't believe it. It's Shannon Callaghan!"

"What's a Shannon Callaghan?" Bobby asks. "Seriously, you should see your face."

"She was a high school friend, like, almost thirty years ago."

I do the math. Twenty-nine.

"She came to our high school just for the last year, then we lost touch. I always wondered what happened to her."

I scroll down. The message part of the Airbnb form says:

Hey Allison, I hope you remember me? So, how crazy is this: I'm doing a painting workshop in Provincetown, and just saw your listing! It doesn't say anything about pets, but a cat's okay, right? Will you be in Ptown then too? Would be so fun to see you again!

"God, Shannon Callaghan. She was such a trip."

"Yeah?"

Bobby actually looks interested, not like when I talk about work.

"Totally off the rails sometimes. Completely fearless. She'd talk back to teachers, walk out of classes, take pretty much any drug she was offered. Go off with all kinds of guys, didn't care about her 'reputation.' But she never took any of them seriously. Just played around."

"That's *so* not the kind of girl I'd picture you hanging out with."

"Right? I mean, she was super smart, even if she didn't care much about her grades. And so funny. But I'd always been such a goody two-shoes, then all of a sudden I'm best friends with this badass troublemaker."

"So you became a badass too? No offense, Allison. That's hard to picture."

"Yeah, no. Shannon didn't take me along for the riskier stuff. But I'd never even cut a class before I met her."

"And then you did?"

"Twice! Well, two classes on the same day. I got detention."

"You wild woman!" he laughs. "I think this story calls for another round of cocktails."

He takes my empty glass, goes to the counter.

Wow. I still can't quite believe it.

I tried googling her a few times over the years, but could never find her. A redheaded, foul-mouthed tornado, she swept through the dreary corridors of my high school and lifted me right out of my previous miserable existence. Brash and pushy, sure, but also protective. She said she'd punch out anyone who messed with me. And she was unpredictable enough, people believed her.

Even better, she treated me like an actual person. Not just the butt of a joke.

I watch Bobby as he's measuring and pouring, squeezing and crushing. He's so much more comfortable in my parents' kitchen than I've ever been.

The other kids used to call me Lurch, like in *The Addams Family*. After all, I was enormously tall and awkward, I had short hair, boys' clothes, and like Lurch, I barely spoke. Whenever I'd tried to talk to people, it only made things worse.

But I was who I was: I no more could have forced myself to wear skirts and crop tops and mascara than my father could have. I didn't understand any of the other unwritten rules of teenage girlhood either. Somehow I missed the memo.

Bobby hands me my drink.

"Thanks." I take a sip. Every bit as good as the first one.

"And so did you sleep with her, this Shannon character?" Bobby asks.

The question sloshes some of my cocktail out of my glass.

"What? God no. She couldn't have been more straight."

"But you wanted to?"

I shake my head as I mop up the spill with my napkin.

We were best friends; I couldn't think of her that way. It would be… like, incestuous. Plus I liked sportier girls, androgynous. Not that I ever approached any—I was a late bloomer.

"Nah. We were really good friends though. You know how intense teenage girls can be."

We spent most afternoons together. I helped her with math homework; even finished some of her essays and reports she'd put off until the last minute. She took me to parties, even if we weren't invited. We'd stay out late, drink forbidden beers. We talked and giggled and shared secrets and dreams for the future. At last I had someone I could talk to besides my mother.

"We told each other everything. She was the only one who knew I was gay."

"Really." He raises his eyebrows.

"Well, she was the only one I told."

Bobby gently swirls his cocktail, watches it rise in the glass, then takes a swig.

"I bet Shannon had some secrets too."

"Sure, she had some really wild stories. Especially from back at her other school. Drugs and boys and stealing things, pranks and silly kinds of vandalism, all kinds of stuff."

Should I tell him? Maybe just some of it.

"But it was kinda sad. There was a reason she acted out so much."

"Yeah?"

He loves gossip. Apparently even if it's thirty years old.

"She had a sister, Maureen, a year older. They were really close. And the two of them were in a car crash. Shannon got pretty banged up, ended up in the hospital. But Maureen died."

"Jesus."

Bobby seems to sense that this isn't one of those times to fill a silence with a joke, and we go back to our plates for a bit. I help myself to a couple more pot stickers.

The thing was, Maureen never should have been driving. She was only fifteen. And she was hysterical that night, some older guy had gotten her pregnant—so young, I was shocked—and then as soon as she told him, he'd dumped her. Told her to get rid of it. She got into their parents' liquor cabinet, was determined to go see him, make him change his mind. Swiped the keys to their mom's car. And Shannon ran after her.

I can't imagine getting in a car with a drunk, freaked out, underage driver at the wheel. Maybe because I never had a sister? But Shannon had been so sure she could talk Maureen down, help her figure out what to do. She felt terrible that she'd failed.

"Poor kid," says Bobby finally. "I can't imagine. No wonder she was messed up. And then she changed schools? That's hard enough in itself."

"Well, she had to. She got expelled from her old one. Her parents didn't know what to do with her, they even sent her to live with her grandmother for a while. Eventually she got a little less wild. But she was still so feisty when I knew her. I mean, she was rich, always had cool clothes, and so pretty—she totally could have hung out with the popular kids if she'd just toned it down a bit. Instead, she ended up with me. The ultimate dweeb."

Back then, everyone just understood: there had to be a bottom rung to the social hierarchy, and if that's where you landed, you got stepped on. Ugly names, practical jokes, shoves in the hallways, dog shit smeared on your locker.

But then Shannon took the seat next to me in English the first day of senior year. And within days, they started leaving me alone. And I had a best friend.

I'll always be so grateful to her.

Bobby's phone reverberates against the table with an urgent frazzle. He takes a look: another potential suitor. This time though, he's porn-star hunky and wants to meet in twenty minutes.

"I can put him off until later…"

"No, you go on ahead."

We've finished our dinner, and I'm ready for some alone time. Lots to think about.

After I walk Bobby out, and thank him for the wonderful dinner, I take the dirty dishes to the sink. It feels good to move around, and I feel a little perkier now, thinking about Shannon coming. I toss the hollowed husks of the limes that gave their lives for our cocktails, scrub sticky barbecue sauce off the counters, wash the plates and glasses, sweep the kitchen floor.

She'll be right here again, staying next door!

I wonder what she's like now? We wrote letters for a year or two, but she took longer and longer to answer. Then my last one came back with "addressee unknown."

I look around, seeing the kitchen through her eyes. How it hasn't changed since she's been here.

The oak cabinetry is stained with years of cigarette smoke. The countertop is ceramic: burnt orange tiles, many of them cracked or chipped, separated by grout that probably used to be white. The dishwasher is harvest gold, and hasn't worked since the mid '80s. The floor is a dingy yellow vinyl, scratched and stained.

I grab the trash and recycling bags, walk them out to the bins in the driveway.

As I come back inside, I realize it's not just the kitchen, it's the whole house. It was just meant to be a summer place; my parents used to laugh about how random and unfancy it all was. Odd knickknacks, clunky furniture, mauve walls. The disorganized décor left by my grandparents, it was actually part of the charm of being here. My parents didn't entertain here, so everything was relaxed, unfussy.

I turn off the kitchen light, head to the living room couch to watch a little TV.

Almost three years since my mom died, and Courtney dumped me, and my dad moved to Miami. And I still haven't done anything to make this place mine, besides put away my clothes and set up a home office.

But I wouldn't know where to start. As I look around again, everything so natural, so inevitable—as though the furniture and decorations just grew here, rising out of the floors and walls, putting down roots like bushes and trees. How do you redecorate a forest?

You can't. Not without destroying it.

CHAPTER THREE

SHANNON

Early morning air slips in through the open kitchen window, cool and delicious. I'm watching a robin on a tree branch, wondering what she's thinking. Brian's finally left for work and I've got the whole luxurious day ahead, completely unsupervised.

I told Cynthia I had an appointment with my psychiatrist and some blood work to get done, which shut off any nosy questions. My mental health, or lack thereof, is a topic she'd rather avoid.

And it's poker night. Once a month Brian joins all his buddies at his friend Pete's house. He goes over straight from work and comes home late, smelling of beer and cigars, then falls straight into bed.

I've felt so much more myself since I stopped taking anything but my antidepressants. It's like stepping out of a murky fogbank into a clear bright morning. If Brian knew, he'd flip out. My shrink wouldn't be happy either, but she doesn't know, because I've also been skipping my sessions.

I've finally started making my own decisions again.

Like going to see my friend Emily last week during her shift at Cumby's. I don't usually get my coffee at a convenience store, but I've missed her, and I worry about her. Her job's just part time. She was my dealer before Massachusetts legalized cannabis and put her out of business.

Brian doesn't like Emily, or any of the rest of the crowd I used to hang with. We'd meet Saturday nights at The Broken Bucket, a bar and grill the next town over that still managed to smell like cigarettes decades after they were banned. True, there was excessive drinking and weed, flirting and carousing. But it was fun. I miss my merry old tribe of troublemakers.

I only went to Cumby's to touch base, see how Emily was doing. I certainly had no idea she'd have 'shrooms to sell.

I sip my tea, savor the promising bitterness.

I've been questioning everything lately. So much brewing inside, darkness and light. I get brief glimpses in my dreams, but they dissolve before I can make sense of them. Mushrooms have always been powerful guides when I've felt lost.

I finish the tea, rinse out the cup. Time for some music! I put on my special playlist from years ago. Trippy and electronic, but also acoustical and spiritual, bells and birds and waterfalls, like being at a rave at a Buddhist temple.

I close my eyes, wait patiently as time gently passes.

Ah yes. Now I feel the music washing out of the speaker, penetrating every pore of my skin. My entire body is filled with swirly patterns.

I open my eyes and the room feels different. Larger and then smaller and then larger again. The walls are breathing! In and then out, in and out, big, deep, nourishing breaths.

But since walls don't normally know how to do this, I realize the mushrooms are starting to work. Yes! My body is pulsing with gratitude and happiness.

I sit down on my yoga mat and just enjoy the music for a long, long, long time.

Eventually I open my eyes. What time is it? How long until Brian comes home?

I look at my watch.

What it says is absurd. There is no way I've only been sitting here half an hour.

I realize I need to say hello to the trees, to be enveloped in their green-scented breath and watch their branches dance.

Out the door, into the yard. They are all swaying, singing their breezy songs, and I sway with them, and try to sing too. But tree songs have tricky melodies.

Something moves. A squirrel looks right at me. And then I realize that it's not an ordinary squirrel. It stares at me with such intensity that I know it has been sent.

Did Maureen send the squirrel?

"She's waiting," says the wind.

I really have to do 'shrooms more often. Normally we can't communicate with the universe, we don't see it trying to tell us so many things.

I am beyond happy to hear that Maureen is out there, waiting for me. That's the answer I was searching for. I have to find her, wherever she is!

Then the light dims, a sudden chill. A cloud, stern and gray, hides the sun.

A warning? Something stirs, dark and subterranean.

But then the cloud passes, and everything feels bright and hopeful again.

I'm feeling a bit tired so I sit down and close my eyes for a moment. When I open them, the sun is in a different place. It feels like time to go back inside.

Where is Niccolo? I go from room to room. There he is! He's curled up on my bed. He raises his head when he sees me.

"Hey sweet boy, there you are!"

Of course I am! I sleep here every afternoon. I thought maybe you forgot about me?

Wait.

His mouth didn't move, but I could swear…

"Niccolo, did you just say something to me?"

His eyes open wide.

I did! You can hear me?

"Yes! And you can understand English?"

These are the best mushrooms I've ever taken!

I can. It's been some weeks now. But when I've tried to communicate with you before, you couldn't understand me.

"Well, I can now. This is so nice!"

His voice is so charming: gentle and cultivated, but not prissy.

I'm quite thrilled as well.

It's not *exactly* like he's speaking out loud—it's more like in a dream. I'm pretty sure no one else could hear him. But it's not just my imagination either. So clear and real, and I'm not doing anything at all to summon it up, I'm just listening.

"Do you mind if we talk for a bit?"

I'd love that, Shannon.

I slip off my shoes and sit next to him on the bed.

"Can I still pet you, is that something you like? I always thought so, but I could never ask you before. I hope it wasn't too presumptuous."

Oh please do. I especially love that exquisite fingernail tickling, right behind my ears.

"Like this?"

Oh yes.

"You're purring!"

I can't help it. I find it embarrassing. Exposing my private emotions so visibly. It's not very dignified.

"But it always makes me happy."

It does? Well, I'm glad of that then.

"I always knew you were smart. I sometimes felt like we were already having conversations."

I've felt that too. But it's so nice having words now.

"Do you miss being outside with the other cats?"

Shannon. The happiest day of my life was the day you took me away from those monsters. But, yes. I do sometimes wish I could be outside.

"I can imagine."

I miss feeling dirt and grass on my paws. The scents. The beetles, the sparrows, the mice. But honestly? None of them are as tasty as you might think. The cans you give me are quite adequate, and not nearly as labor-intensive to eat.

"I'm so glad to hear that."

And I truly appreciate how attentive you are to the litter box. My previous owners let it become completely soiled and unusable.

"Do you remember much about them?"

I prefer not to. I've managed to forget almost everything about that life.

The lady at the shelter hinted that he'd been abused.

"But you're safe now, you know. I promise to always take good care of you."

I know you will, Shannon. And I promise to always take good care of you, too.

* * *

I'm standing at my workbench out in the garage, staring at a fresh denim jacket, waiting for inspiration. I'm not quite as high anymore, but I can still feel the 'shrooms swirling, inviting creative chaos, dissolving barriers.

But the jacket is just staring at me, it doesn't know what it wants to be yet.

My creations start as thrift store finds, cheap jeans or jackets, but then I go to town on them. Paint, decals, braid, burns, bleach, sequins, feathers, spikes, whatever I can think of. I don't sell a ton, but I've done some experimenting: the people who appreciate my designs seem reassured by ridiculously high price tags.

I used to paint and draw, but no one bought my art. Clothes are an easier sell. People feel like if they're wearing something arty, then they become the artist. They become the cool person who is expressing themselves by wearing the art. That's fine. I know who the real artist is.

I look up just as Niccolo comes through the door I left open to the kitchen. He's carrying something in his mouth. He approaches and drops it at my feet.

It's one of Brian's boxing gloves, still recognizable, but very chewed up.

I brought you a gift, says Niccolo.

"I see!"

Brian is going to shit.

It smells quite wonderful, and I've softened it up for you. And look at all the pretty white fuzzies popping out of the holes!

"Well thank you!"

I had the feeling you might need it for something.

I laugh. What does he think I'd want it for, a snack?

But then I think on it a moment. Oh my God. Yes.

"It's such a powerful metaphor."

I'll have to flatten the glove quite a bit, take out more stuffing. It's the oversized right fist of a cartoonish brute, just spoiling for a fight. I'll also give him one of those old-fashioned round bombs with a lit fuse. Maybe a machine gun. A snarling bulldog in a spiked collar.

But confronting him will be a little pig-tailed girl, arms crossed in front of her, unafraid. Not about to be menaced. Maybe a little like Pippi Longstocking?

I sort through my fabric scraps. I'll want lots of bright colors to draw the eye. Blue for her dress. Orange yarn for her hair. Red and yellow sequins for the lit fuse.

"Thank you Niccolo, that really helped!"

Anytime you need me, Shannon.

Hours later, I put down my scissors, put the caps back on to the paint and the glue, tidy up the scraps, and stand up straight, stretching out my cramped muscles. The 'shroom's have left me now. The garage is completely still, nothing swirls or throbs, my mind is quiet and clear.

I feel a little sad. I've always struggled with endings, clinging too tightly. Chasing the highs—drugs, the thrill of easy, not-strictly-legal income, hopeless schemes, doomed romances. I'd keep going and going, even if it eventually meant running off a cliff.

To be still, in the moment? No thank you.

But I understand now that some gifts are meant to be ephemeral. I try to just feel grateful to the mushrooms, for the amazing day they gave me, for the miracle of Niccolo.

I remind myself that there are other cats who need me too. I'll get them fed first, then go find Niccolo. As I step outside, the soft early-evening air refreshes me, restores me after so many hours of concentration.

I scoop the cats' boxes and fill their bowls, trying to open my heart to them. Even though they're just ordinary cats, wordless, crunching on their kibble.

I'm barely two steps away from the shed when I hear the rumble of Brian's truck coming up the driveway.

He's supposed to be at poker!

Still, there's no need to panic. I've come down now, he won't know I've been tripping.

But something's off. He doesn't even pull into the carport, just parks, slams the door, and walks toward me, steely.

"Hey Bri, you're home early!"

"Pete had to cancel. He and his wife got the flu."

"Oh no! Sorry, I know you were looking forward to it."

"Thing is, I stopped by Wombat's. To see if you felt like going out for dinner tonight. But you didn't go to work? Cynthia said you had some medical appointments. That was a lie, right?"

I feel my cheeks starting to flush.

"It's just been so slow at the shop; I knew Cynthia could handle it. I really needed a day to catch up in my workshop. I've got all these great new ideas, and I wanted to build up a little more inventory."

His arms are folded across his chest and his face is stone.

"And she said something about you asking for time off during the summer. For a painting workshop? You didn't go ahead and sign up for that, did you?"

"But I told you I was going to."

"No, you didn't. You said it like 'someday.' I thought you came to your senses."

"What's that supposed to mean?"

"Shannon. There are painting classes everywhere, but you wanted to go all the way to Provincetown for this one? I figured maybe you were up to something. So I went to the website. And I'm supposed to think it's just a *coincidence* that Grant Pritchard is teaching a writing workshop there, at exactly the same time?"

Shit.

"What am I supposed to think, that you're *not* stalking him again?"

I so wish I'd never told Brian. I could never explain it very well, the desperate urge to keep Pritchard in my sights, to find out where he was and what he was doing. So despicable. So irresistible. I still can't help but feel drawn to him, he's a black hole sucking me in, a curse I can't escape. The man who killed my sister is the strongest link I have to Maureen herself.

"He's going to be there the same time? Wow, I didn't know that!"

Brian just laughs, a dismissive snorty sound.

"So Cynthia also says you've been coming in late again. Acting a little hyper. Laughing at things that aren't that funny. And honestly, I've noticed the same thing."

It feels like a slap. I can't even be in a good mood anymore without getting grief for it? The two of them trashing me behind my back, commiserating, making me sound like a crazy person—it's infuriating.

"Did you stop taking your meds?"

"No."

Not all of them, anyway.

"Are you even still seeing your therapist?"

How does he feel so entitled to grill me? I don't ask him to account for every minute of his day.

"None of your business!"

He shakes his head, unfolds his arms, then puts them on his hips, posed like a dictatorial teapot.

"You're right, Shannon, it's none of my business. Not anymore."

He starts walking toward the house.

I go into the garage to put away the kibble bucket, and dump the cat box leavings in the trash. A few seconds later the door from the kitchen bursts open.

"Really?" he says. "You don't even care that I'm thinking of leaving? Instead of talking things through, you go hide out in the goddamn garage?"

"I was just putting these away. You'd prefer we have a serious conversation while I'm chasing you through the house carrying a bag full of cat shit?"

His eyes fall on the denim jacket. His ripped boxing glove, transformed into art.

"Is that my…? What. The actual. Fuck."

He slams the door on his way back into the house.

I take a deep breath. I realize I'm shaking.

But it's okay. I know I can stop him from leaving. He's pissed off right now, but if I apologize, swear to do better, get back on my meds, go to my shrink, stop showing up late for work, buy him new boxing gloves, "behave myself," I know he'll stay.

Back into the kitchen, I pour myself a glass of iced tea, then go sit on the couch in the living room. I can hear Brian upstairs, stomping around. I need to give him the right amount of time to cool off, but not so much time he thinks I'm ignoring him. Then I'll do the clean-up work. Take my meds with him watching me, tell him how important he is.

It'll all be fine.

I see Niccolo at the door. He crosses the room, jumps into my lap. The feel of his soft warm coat as I pet him, his unfailing loyalty, it's so comforting.

Are you okay, Shannon? I know it upsets you when Brian starts yelling.

Wait. He's still talking to me?

"You're right, baby, I hate it. But I'll survive. I'm going to have to go up there soon, apologize to him. Even though I don't feel the least bit sorry."

I don't understand. If you're not sorry, then why do you have to apologize?

"Well, if I don't, he'll leave me."

And that would be bad? Things are so much more peaceful when he's out of the house.

He's got me there.

"Well, he tries his best. Keeps me company. Doesn't let me get too… I don't know. Inappropriate."

Oh. So you like it that he tells you what you should and shouldn't do?

"Actually, I hate that part! It's just… I'm not sure I want to be single again. On my own."

With Brian, at least there's another person in the house. Occasional sex. Non-demanding dinnertime conversation. Someone who's tall enough to reach the top shelf in the kitchen cabinet when I want to use the crockpot.

Although surely there's got to be more left to "us" than that? It's just a little hard to remember right now.

But Shannon. You wouldn't be on your own. You have me!

Niccolo. My little angel! Not much help with the crockpot, but it's true: he's a wonderful companion.

I put on an episode of Vera, a British police procedural. The crisp accents and melodramatic soundtrack help muffle the stomping upstairs as Brian packs his suitcases.

I should go up there pretty soon. Shouldn't I?

Niccolo sleeps beside me; his paws twitch when he dreams. His breathing is gentle and rhythmic, but it's not human—much faster, not as deep.

How long will we be able to keep talking to each other? I dread the thought of going deaf to his voice again, guessing instead of knowing what he's thinking.

Would I need to keep taking mushrooms? Tripping occasionally is one thing, but being in a hallucinatory state 24/7 would be pretty unworkable. Maybe microdosing would be enough? After all, I can still hear him now, even with only trace amounts of psilocybin left in my system.

Then it hits me. Those pills I've been skipping—it's probably no coincidence. If I decide to go back on them, will they put a complete end to our conversations?

Of course they will.

Now Niccolo is waking up. He rises, arches his back, stretches, and sits up straight.

So now that we have words, please tell me more about our trip to Provincetown. I'm so excited!

"I don't know, sweetheart. If Brian stays, he won't let me go. And if I don't stop him from leaving, there's too much to take care of around here. I'm not even sure where I'd find a house sitter, we live so far out in the boonies. The outside cats, the bird feeders, all that watering every day… I can't just up and leave everything."

But just suppose you figure that part out. What's it like there?

How to describe it? I feel a pleasant wash of nostalgia, remembering my summer there. A quaint New England village by the sea, with stunning beaches. But it's the vibe: charming and historic, but edgy. For centuries it's drawn creative rebels and outcasts. Poets and pirates, painters and musicians, drug runners, drag queens. It went from a Portuguese fishing village to an arts colony to a hippie haven to a gay utopia where everyone is welcome to join the party.

But how much of that would make sense to a cat?

"It's very pretty there, and the people are fun. Tons to see and do."

So you'd be happy there? I love it when you're happy.

"Happy? I think so, actually. I'd be energized. More aligned with my true destiny."

Allison and I have traded a couple of emails—mostly just logistics, but I was touched by how excited she was to see me again. And I realized she could even help me with Pritchard. We could be like Scott and Bailey, or Cagney and Lacey: teaming up to bring a heinous killer to justice.

I googled and she works at a big company now, with an impressively incomprehensible job title. I bet she hangs out with other overachievers, not like the Broken Bucket slackers I gravitate toward. Provincetown is quite popular with media types—columnists, reporters, producers, influencers. If I wanted to ruin Pritchard's reputation? I bet Allison knows people who know people.

I just wish Brian hadn't gotten wise and ruined everything.

Niccolo's paws poke into my thigh; he's moving into my lap now.

So Shannon, he says, *what about that nice lady who gave you the mushrooms? If Brian's not here anymore, couldn't she help us out?*

Emily?

Emily, of course! She adores animals, and can always use some extra cash. Why didn't I think of her?

Because of Brian. I never should have let him banish her from my life.

Vera is now interviewing her fourth or fifth suspect. And I'm still lingering on the couch, petting my cat. Pondering my options.

Brian thumps his way downstairs with two suitcases. He stops at the bottom.

The way he looks at me: like I'm a naughty terrier who's just pissed the rug and shredded all the furniture.

As though the chilly distance between us is all *my* doing.

He says nothing. I say nothing right back.

I turn back to the TV as Vera finally confronts her final suspect: the real killer.

The front door slams shut.

It doesn't take long before I can sense the first soft edges of loss. I'll miss him. This is going to hurt.

But the Brian I'm going to miss? He already left, a long time ago.

CHAPTER FOUR

ALLISON

It's Saturday of Memorial Day Weekend, only seven in the morning, but I'm already showered, dressed, and fully caffeinated. For so long now I've been feeling like an inmate in a dreary cell, serving a long sentence. But I finally realized: there are no locks on my door! No armed guards. Nothing is keeping me imprisoned but my own defeatist attitude.

When I found out Shannon was coming, it shook me up, imagining how pathetic my life would look to her. But it also got me thinking: maybe her arrival could, once again, change everything? I guess I've always thought of her as larger than life, like some sort of mythic figure.

But how did I think that was going to happen: by magic? The only person who can change my life is me. And I can start today.

Here in Provincetown, Memorial Day Weekend often goes by another name. Even Alba, who's 84, asked me on the way to her cardiologist appointment: Did I have any plans for Baby Dyke Weekend? A tradition for ages: feral packs of young lesbians come here to party, often hauling their own beer and snacks, starting the occasional drunken brawl. Many business owners dread their arrival. They cram way too many bodies into their hotel rooms and rentals; they don't tend to buy art or expensive dinners out like the affluent older gays. Plus they're much louder than the culture vultures who theater-hop during the Tennessee Williams Festival. But I've always enjoyed their scrappy what-the-hell energy. And since the weekend is the official start of the summer season, it seems a perfect backdrop for new beginnings.

There are two items on my agenda for today: The first is to make a start on fixing up the house. And the second is to do something social tonight. There are tons of women in town, and many of them are no longer "baby" dykes. Lots of parties and dances scheduled.

It's time to stop mooning over Chloe. I'm hoping we can at least be friends, eventually, the intentional kind where you trade numbers and make plans together. But she's not showing any sign she'd want that, let alone anything more serious. We talk, sure, but we're also working, so as soon as we start to get deeper into anything, we end up pulling back. I keep thinking "well, we'll just have to finish this conversation later," but there's never a later, and I finally realized it's because Chloe doesn't want one.

She's out of my league, that's the problem. She works for a chain of hospitals, a director of something. It sounds important and stressful. I hear the beginnings of her phone calls, before she takes them outside: she's decisive, a leader. I'm at best a "team player." Not exactly a nobody, but not a somebody either.

I look around the living room. Time to cull the herd.

Like that ugly lamp. It's probably sixty years old, bulbous and lime green. And the ceramic clown collection! It was a running joke between my parents, they'd give them as gifts for each other's birthdays, the tackier the better. Or maybe I'll keep one or two. A few. They're all so perfectly hideous, all the different variations of cringe. When I look at them I can almost hear my parents laughing.

In my office, which used to be the den, it's mostly family pictures. Those can stay. My mother on the ferry from Boston, hair blowing every which way, sticking her tongue out at my dad, that's my absolute favorite. Or it might be the one with the three of us grinning at my graduation from UMass. I didn't want to go, formal ceremonies make me nervous, but it was the right call: my parents were deliriously happy that day. Neither of them finished college. My dad was studying biology, hoping to become doctor, but my mom got pregnant with me their junior year. Knowing it would be years before he could make a dent in his student loans, my dad quit and went to work for his father, selling mattresses. My mother stayed home to take care of me. But they always said they had no regrets.

There's a shiny blue canister on the side table, that obviously stays too. My mom's in there. I was supposed to scatter her ashes off the jetty at her favorite swimming spot, but I haven't yet. I just can't.

I go through the house and finally fill up three cardboard boxes. But when I look around, nothing looks very different.

But it's a start.

* * *

I'm poking around the thrift shop at the Methodist Church, reminding myself that I'm here to get *rid* of clutter, not come back with more of it. But these binoculars, they're in great shape. I like the solid weight of them in my hands, the smooth but steady resistance of the dial as it brings everything in and out of focus. Should I take up bird watching? People seem to like it.

"Allison?"

I turn around, and oh my God. It's Chloe.

What is it about her? She's not conventionally pretty, her jaw's too strong for that. Her cheeks have some acne scarring; her glasses are clunky. But she has presence. She barely smiles or laughs… until she does. And then she just beams, unforced and unfiltered, radiating delight. She's Asian, about my age, maybe a year or two younger. But we look so different: she's petite, graceful, self-contained. I'm over six feet tall, with elbows, knees and feet that always seem to be in someone's way. Standing this close to her I feel a bit like King Kong.

"Hi, Chloe!"

Even my voice is too much. I sound way too excited.

"Planning to do some spying?" she asks.

"Um, no?"

Does she know I have a thing for her? Does she think I'm going to follow her home?

She points at the binoculars in my hands.

"Oh, right. Those. No, not for spying! At least not on people. More like on birds. Hypothetically."

"Oh okay."

"But then hypothetical bird-watching, that's probably the best kind, right?" I keep yammering, somehow not able to stop myself. "My dad did that for a few weeks, until my mom figured out he was really just going outside to sneak cigarettes. Actual bird-watching, that might be kind of boring."

Then Chloe laughs, suddenly, as though her amusement just escaped from some buried vault where she'd tried to lock it down.

"Like we need more things in life to keep track of?" she says. "All those different kinds of beaks and wings and feathers?"

"Right?"

We both fall silent.

"So Allison," she says, "I've been meaning to ask you, would you have any interest in …"

And then suddenly we're interrupted: a symphony begins to play something joyous, getting louder and louder. And while it's the perfect movie soundtrack for how I'm feeling right now—she's asking me to do something! —it's also problematic. Because it's her phone.

"Oh shoot, it's my mother, sorry I need to…"

And she's heading outside to take the call.

But I'm swirling. *Would you be interested…* Why yes I would be interested! In whatever you're proposing! I wander the aisles, picking up and putting back down random vases and paperbacks and shot glasses. Still no Chloe. I make another round, examining used furniture, holding up jackets I'd never wear to see if they'd fit.

Damn. I'm realizing I may have let: *Would you be interested…* get way too big in my head. It could be: *Would you be interested… in any of the old DVD's I have out in my car? I was just coming here to donate them.*

It's been what, almost ten minutes? At this point, will she think it's weird if she comes back and I'm still here? Like I'm someone so desperate and needy that I'd wait indefinitely just to hear the end of a sentence?

I *am* that desperate and needy. But I'm not sure I want her to know that. I'll give her to the count of one hundred.

When I hit a thousand I look out the window again and she's still talking. The fantasy that she was about to propose some future get-together is getting harder to sustain. I go out the back door, get in my car and go home.

* * *

Usually at nine o'clock I'm at home on my couch. But tonight I'm walking down Commercial Street, the main drag in Provincetown. There's a dance at the Crown and Anchor. Anxiety claws at my chest, but I try to reframe it as "excitement." Maybe I'll meet someone new? As my mother would have said, "Chloe's not the only fish in the sea, Allison."

She used to say that a lot about Courtney. I just wish I'd listened. We fought all the time. Or rather, Courtney got mad at me a lot, and eventually accepted my apologies. It did get easier when I finally stopped having opinions. We were together eighteen years, got married when it became legal, and I'd probably still be stubbornly hanging in there if she hadn't left me.

It was three months after my mother died that Courtney said she wanted out. I could tell she didn't know what to do with me. She said I'd changed.

Of course I had.

The good thing about her brutal timing: my every cell was already grieving my mother's death, so her exit left me strangely numb. We got divorced, sold our condo, and I let her have everything in it. Then I came here. Our family's "happy place."

I can see women are starting to congregate as different events are starting. Dancing, cabaret, comedy. So many of them look straight to me, with their long hair and make-up and general flounciness. But there are also plenty of us who kick it old-school, from the soft-butch types to the hard-core gender-rebels.

There's quite a line when I get to the Crown and Anchor, and everyone in it is part of a couple or a group. They're all bubbly, talking loudly, laughing—their parties have already started. I feel conspicuous, standing there by myself.

So many people, will it be super crowded inside? I have my mask in my pocket. I still wear it in crowded indoor spaces, but almost no one else does, not anymore. I don't want to pass anything on to the vulnerable old folks like Alba who I give rides to. And I've checked the numbers; Covid has *not* disappeared. Will it ever?

I can picture it clearly now: a tall awkward figure standing alone, her face shrouded by a black KN-95, staring out at all the happy partying women, their naked faces full of joy, unafraid to breathe deeply and dance. I try to imagine a scenario that starts this way, but ends with me having an animated conversation with a charming single woman who finds me attractive.

I step out of the line and start walking home.

What was I even thinking?

CHAPTER FIVE

SHANNON

It's still dark when I open my eyes. Niccolo is standing on my chest, his face barely an inch from mine.

It's today, right? I can't wait!

"I can't either, sweetheart!"

I love waking up to hear his voice. My microdosing routine is working even better than I thought it would.

I prepare him a special breakfast: a mix of anchovies and tuna with a generous eyedropper of kitty sedative. What he doesn't know won't hurt him.

My goodness, Shannon, this is exquisite!

"Well, it's a special day."

What a lovely bon voyage feast, he says, diving back in.

I'll be gone for two weeks: one week for the workshop, and a few days on either side. And I know I've left the place in good hands. Emily asked so many great questions: about the irrigation system, the composting, the emergency generator, the bird feeders, the nearest vet in case anything happened to one of the cats. She took the notes I'd made for her and added her own clarifications, printing her letters slowly and carefully, like a fourth grader.

Would Brian have taken his head out of his ass long enough to pay such close attention to all the little details?

Ha!

I do miss him sometimes. Evenings are the hardest. Time gets tired of ticking, slows to a crawl, and it takes more effort than before to divert myself before I finally get to go to bed. But I don't miss living under Brian's smothering supervision. My freedom was worth it.

I eat a quick breakfast, start packing up the truck. Then I open the Amazon delivery that arrived last night, just in time. *Nom de Guerre*, the graphic novel by Wylie Buckner.

It's soft-cover, tall and wide like a workbook. I flip through the pages—something about World War II and the Holocaust, with obvious literary pretensions. And yet every page is full of colorful cartoon panels. I'm not sure I get it.

How many times had I visited the workshop website before I finally realized? Her workshop, *Getting Graphic*, is happening the same week as Pritchard's. And she just happened to have earned her MFA from the same university department where Pritchard teaches. She did win some sort of an award as a "promising newcomer," but she's only published this one book and it didn't do well. I'm sure it was Pritchard who got her the spot. She's not only a former student, but now she's some sort of assistant too—she's listed as a contact person for his PR inquiries. Internet photos confirm she's been tagging along with him a lot, at writers' conferences and other events.

I wouldn't be surprised if she's sleeping with him. Even though she's half his age.

I switched right out of my oil painting class and grabbed one of the open spots. While I couldn't have faked being eligible for Pritchard's "advanced" level novel workshop, Wylie's doesn't require any particular experience. I already know how to draw. I've taken literature classes, read a lot of books. I can bluff my way through for a week.

Wylie Buckner. I look at her photo on the back cover. She's not striking, but she's pretty enough. Slim build, fair skin, auburn hair. She's been in his orbit for years now. What does she know about him? Misdeeds, habits, haunts, peculiarities, vulnerabilities? I'm good at striking up quick friendships. I know how to coax gently, innocently, lending a sympathetic ear. And I can hear what people are saying when they don't realize they're saying anything at all.

In order to nail Pritchard, I need to dig up fresh dirt. Maureen didn't tell anyone but me that she got pregnant by her English teacher, and it happened thirty years ago. Pritchard was nowhere near the scene of the accident when she drove us off the road. Plus, as an accuser, I couldn't look less reliable: I've got a criminal record. Hospitalizations. An erratic employment history.

I put the book in my daypack, and double check that the Ziploc is in there too. I'm so grateful Emily came through with my request for more 'shrooms.

Should I bring along the Glock? I've never shot it outside of target practice.

An ex-boyfriend with soulful green eyes and an expensive cocaine habit gave it to me for my twenty-seventh birthday. Not so romantic maybe, but I was pleased. We did business with sketchy people back then, and it seemed quite possible I'd need it to scare someone off. I hid it in a toolbox in the garage when Brian moved in, inside a big cardboard box full of art supplies.

If I make too much trouble for Pritchard, would he actually try to come after me? Or maybe send someone to do it for him?

It's unlikely. But you can't be too careful.

I finish packing up the truck, and then put my very drowsy cat in his carrier, and we head out into the cool still morning. The air smells of damp earth, fertile, full of promise.

* * *

It feels good to be on the road again. On a quest, an important mission. I don't even need the radio, just the ambient rumble and swoosh of other vehicles, fellow travelers.

I find myself thinking back to high school. Not the public one where I met Allison, but the first one. A tony private enclave of stone buildings, lush landscaping, abundant resources, long waitlists. Poor Maureen, she'd been so happy there. Before everything changed.

She and I shared a superficial resemblance; people could tell we were sisters, especially with our strawberry-blonde hair. But Maureen got the more refined version of all our features. She was beautiful, and Pritchard definitely noticed. It started towards the middle of her freshman year.

At first, Maureen giggled and bubbled and sighed with happiness, floated rather than walked to school. He was so smart and handsome, she told me. She was so flattered that he'd chosen her.

I kept her secret of course. It was always that way between us. And when it started, it didn't even bother me that Maureen was only fourteen, and that he was so much older and married. It was like she'd gotten an unexpected promotion, had skipped ahead of everyone else and achieved adulthood ahead of schedule. It made me feel more grown-up too, being trusted with such a scandalous secret. Maureen was always the first one I'd turn to when something was bursting inside me, whether thrilling or terrifying. I was more than eager to return the favor.

But who was this man who cast such a powerful spell over her? The next year, when it was my turn for high school, I signed up for his freshman English class. Lush black hair and blue eyes, tall and lean, witty, slyly subversive. He didn't break a sweat trying to be "relevant" like so many of the others. In fact he seemed slightly mystified as to how he could have landed himself in a classroom full of teenagers, taking roll and devising quizzes. But his passion for literature seemed so pure, so unforced, that he swept us along with him. He was actually a good teacher. Inspiring his students during school hours, even as he was destroying one of them after the last bell rang.

By then Maureen's radiance had faded. She was losing weight, dropping her old friends, struggling in subjects she'd had no problem with before. Yet Pritchard always seemed the same: amused, detached.

I couldn't bear to lay eyes on him after Maureen died. Couldn't bear to go to school at all. It didn't take long to get myself kicked out. And it was so much better down in Key West, home-schooled by my grandmother, a real radical in her day. She always understood me so much better than my parents did. She helped me heal.

Not that I've ever healed completely. For that, I need justice. It's long past time. And I've got Allison and Wylie Buckner to help me, even though they don't know it yet.

I feel more alive than I have for years.

* * *

Allison isn't expecting us for more than an hour, so I pull off Highway 6 an exit early, taking the more scenic coastal road from north Truro into Provincetown.

The "Welcome to Provincetown" sign is done like an old-style painting, a group of fishermen bringing in their catch, giving no hints at all about the carnival atmosphere to come: the parties, the parades, the music, the performers. Well played, Provincetown! Let it all come as a surprise.

Across the road is stunning sandy beach with enticing blue-green water, under a vivid blue sky. A few cheerful whipped-cream clouds float above. In the distance is the harbor and piers and monuments of the central part of Provincetown.

It's a postcard come to life—improbably spectacular.

I've got time, and I don't want to show up at Allison's feeling ravenous and cranky. Maybe a lobster roll, with a cold draft beer? A Cape Cod tradition.

Commercial Street is where all the action is. The sidewalks are narrow, so pedestrians just take to the street, forcing cars to creep along behind them. Daredevil bicyclists whip in and out; huge trucks stop in the middle of the road to make deliveries. So it makes no sense to drive this way, it would be so much saner to take Bradford Street.

But how can I come back to Provincetown after all this time and *not* drive down Commercial Street?

Sure enough, after a few quiet blocks on the far east end, traffic backs up. But driving through it all at a snail's pace, I have time to take it all in. Carefully preserved buildings from centuries past, freshly painted and meticulously landscaped with glorious gardens, one after another for miles. And there are so many hip-looking restaurants and bars and clubs, and so many galleries and funky shops. I feel like I'm in Disneyland, but a Disneyland for grown-ups. Sure, there are candy stores and hot dogs and ice cream, but also sex toys on display in shop windows, pot shops, sassy T-shirts with racy slogans, thongs and bongs and whips and leather and rainbow flags everywhere. Revelry and rule breaking and freedom and fun.

But, I have to remember: this isn't a vacation.

* * *

Niccolo is still conked out in his carrier next to me on one of the public benches in front of town hall. I'm trying to convince myself that I'm just as happy sitting here with a burger and an iced tea as I would have been sitting on a restaurant terrace overlooking the harbor. But parking cost me forty dollars, and the restaurant was asking thirty-eight for a lobster roll and ten bucks each for a coleslaw and a beer, plus tax and tip. Better to be thrifty.

Money's tight at times, but I always get by. I haven't had to ask my mother for help since my twenties. I don't want her in my business. But I do get a modest monthly check from the trust my grandmother set up for me. She didn't "trust" me not to have a manic spree and blow my entire inheritance on something like an ostrich farm or a petting zoo. But her will also left me enough to buy the house I live in. So, no rent to pay.

Plus I have the part-time gallery job. That is, unless Cynthia decides to fire me.

I told her I'd be gone a week, and she wasn't happy. Then, for the second week, I'm planning to have an issue with the truck, some broken part that's impossible to find. Will that put her over the edge?

It's a risk I'm willing to take.

As I eat my burger, I'm keeping an eye out, because Pritchard is probably here already. When the school year ends, he chooses an upscale coastal town to spend the summer to write. And to fish, and drink, and carouse. He likes to mix it up. Back before Brian, I followed him to Bar Harbor, Rehoboth, and Newport. But I've never been able to afford to stay very long. One time his wife actually joined him for a couple days. Her bright clothes and floppy hats said "vacation," but her face was all business, tense and vigilant.

A giggling gaggle of bachelorettes approaches, already shit-faced and stumbling. Then the town crier, dressed in his official period costume. A group of churchy looking older Black women wearing lanyards, must be here on a bus tour. And quite a few ordinary day trippers just off the ferry. But this being Provincetown, mixed in there are a ton of gay guys and lesbians and gender-fluids of every stripe, star, and polka-dot.

Allison must feel so much more comfortable here than she ever did at that conformist, gossipy, soul-sucking suburban high school where we met!

A rustling sound from Niccolo's cage. I look in. He stretches, moves to the front, and pokes his nose through the wires.

What a long nap I've had! Where are we now, Shannon?

"Hi baby boy, oh good, you're awake!"

People are tolerant of eccentricity here, but I don't want to be overheard having serious conversations with a cat.

Are we in Provincetown already? There are so many people.

"Almost ready!"

Shannon. Do you not understand that you can answer me without speaking out loud?

I look at him. Why had that not occurred to me?

Just direct your inner voice to me. You can hear me, can't you, even when no one else does? It's because I'm speaking into your mind directly.

Like this? I ask him, sending only my thoughts.

Exactly!

Excellent, it works perfectly!

Okay, so yes, we're in Provincetown. And we'll be going to our cottage at Allison's just as soon as I finish my burger.

I take the last few bites, collect my trash. Then I see him. Talking to one of the traffic cops. Pritchard!

He's with the comic-book girlfriend, Wylie.

My body swings into high alert, I can feel the adrenaline pumping.

It's him! I direct my inner voice to Niccolo. *Over there, with the white pants and blue polo shirt.*

It's so annoying: he never seems to age. He still looks fit and vigorous. His hair is full and thick, with just enough grey to look distinguished.

They finish their conversation and continue down the street.

Don't you think you should follow them? asks Niccolo.

I do.

I hang back about twenty yards as they take a left towards Bradford. Then they turn right, and this is convenient, because it looks like they're heading to the same parking lot that I'm parked in, next to the CVS. I keep my eye on them as I hurry to my truck. They're getting into his white Jaguar convertible—vintage of course, no doubt worth a fortune.

I settle Niccolo's carrier in the passenger seat, start my engine, follow them out of the lot. We make a left on Bradford, heading east.

Allison won't mind if I'm a little late.

This is exciting! says Niccolo. *It's been so long since I've been on a real hunt. I do miss it, Shannon. I especially love the part where you know you have your prey cornered, and you can play a little first before you go in for the kill!*

I laugh.

"Well, he's a long way from cornered, but I do finally have him in my sights again."

I can use my real voice now, no one can hear us.

We do get to kill him in the end though, don't we?

He must think the human world works just like the animal world.

"As satisfying as that might be," I explain to Niccolo, "the legal system takes a dim view of that sort of thing. And I'm not sure I'm the murdering type."

Okay, so it's not like I've never thought about it. But only as a fantasy. I've imagined aiming the gun, seeing the terror in his face as he realizes what's about to happen. Pulling the trigger, feeling a rush of satisfaction as he crumples and falls.

But that's only harmless mental entertainment. It's never been a plan.

So then what are you doing to him instead?

"I'm going to expose him! Embarrass him! It may be too late to put him in jail, but if people knew all the terrible things he's done—the statutory rape, the harassment, the way he forces women to go along with him—it could really hurt his reputation. Maybe he wouldn't sell as many books. He might even lose his teaching job!"

Oh.

Niccolo goes quiet for a moment.

May I be honest, Shannon? That doesn't seem like much. For killing your sister.

"Maybe not. But it might be the best I can do."

But I feel myself deflating as I think it through again. Niccolo's right. Even if Pritchard's university did fire him, which is a big "if," he could still live off royalties and residuals and his wife's salary, and just keep pumping out books. A scandal might even boost his sales, the way this crazy world works.

But that crazy world is the one we live in. Powerful men accused of rape or sexual assault still get elected, confirmed, promoted, appointed, anointed, elevated.

I take a deep breath in, let it out slowly. Remembering what he did to Maureen. So young. Gone forever.

The white Jaguar slows; Pritchard has come to the junction where Bradford ends, and he makes the sharp right back onto the far east end of Commercial Street. He parks a block or so later. There are very few garages in a town built before cars were invented, so he has to park his fancy car on the street.

I pass by, turn off onto a side street and pull over.

"Be right back."

I lurk behind a hedge, watch as he and Wylie get out of the car. They walk towards a building right on the water. He goes upstairs; she goes around the back.

Lovers? Not lovers? Same building, different apartments. Could go either way.

I notice that he's positioned the Jag so it takes up two spaces. As one does, if one is an asshole.

How fun would it be to come back in the middle of the night, with a can of gasoline and a lighter? I imagine the intoxicating smell as I swing the can and splash the hood, the tires, and especially the leather upholstery. A huge roar as the fire catches, my absolute joy as I scurry away, undetected, laughing uncontrollably.

Probably too risky. But thrilling to think about.

CHAPTER SIX

ALLISON

I peek out the living room window yet again, willing Shannon's car to pull into the driveway. I wonder what she drives now? My guess would be something cool like a Mini-Cooper, but I know so little about her now. Even an Oscar Mayer Weinermobile wouldn't totally surprise me.

What will she think of me, of how I live? So of course I didn't manage to upgrade my entire life in time for her arrival. I couldn't even make a decent start at it. But at least I got the cottage ready. I scrubbed it clean, made up the bed in the loft, stacked up the fresh towels and washcloths, stocked the little fridge and the kitchenette with all the basics. I'm not charging her anything—how could I, she's Shannon! But Bobby's right, the place isn't very fancy. I hope she's comfortable enough.

Finally, a blue pickup truck pulls up and a red-haired woman gets out.

Is it her? It must be.

She walks around to the passenger side, grabs the handle of a gray plastic crate. I open the door just as she reaches the top step.

We stare at each other for a few seconds.

Shannon, the sexy rebel with the gorgeous face and curvy figure, the girl who got the boys so hot and bothered: she looks more like one of the cafeteria ladies now. Not unattractive, but, well, regular. Pleasant looking, overweight, middle-aged. I like that, actually. She seems approachable.

She's still stylish though: she's wearing leggings and a flowy top, and something about the pattern and fabric looks sophisticated. Especially compared to my cargo shorts and Boston Bruins T-shirt.

"Alley Cat! It's been way, way, way too long."

How had I forgotten she used to call me that?

"Shannon, oh my God, you're really here!"

She's got a huge smile, like she's genuinely happy to see me. She puts down the carrier and gives me a big hug. We just stand there grinning at each other. Her body is different, her face is different, but there's something about her eyes and her smile and her voice. She's still Shannon.

When she looks at you like that, it's like she's totally *there*, appreciating you. You feel special. You feel chosen, singled out.

But what now? I'm not good at being a host, at figuring out social next steps.

"Okay, first off," says Shannon, "I totally have to pee or I'm going to explode!"

At least that one's easy.

"It's down the hall, past the…"

She's already on her way. "Of course I remember where the bathroom is, doofus!"

I kneel down and peer into the crate.

The cat is fancy-looking, like it's an actual breed, and it has beautiful blue eyes.

"Hi there," I say, "aren't you pretty."

I curl my fingers inside the metal bars, and the cat approaches cautiously. Sniffs at me.

I hear the toilet flush. Shannon will be out soon; I should figure out whether to offer her something to eat or drink. Or maybe she just wants to get to the cottage and unpack?

I can feel the cat's warm breath against my knuckles. Then a wet nose.

"Are you a boy or a girl kitty?"

"He's a boy. Niccolo."

I feel silly: Shannon has just returned in time to catch me in the act of asking the cat a question.

"Oh crap," she says, "I totally forgot! You're allergic, right?"

"No, that was my dad," I say.

"Oh yeah, that's right."

She looks around the room. Taking in the unchanged state of things, probably, but she's being tactful, not saying anything.

"So how *are* your folks?" she asks. "They were always so nice to me. Even though they couldn't have been thrilled we were friends."

I've been dreading that question.

"So my dad's good, he moved to Miami. But my mom died a few years ago."

"Oh Jesus."

She looks stunned, her face goes slack. Then when she's taken it in, there's such a heavy sadness left in her expression. She spent so much time with my family that year, and she really did like my parents, especially my mom. I can tell she gets it.

"Covid?"

I shake my head. "Aneurysm. Totally out of the blue."

My mom never missed a check-up, ate more roughage than a rabbit, fed her greedy Fitbit well more than its 10,000 steps every day. She was supposed to live to be at least a hundred.

"I'm so, so sorry Allison. She was really special. And you guys were so close. That must have been so hard."

"Yeah."

I don't want to elaborate, to try to put it into words how ripped apart I've felt.

"How about your parents?" I ask. "Do they still live in that big house in Newton?"

It's the only "mansion" I've ever been in; so many rooms for one small family.

"Nah, they divorced, moved away a long time ago. And then my dad died a few years ago too, a heart attack. He was just your basic rich corporate fuckhead, and I hardly ever saw him, but even so, he was my dad, you know?"

It used to shock me how Shannon talked about her family. But it doesn't seem as shocking now, the world has changed so much.

"Sorry to hear that," I say.

"It's just weird not to get that Hallmark birthday card every year," she says, "the one his third wife would pick out for me and sign his name to."

I'm not sure whether to laugh or sympathize. When I knew her, her dad was almost never around. Shannon said when he was, he was distant and disagreeable.

"You want to sit down?" I ask.

"Sure. Oh, and can I let Niccolo out for a second so you can meet him? He's a real gentleman, he won't misbehave."

"Okay," I say.

I'm a little nervous around cats. I'm not sure how to interact with them.

She opens the door to the carrier.

The cat steps out, looks around. Should I pet him? You're supposed to, right? I reach towards his head, but he jumps back. I must not have done it right.

"And how's your mom?" I ask her.

"The Ice Queen is still very much alive! She's down in Florida too, in Saint Pete. And as far as I know, doing well. We don't really talk much."

And now I'm remembering: I learned pretty quickly never to say anything nice about her mother. Shannon wanted me to despise her just as much as she did. So superficial and fake, Shannon would say, how could I possibly fall for her act?

But I'd found her mother fascinating. She'd worked as a reporter for *Time* before she got married, and they'd sent her to exotic places all over the world—not very common for women back in the '70s. When I knew her, she still worked, closer to home, writing for a New England lifestyle magazine, big and glossy. I remember she cared a lot about words. She'd correct our grammar, but she'd also swear in front of us, like we were adult enough to take it in stride. She seemed bold, risqué.

The cat is making a production of sniffing at the carpet. Then he digs at it with his paws, rubs his face in it. It's the spot where I spilled a bowl of chicken noodle soup a year or so ago. I'd tried to soak it up with wet paper towels and dish soap, but apparently not successfully.

"She always liked you," Shannon says. "Kept wanting me to invite you over more often. You were so polite and reasonable and well-behaved. I guess she was hoping some of it might rub off."

"And Michael?" Her younger brother. All I remember is that he whined a lot and his nose was always runny.

"Okay, so get this: he's a Jehovah's Witness now."

"A Jehovah's Witness?"

"I haven't talked to him in years."

So it sounds like she's got no real family.

At least I have my dad. We only talk a couple times a month, and he's got a whole new life in Florida now—he's even started to date again. Which is normal and healthy and appropriate and completely horrifying. But even if we don't see each other much, I know my dad loves me, and he cares how I'm doing, and he'd be here for me in a heartbeat if I needed him.

The cat finally stops obsessing over carpet and goes over to Shannon, rubs against her legs.

"Okay," she says to him, "let's get you settled then."

"So," she says to me, "I'll just go get unpacked, take care of Niccolo. But after that, let's catch up a little more, okay?"

Shannon smiles again, looking right into my face like she's drinking me in.

"*So* good to see you again, Alley Cat."

* * *

I'm halfway through my Blue Moon, and Shannon's on her second IPA, when Bobby stops by. He's got a tray of stuffed grape leaves and an assortment of colorful cupcakes.

He puts the tray on the table. "Don't mean to interrupt, just some leftovers from a birthday party. I'll leave them right here and…"

"Wow, how festive, thank you!" says Shannon. "So sit down, join us! You must be…"

"I'm Bobby! The nosy gay neighbor."

"Well, I'm Shannon! The delinquent high-school friend. Want a beer or something?" she asks.

"One of those IPAs would be wonderful."

I get up to get Bobby the beer. It's my house, I know I should have been the one who asked him to stay, but I was too slow. Courtney was always the one inviting people over, taking the lead. I never had to figure that stuff out.

"These are to die for," Shannon says, eating one of the stuffed grape leaves.

I tried one once, so slimy and bitter, how can people eat them on purpose? I take a couple of cupcakes instead.

"So Allison may have told you that in addition to being the world's most fabulous bartender, I also have a catering business?"

"Allison hasn't said a word about you. I guess she must not like you very much."

"Shannon!"

"Just kidding, obviously. Mostly I've been yammering on about myself. But when I did let her get a word in edgewise, you seem to be among a very select few people she knows in Provincetown. Despite having lived here full-time for what, five years now, Allison?"

"Not even three! And some of that was during the pandemic. Which made it pretty hard to meet people."

Bobby shakes his head. "I do my best to try to get her out there, Shannon."

Shannon's been asking me about my friends, how I keep busy, what events and parties I go to in town. So embarrassing, because I have nothing to say. She was also curious about all the rich and famous people who have summer homes here, or come for festivals. Like she was hoping I'd gotten to know some. But I only catch glimpses now and then, it's not like I'm friends with any of them.

"We'll have to join forces while I'm here," Shannon says to Bobby. "See what kind of trouble we can get her into. That was always my specialty."

"Excellent idea," Bobby says, rubbing his hands together like some kind of cartoon villain.

"Oh my God, look at her face, we're scaring her!" says Shannon.

They are, a little.

"I mean, she does leave the house for groceries," Bobby says. "And she's one of those do-gooders, she drives old ladies to their medical appointments, picks up trash on the beach, that sort of thing."

"She was always like that," says Shannon. "She'd give a hungry stray dog her lunch, talk to the old one-legged guy at the bus stop. Always the designated driver, the mopper-upper of messes. Saved my sorry ass a few times."

"I did?"

"You did! Like that party where I got totally wasted and was about to head out the door with those biker guys? Going to some party at a warehouse because they said Madonna was going to be there, and I totally believed them?"

I'd forgotten all about that. They were so rough looking, already high on something. "Oh God, you're right. I was petrified I'd never see you again!"

"She lured me away from them with the promise of a Dunkin' Donuts run," Shannon explains.

It was sweet of Shannon to share that story, but we both know the truth: *she* was the one who saved *me* during high school.

After we share a few more memories, Bobby drains the last of his beer.

"So, time to get ready for tea. You're coming with me, right girls?"

"Tea?" asks Shannon.

She wouldn't know; we were too young when she was here.

"Tea Dance at the Boatslip. It's a great party. Everyone goes. I keep telling Allison how fun it is, but I can never get her to come along."

"Sounds fun! Count me in," says Shannon.

"I don't know," I say.

All those people, the noise, the chance of Covid; a terrible idea.

"I'll swing by in half an hour, we can all walk over together," says Bobby. "You work on her, Shannon."

But when Bobby leaves Shannon doesn't even mention Tea Dance. Instead, she asks the other question I was afraid might be coming.

"So, Alley Cat, you seeing anyone?"

CHAPTER SEVEN

ALLISON

"I can't believe this, it's so fucking fun!" shouts Shannon, or at least I think that's what she's shouting.

"It totally is!" I shout back, *dancing in public*, of all things, with Shannon and what seems like a thousand other people on the dance floor.

I'm getting slimed by sweaty shirtless men and doused with spilled drinks. Probably catching Covid, because I never took my mask out of my back pocket. Setting myself up for possible hangover tomorrow with a potent rum punch.

But it's not tomorrow yet, and we're all like one big amoeba together, me and Shannon and all these random people. Swinging and shuffling and pumping and swaying and spinning and jumping up and down, up and down during the choruses, shouting out lyrics to songs we've heard a hundred times before. It took me a song or two to loosen up, let the beats in, surrender. Watching Shannon helped. Such wild, hilarious moves, like it's all in quotes, she's laughing at herself—but at the same time she's blissfully enjoying every gyration.

The song ends and Shannon motions like she'd like to take a break and I'm ready for one too, it's been so many songs in a row. A little fresh air would be great.

We have to push our way through so many people to find a good spot to chill, on the railing overlooking the water. I scan the crowd for Bobby and finally spot him in line at one of the bars, talking with a tall bald guy nearly covered in tattoos. Every time I've seen him he's been talking to a different guy; he sure gets around.

But that's okay, I don't need him to babysit me. I have Shannon. Who knew this would be so entertaining?

I'd pictured the crowd being all young and trendy, but maybe because Tea Dance starts in at four in the afternoon, there are millennials and Gen X and even boomers here. A big group of people dressed like bunny rabbits from some private party, quite a few men in drag, some bachelorettes dressed like cowgirls. On the dance floor, a couple of earnest looking men were doing an elaborate flag routine like high school cheerleaders, and a stubborn pair of older lesbians kept swing dancing like it was some '50s sock hop, looking miffed whenever anyone bumped into them. And the two straight couples right next to us were so cute, looking fresh off a bus from Milwaukee.

I return my gaze to the water, half-listening to the party atmosphere behind us. Shannon does the same, but our silence feels companionable, not awkward.

After a few minutes, she decides to go get us another round of drinks.

"Just a water," I say, and I turn around to watch her thread her way through the crowd. Eventually she runs into Bobby, also in line for a drink. They're laughing, faces close together. It looks like she's teasing him about something, and he's dishing it right back. They're both so handsy with each other too, especially for people who've just met.

I love that they're getting along, but at the same time it stings a little, to see them bond so easily. They both belong to a different, hardier species than I do, able to adapt and thrive in any social climate. I'll never be like Shannon.

But… could I become a more Shannon-like Allison?

I couldn't quite do it on my own. But her being here, I already feel something shifting, opening up. That was *me* out there on the dance floor, shaking and shimmying like a wild woman. Maybe Shannon brought a little magic with her after all?

"Drink up!" says Shannon. She's back with Bobby, my water, and Mai Tai I didn't ask for. "We gotta get back in there. Bobby says the last half hour is not to be missed!"

And Bobby is right. I've never tried ecstasy, but I imagine this is what it must feel like: a tremendous rush of excitement and a floaty feeling of goodwill, even love, for everyone here as we all move together to the same propulsive beats.

Then suddenly it's seven o'clock, time to go. We all head out to the street, tired but happy and buzzy, part of the nightly Great Tea Dance exodus.

How many times have I seen this same sweaty mob streaming out of the Boatslip? Everyone talking at the top of their lungs because of all the drinks and the music-induced temporary deafness, acting unreasonably giddy and gleeful.

And now I am one of them, they are my people!

* * *

"Wow, look at that humongous line!" I say.

Four days after our initial Tea Dance adventure, we're all back at the Boatslip again to give it another go.

We can see out to the crowded deck behind the entrance: every square inch is packed with gorgeous young gay men, many of them shirtless, crammed so closely together it looks like they've been superglued.

"Oh sorry," says Bobby, "I should have mentioned. Fourth of July weekend, the Twinks all come to town, things can get crazy. I've got a season pass, so no line for me, but if you want me to wait with you…"

But Bobby doesn't seem to mind at all when Shannon tells him we'll head somewhere else for a cocktail. And I realize I'm glad too; instead of shouting over the din of a packed dancefloor, I'll get to have one more "girls night" with Shannon before her workshop starts. I've gotten spoiled: we've been spending every evening together, strolling down Commercial Street. And Shannon's been doing this whole *Queer Eye* makeover with me. But backwards I guess. Straight eye for the queer gal?

At first I was reluctant. But she talked me into going to a trendy salon, and I ended up with a very cool haircut, much closer on the sides. And next some new sunglasses, and after that it was shoes, and by then I trusted her enough to take on the whole wardrobe issue. We go to the men's stores, because Shannon gets it. Tonight I have on a retro-style bowling shirt, and snug but flattering shorts in a fancy fabric, and some super fun boat shoes. A total upgrade from my usual baggy T-shirts and cargo shorts.

Then, after shopping, we go out for drinks, then dinner, talking and giggling the whole time, catching up on the last thirty years. Finally we walk back home, appreciating the crazy nightlife, everyone in good spirits. Courtney didn't like the crowds, found the buskers and street musicians tiresome. But Shannon loves the party atmosphere. In fact, she even goes out again just as I'm getting ready for bed. She has so much energy!

She suggests Harbor Lounge for drinks, which sounds perfect, so we thread our way eastward against the tide of hot hunky guys heading to Tea.

Then I see her.

Chloe is heading our way! She's walking by herself, headphones on, absorbed in her own world. That's the thing about Commercial Street, eventually you run into everyone in town.

"What?" asks Shannon. My face must have given me away. "Is that Chloe?"

I nod.

Chloe glances around like she's looking for something. Then veers over, heading for a bench. I notice the dangling laces on her right shoe, and sure enough, she props up her foot.

"So wait," Shannon says, stopping in her tracks. "You're not just going to walk right past her, are you?"

Shannon opens her purse, searching for something.

"Lose your phone?"

"No, silly, haven't you ever spied on anyone before? I'm just pretending, giving us a reason to hold up."

As Shannon paws through her purse, I look over at Chloe, watching the meticulous way she double knots her laces, then starts on the other shoe for good measure. How could that be something that makes me melt?

I've told Shannon all about my pathetic false hopes, how the interrupted "would you be interested" conversation never got finished. She couldn't believe Chloe and I just went right back to chatting at the coffee shop about nothing in particular, not mentioning it, not making any plans together. And then Chloe started traveling more for work; I've hardly seen her.

My theory is that Chloe's not interested in dating me. And so I don't want to ruin a potential friendship by putting her on the spot. Shannon's theory is that we're both just chicken. "Straight people have a default asker-outer," she said. "It may be sexist, but it comes in handy. You can't both be dainty princesses too fragile to risk rejection. Someone has to step up!"

Her laces secure, Chloe is now walking right toward us.

"Allison, c'mon," says Shannon. "You can do it. At least ask her if she wants to come join us for drinks. You got this."

Chloe catches sight of me. She smiles in surprise. A big, beautiful, happy-to-see-me smile. And what makes me especially ecstatic is the surprised part. She sees me unexpectedly in the wild and is genuinely happy about it!

She takes out her earbuds. That seems like a good sign too.

"Hey Chloe, you're back in town, great to see you!"

"Yeah, the nurses' strike finally settled, thank God."

"Oh good."

Shannon lifts her eyebrows, cocks her head impatiently, the equivalent of an elbow to my ribs.

"So this is Shannon, my old friend from high school."

"Oh right! I didn't know that was this week."

I'm actually glad to run into Chloe during the rare moment when I appear to be someone with friends, who does things outside the house. Chloe has mentioned parties and gatherings, so I know she's not as socially backwards as I am.

I take a deep breath. It's time to try to channel my new alter ego, the Allison who's more confident and proactive. Like Shannon.

"We were just going to Harbor to get a drink. Any chance you want to come along?"

But her face falls.

"Oh shoot, can't, I have this beach fire thing to go to. The string people. And their significant others and kids and everything."

"The string people?"

It's hard to picture.

"I guess I didn't mention. I'm in a string quartet. We're not good or anything, we just get together every couple of weeks for fun. We do this bonfire every summer. But maybe another time…"

"Cool," I say. "Another time then."

I give her my best cheerful "whatever, I'm not crushed but it would have been nice" smile. Though I'm actually kind of crushed.

"Wait," she says. "Would you like to come along?"

She says it to me, but then looks over at Shannon as well. "I mean you'd both be welcome."

"Sounds like fun," says Shannon, not faking it particularly well, "but I'm afraid I can't. I've got a workshop starting tomorrow, I should really get prepared. But Allison, you should totally go!"

What? By myself?

A beach party full of complete strangers. Musical strangers, who've known each other for years and are probably all very sophisticated.

Shannon gives me a death stare, like if I blow this she'll never speak to me again.

"Um, sure, I'd love to!"

* * *

"So I have to warn you, it's a mess, I didn't know anyone would be coming," says Chloe, as we approach her condo building.

We didn't have enough time for me to go home first, so the plan is to go to her place, and she'll lend me a jacket, because it gets breezy when the sun goes down, and we'll also pick up the food and beach supplies. Then take her car out to Herring Cove and meet her friends there.

I'm a foot taller than she is, so I have my doubts about how this jacket is supposedly going to fit. I'm hoping she has an extra towel or a blanket that I can drape around myself as a plan B.

The condo is in a newish complex, five or six buildings densely packed together, outside the historic district. Her ground floor unit looks basement-y, because the back side of the building nestles into a sandy hill. Sure enough, when we enter, only one side has windows and they're not very big.

"It's tiny," she says, "and gloomy, and it came with this ugly generic furniture. And it cost me a fortune. But then, that's Ptown, right?"

"But wow, everything looks so nice and new. And I don't know what you mean by 'it's a mess.' What, you've got one neatly stacked pile of mail on the counter?"

But she's right, it's gloomy. And sterile. I've watched enough HGTV to know how horribly worn down my place looks. But this condo seems equally depressing, just in the opposite direction. The floors are that gray-tinted fake wood that everyone's using these days. The furniture is all cold metal, dark leather and glass, like office furniture. Stark white walls, probably to compensate for the lack of windows. No pictures, just a couple of artificial plants.

"I don't spend that much time here," she says, as though she knows what I'm thinking. "My 'remote' job turned out to be a lot less remote once the pandemic started easing up. I thought I'd get to spend more time here and fix it up. Hopefully eventually."

"Yeah, no, it's great."

She opens a closet door, takes out a couple of sweatshirts and jackets that look to be as tiny as I was fearing they'd be. A cooler, some mosquito spray, and a beach chair.

"So I only have one chair. But you can sit in it, I'll just sit on a towel."

"It's your beach fire! I'm totally good with a towel."

"No way, you're my guest. My mother would die if she knew I invited someone somewhere, and then took the only chair. You don't want to kill my mother, do you?"

I try to laugh, but I don't do it well, and then suddenly her expression shifts into a look of horror.

"Oh my God," she says. "I forgot; you lost your mother. Such a dumb thing to say!"

"No, that's okay! It happened a few years ago. And I only mentioned it, like, once."

I feel for her, because who remembers all the details? And she has no way of knowing I'm still sensitive about it.

"I can't imagine," she says. "My mother drives me crazy sometimes, but mothers… they're always there, right? That's their thing. The good ones anyway. To not have that anymore…sorry. I'm not making sense."

She's totally making sense.

And her face, compassionate, like she gets it.

"My mom and I used to talk on the phone, practically every night." My voice is a little husky, so I clear my throat before I go on. "And so I still find myself mentally narrating my day, you know? Compiling these boring little stories about how my banking app locked me out, or that I saw a huge coyote run across the road, or that I found a twenty-dollar bill in an old pair of jeans. And I keep doing it, even though she's the one the stories are for. But… she can't hear them anymore."

Oh goddamn it, now there are tears. I'm crying, and I never do that.

Chloe looks stricken. There's such a sweet pained look on her face. I'm afraid she might try to give me a sympathy hug; I'm never sure what to do with those. Plus I'm all snotty.

She digs a Kleenex out of her pocket and hands it to me.

"Thanks," I say, wiping up. "Sorry."

"No!" she says. "My fault. And it's supposed to be good, right? Feeling stuff?"

"In theory." I try to smile.

The silence gets too awkward and so she takes the cooler over to the refrigerator. I'm not sure if I should follow her—would it be more normal to wait for her here in the living room?

"So what's it like, having Shannon here? You said you hadn't seen her since high school?"

I guess this is my cue to go ahead and join her in the kitchen. I'm glad we've moved on to other subjects.

"Pretty cool, actually. So many years, but then in some ways, it's like no time has passed at all!"

She starts taking Tupperware out of the fridge. "Sushi, teriyaki chicken, and seaweed salad."

The chicken sounds good. I'm hoping I can discretely pick out the icky things from the sushi and just eat the rice. But there's no way the seaweed salad is happening.

"She always was pretty inspirational, in her own crazy way," I say. "She's helping me get out of the house a little more, I think it's good for me. She's this major extrovert, and I'm, well… basically a hermit."

"Same here! Actually, that's why I make myself do the string quartet."

"You? But you seem so much more comfortable, like, socially."

"What?"

"No, seriously, you're so easy to talk to. You're good at it. You make such great observations, ask such good questions."

"You're so funny. You're the one who's easy to talk to! Comfortable to be with. Such a great sense of humor. And you actually listen to what people say, you're not just waiting to talk about yourself."

Me? Comfortable to be with? No one ever says that. I've always been the outsider, the derp, the freak, trying to fake being normal but never quite pulling it off.

"But you've got lots of friends," I remind her. "I hole up; you go out and do things."

"I've got work friends. I've got brothers and sisters and cousins, so lots of family events I have to go to. Back when I was with Eileen, we had our couple friends. But then once we broke up, it was really clear they weren't really *our* friends. Just hers."

Same with me and Courtney. Courtney was the one who picked our friends, so I wasn't surprised when she took them all away with her, along with everything else we'd accumulated together.

"Their loss," I say. "I mean seriously. Who *wouldn't* want to hang out with you? You're awesome. You're smart, and funny, and kind, and so pretty. You must know that, right?"

She looks at me, just staring, not laughing or smiling.

Oh crap. What just got into me?

I've gone way too far. I especially didn't need to add the "so pretty" part.

But the more I get to know Chloe, the prettier she seems. That smile. The way her face is expressive, but not in a showy way. Like she's always thinking about things, but meaningful, personal things, and doesn't always need to tell the world about them.

"Allison," she says.

Damn.

It's already time for the Talk. And I know she doesn't want to have it with me any more than I want to hear it. It's the "You're really nice but I don't think of you that way" talk.

"Allison," she repeats, taking a deep breath. "Oh God. I'm really not good at this. But, are you okay if we skip the beach fire thing?"

"Yeah, no problem."

"And, um, can I kiss you?"

I nod. I'm actually shaking a little as I reach over, put my hand on her upper arm, lean in and try to remember how to do this. It's been a long time. Courtney was never big on kissing.

But wow. It seems I'm remembering just fine.

CHAPTER EIGHT

SHANNON

The ten-minute walk from the Fine Arts Center to the cottage isn't nearly long enough for me to clear my head. Storyboarding, thumbnails, inking… my brain is still back in the classroom, absorbing, assimilating. There's just so much to learn about writing a graphic novel! To create an entire narrative, gradually unfolding with layered complexity over hundreds of pages—what a huge challenge, compared to painting a single still image.

But I have to say I'm intrigued.

I open the door and Niccolo dashes across the room, rams his head against my legs over and over, welcomes me with adorable feline enthusiasm. I try to imagine humans greeting each other the same way: bashing the tops of our heads against the bodies of our loved ones. Makes me smile.

Shannon you're home! Hooray!

I pick him up and we snuggle. Then I lower him to the floor, go grab a beer from the tiny fridge and sit down, trying to relax.

I don't love it here, honestly.

The recliner I'm sitting in smells of body odor and stale tobacco. I know Allison tried her best to clean up, I could smell the Windex, but the cottage is a dump. Decades of dirt, spills, and excretions have settled into every pore of the fabrics. The walls have chips and smears and spatters. Mold creeps into the sleeping loft from the leaky roof—where spiderwebs have already appeared, with active inhabitants. I bunk downstairs on the saggy sofa bed instead, making it up every night with scratchy sheets and a musty hand-quilted bedspread—probably an heirloom, but in dire need of dry cleaning. I didn't tell Allison, but after the first night I found a deal for new sheets and a fleece blanket online—I can't wait for them to get here.

I take a long swallow of my beer.

And poor Allison. Still sweet and earnest, so easy to be around, but so different than what I was hoping. Stuck and floundering. And so timid. As smart as she is, I thought she'd have life figured out better by now.

I wonder, if I hadn't given her a push—would she and Chloe have ever gotten together? Or would they have stayed in coffeeshop purgatory for all eternity, sipping French roast pour-overs and sneaking sad, longing looks at each other?

They're sure together now, though. Allison is besotted, it's Chloe this and Chloe that. Bobby and I had a beer last night with the two of them, and I honestly don't get it. Chloe's so serious and uptight. Didn't laugh much at my jokes. I don't think she knew what to do with me.

It's been frustrating. I'd thought I'd be trailing Pritchard around the whole time, finding out where he prowls and what he gets up to.

I got myself sidetracked, is the problem, trying to jumpstart Allison's stalled social life. But how could I not? She was so appreciative! She insisted on paying for our dinners, keeping me out of bankruptcy given the prices here. And, unlike Brian, she loves hearing my stories and appreciates my weird sense of humor.

It's too bad though. I'd planned to tell her everything by now. I'd thought she'd be my co-conspirator—dialed-in, useful. So much for that. Especially with my intentions so murky, still evolving. I need to leave her out of it.

Mind if I join you?

"Sure, c'mon up!"

Niccolo lands heavily onto my thighs. Then circles, tickling my nose with the tip of his tail before finally settling down into my lap.

How did it go today? Better than last night?

We'd both had such high hopes for the opening reception, attended by students and teachers from all the various workshops. My first opportunity to meet Wylie and chat her up, as well as see what I could learn about Pritchard.

But I couldn't get anywhere near her. She was standing next to Pritchard the whole time, surrounded by sycophantic students, all competing for his attention. He'd even put a proprietary hand on her arm every now and then. Pritchard was in his element, slathered in admiration. Watching him, I felt an electric sizzle: like spotting a demon escaped from the underworld, visible only to an unfortunate few. But all I could do was drink my wine, eat my Brie and crackers, and listen to the frustrated artistic dreams of a retired orthodontist from New Jersey.

I did tense up when Pritchard glanced around the room, but his gaze paused only twice: to take in another well-known author, then to rest appreciatively on a young blonde in a mini skirt. His eyes slid right over me. It's been decades after all; hundreds of students passing through his classrooms. I needn't have worried.

I just wish I had more to tell Niccolo. I know he's eager for me to put things in motion, to finally close the books on this despicable man who's haunted me for so many years.

"Afraid I still didn't get the chance for any one-on-one with Wylie today," I tell him.

She was in a hurry, left right after class, and I couldn't very well chase after her, not without seeming like some kind of weirdo.

"But at least the class was pretty interesting. Five other students. And I'm the only one who hasn't written a graphic novel before. But you know what? It's actually something I might want to try out! I think I could be pretty good at it."

Niccolo yawns, starts licking his paw. I suppose concepts like "graphic novels" aren't all that relatable to a cat.

"Wylie's different than I thought, though."

He stops licking and looks up. *Is she?*

"Friendly enough, but not coy, more matter-of-fact. Not a lightweight. Probably about thirty? But she seems seasoned. Like she's been around; seen some things. I'm surprised Pritchard went after her. I expected someone perky, naïve. More malleable."

Is that a good thing, do you think? Or a bad thing?

"I guess it cuts both ways? She's more likely to see through him, so maybe that gives me more of an opening. But then she'd also be more likely to see through *me*. So, harder to manipulate."

Have you decided what you're going to do to him yet? I do so hope we get to kill him!

I laugh, though a bit uneasily. Niccolo still thinks that's the simplest answer. And there's a part of me that sometimes wonders…

"I haven't decided yet, sweetheart. It's complicated."

My original plan, to somehow get the goods on Pritchard and expose him, is turning out to be a lot harder than I thought. And it might not even do him much damage. But it's by far the least risky.

The problem is, every time I remember what he did—laying hands on an innocent fourteen-year-old girl, violating her, corrupting her, then abandoning her to die a pointless death—I can barely contain my rage. I want him to suffer. To know what it feels like to be the victim for once, instead of the perpetrator.

I keep imagining the charred husk of his once-sleek white Jaguar. Or his rental on the water: ransacked and trashed, with all of his clothes and electronics and fishing gear and everything else I can find tossed into the bay, carried away by the tides. A roofie slipped into his drink, and when he's passed out and defenseless, a dozen vigorous blows from a tire iron to his kneecaps. Nudged off a pier, pushed down a steep stairwell, jostled in front of an oncoming car, shot right between the eyes…

Whoa there. I need to get a grip.

Good people don't let themselves go there, do they?

Especially not women.

We feel grief and rage. But we look to the authorities to make things right again. We don't take justice into our own hands. In every Hollywood revenge fantasy I've ever seen, that's a man's job, not a woman's.

What would it feel like to commit a daring, dramatic, irreversible act? The triumph! The panic! The thrilling horror of it.

My heart is beating fast; I've gotten myself too riled up.

I take a slow deep breath. Remind myself I haven't done anything wrong. I've committed no actual crimes. No one can see inside my skull at the movies playing inside.

But it might be a good idea to dial it back a bit.

"So how are you doing, Niccolo?" I refocus on my precious baby boy. "Are you happy here?"

I am, Shannon! I have my favorite window to look out of, and sometimes I see dogs and squirrels and chipmunks!

I'm glad at least one of us is enjoying this funky little rathole.

And there are so many interesting smells. Not like at home where you're always wiping spills away before they even have a chance to decay. Plus the loft! It's high up, so I can see everything, and it reminds me of my old days in the woods. That lovely damp, mossy aroma.

"You don't mind the spiderwebs and the spiders?"

Of course not Shannon, I am a cat! And all kinds of other insects come in through the holes in the window screens. At home I hardly ever get to kill things.

"How nice for you."

There's just one thing lacking, Shannon, something that would make this whole experience absolute perfection. If you could just consider…

"Afraid not, Niccolo. I'm not letting you go outside."

But it's my only chance! The other cats aren't here to attack me like at home. I promise I'll stay very close by.

I feel for him, poor guy. Animals should be free to go outdoors now and then, where they feel more truly themselves. I hate to be a Brian—his jailer.

"I'm sorry, sweetheart. But there are coyotes here. I just can't risk it, you're too important."

I do hope you will reconsider, Shannon.

He looks so disappointed.

There's a loud knock at the door; Niccolo leaps off my lap and dives under the sofa.

"I come bearing gifts," says Bobby when I answer.

"Is it what we talked about?"

"It is! I thought I'd stop by while Allison and Chloe are off to get groceries. You're going over for the Fourth?"

"I am. Come on in," I say, motioning him inside.

Bobby breezes through the door, crisp and bronze and muscular, tightly packed into a pair of teal shorts and a multi-colored flowered shirt, smelling of cologne and minty mouthwash. How I've missed gay male energy! Naughty, stylish, hormonal, creative. It's been so long since I've lived anywhere that gay men cared to congregate.

"How about you?" I ask. "I don't want to feel like a third wheel."

"Yeah, I'll be there too, as it turns out," he says. "Had a catering gig for some old-money queens up from Savannah, but with the shitty weather, they canceled."

"So what do you think she'll serve? Unless Chloe can cook, I'm predicting, what, hot dogs, Doritos, and Hostess cupcakes?"

"Right? I've never seen Allison cook. Or eat anything green, unless it was guacamole or an M&M."

Niccolo crawls out from under the couch.

"Hey buddy," says Bobby.

Niccolo greets him with a cheerful meow, and even rubs against one of his legs.

So you like Bobby? I ask Niccolo.

I do! He has very hairy calves and he smells nice, like a deer.

Now that Niccolo mentions it, I do notice a hint of musk in Bobby's cologne.

I go over to the desk in the corner, cheap particleboard with the white veneer coming loose on the sides. I wrench open the sticky top drawer to take out my cash.

"Really appreciate it. I'm only microdosing, but I just wanted to make sure I don't run low."

He hands me the baggy and pockets the cash.

"They seem to level me out," I explain. "I've even been able to drop a couple of prescriptions."

"Natural remedies are so much healthier," he says. "And we can keep this just between the two of us, right? Allison doesn't know about my little side hustle. It would totally stress her out."

"She's so wholesome, it's adorable. And yeah, she thinks every time you talk to some guy or get a text that you're trying to hook up with him."

"Well, *sometimes* I am. But I'm not seventeen anymore. I'm super small-time though. Just psychedelics, X. Maybe a little off label help for anxiety, depression, ADHD, that sort of thing."

"Providing essential public services without all the bureaucratic hassles?"

"Exactly!"

After Bobby leaves, Niccolo nudges my calves.

I'm wondering if I can get my dinner now? A green can would be lovely, he says.

I glop the can into his bowl, it's a stinky beef stew, one of his favorites. But when I put it down, he just stares at it.

"What's wrong, sweetheart?"

He looks up at me.

Shannon, he says, *I realize I'm a bit confused about something.*

"What about?"

What happens if you haven't managed to do anything about that horrible man when it's time to go? Do we just go back home, and let him go unpunished?

I've been wondering the same thing.

"I sure hope that won't happen. But I don't have a lot of time. And I'm not even sure what my next move should be."

Why did I think it would be easier than this?

He looks down at his bowl, but he's still not eating. He looks back up at me.

I guess sometimes I forget that you're… well, just human.

I ease myself down, sit cross-legged on the kitchen floor so I can see his face better.

"Just what are you saying?"

I mean no offense! I can't open a can of my own food, let alone use computers or cars. But we cats are experts at hunting. We're fearless. And ruthless. We stalk. We obsess. We pursue our prey with endless patience. We take risks. We see things through to the very end. That is, if we are truly hungry.

He's looking right into my eyes.

But other times, we might bat our prey around a bit. Then lift our paws back up and let them escape, just so we can nab them all over again. Just for fun. And maybe that's what this is? Maybe you just want to play with him a little, because you're not very hungry?

Wow. So unfair.

Because I *do* feel a hunger for revenge. In fact I'm starving for it. But it's so much harder than he realizes. It's not like I can just pounce on Pritchard and bite his head off, the way Niccolo could dispatch a rodent.

"You think I'm just… playing around?"

I'm so sorry Shannon! I didn't mean to make you mad. It's just… I'm afraid if I don't encourage you, remind you why we're here, then nothing will happen to that terrible man.

I still feel a bit sulky. But after I sit with it a minute, I have to admit, he's got a point. In all the times I've come after Pritchard, I've never even batted him around, let alone "finished the kill." I just leave. No justice for Maureen. No closure for me.

Still haunted.

I pet Niccolo a couple of times to let him know that I'm not angry with him anymore. He's only trying to look out for me, after all.

* * *

The classroom is so quiet. My neck is starting to ache; we've been at it for hours. Only the second day of class, but we're already deeply into the work. I look up from my drawing: Six heads, all bent over the big round table, everyone scratching away on their sketchpads, including Wylie. But I guess it would be strange if she were just sitting there staring at us.

Outside it's drizzly and gloomy, but not pouring yet. Big rains coming later. Poor Allison. It must be Chloe who's pushing her to do something for the Fourth. Allison will be totally dreading this, even though it's only the four of us.

I return to my sketches. Our exercise for today was to try to capture an "in-between time" for a character: a few quiet moments of transition, reflection, or transformation. But we're supposed to try to use images instead of words.

At least now I have a little more sense of where I'm going with all this. But it wasn't until this morning, on my way to class, that I realized what my book will be about. My sister, of course!

I'm calling her Colleen instead of Maureen. She's a high school girl in an elite private school back in the '90s, coping with intense academic demands, a predatory teacher, and unsympathetic classmates. But because the real story is too depressing, I'm embracing the comic-book possibilities of the format. Instead of having a younger sister, who loved her but was incapable of saving her, Colleen will discover she has some sort of superpower. She'll ultimately triumph over the villainous teacher, and will save herself and other girls from his heartless exploitation.

I'm pleased with my progress so far. The three panels are only supposed to be rough sketches, and I'm almost finished with the last one. In the first, we see Colleen from middle distance, sitting on a bench outside the school library. Her shoulders are hunched, her hands limp in her lap. Her eyes stare vacantly and her face looks slack, like she's in shock.

Then next, from closer up: we can see the tear stains, the red swollen eyes. She's squinting slightly now, and her hands have closed into fists.

In the third drawing, the shadows have changed, the sun shines from a different angle. Something has caught Colleen's eye. She's turned her face, tilted her head slightly. Intent on what she sees. She's sitting up straighter, her body more energized, her hands on the bench now, as though any moment she might use them for leverage, rising up and…

Doing what?

What is it that she sees?

The fun part is that I don't know yet. But whatever it is, it will change her life.

I use the last few minutes of class to do some shading, correct and refine some of the roughest parts of my sketches.

When her phone alarm goes off, Wylie looks up from her sketchpad and fumbles for it, a little dazed. Like the sound has rousted her from a world she was fully immersed in.

"I guess it's time then! Have a great Fourth, everyone. If you've finished, I'll take your drawings, give you some feedback tomorrow. Or you can hang on to them if you're still working on them."

Two others besides me have finished. They hand over their drawings.

I "accidentally" elbow a couple of pencils off the table, sigh, then awkwardly lower myself to retrieve them. When I'm back in my chair, I look at my phone, frown and shake my head, as though I just got an important but inconvenient text. I pretend to reply. I put my phone back in my purse, fumble around getting my papers together, and make a big production out of gathering up my supplies and putting them in my satchel. Now everyone has left but Wylie.

She's not in such a rush today, she's returned to her sketchpad. A dragon, artfully drawn, with a sensitive, intelligent face.

"Wow. So different from *Nom de Guerre*," I say.

This looks more accessible. Probably a smart career move.

"Ah, you read my bio," she says, drawing a few more scales on the dragon's tail.

I finished the book late last night; I got totally caught up in it. It was about a French family during World War II. The mother and teenage daughter were secretly working for the resistance, while the father, an official in the Vichy government, was too busy trying to appease the Nazis to realize it. The harrowing tension of keeping up a false front, living one life on the surface while secretly risking everything—I found it inspiring.

"I didn't think I'd like it, actually," I say. I'm pretty sure she's the type who prefers bluntness to bullshitting. "War and genocide? I figured it would just be depressing. But something about it drew me in, made me keep going. And the ending… I mean so bittersweet, right? But also, well, beautiful."

"So you actually found a copy, and read it?" she asks, putting down her pencil.

She looks up at me curiously, like only now is she actually seeing me standing there.

"It was cool," I say, "the way you used the family dynamics as kind of a shorthand for the political stuff. With all the right-wing fuckery going on in our country, it seems kinda relevant."

She closes the cover of her sketch pad.

"So not only did you find a copy, and read the whole thing, but you understood what I was getting at?"

I shrug.

"That makes, like, four people. You. Me. The guy on the awards committee who talked the rest of them into calling me 'promising.' And the poor editor who actually paid me money to publish it. I wonder if she still has a job now?"

"Well, it was your first one. Probably takes a while to get traction, huh?"

She gives me a sad smile. "So they say."

I hand her my drawings.

"I hadn't actually read any graphic novels before. So I thought I might as well start with yours."

She tilts her head, and almost starts to say something. But doesn't.

She glances at my drawings. But instead of putting them in the pile with the others, she lays them out on the table, looks them over.

She takes her time. Her face is unreadable. I feel myself coiling up, already defensive.

"Hmm. Not your first rodeo. What, MFA? Or did you go the more commercial route?"

I exhale, relax again.

"Neither. But yeah, I've had some classes. I wasn't sure if I was going to major in art or literature in college, did both for a while. But didn't end up graduating. I was… kinda fucked up back then."

"Yeah, well. I may be biased, but people who've had a smoother ride… they're not as good at this. I mean, look at this girl's face: Pain. Numbness. Repressed rage. So much seething below the surface. And this last panel, the sense of suspense… what is it she's looking at? The reader's got to be curious about that."

"Oh good, that's what I was hoping. But I wasn't sure if…"

Something moves in my peripheral vision and Wylie's face shifts in the same moment. I turn my head.

And there he is at the door.

Grant Pritchard.

I'd forgotten how tall he is. It's more obvious now that he's up close, looming.

I feel like the ground under my feet has turned into ice, and he's cracked it wide open and I'm falling into frigid water. I feel a panic all out of proportion to the situation. I don't know if my legs will even work to propel me out of there.

I turn back to Wylie, try to breathe, focus on her face, be appropriate.

"Sorry to interrupt," says Pritchard. "When you're done, Wylie, if I could have a moment of your time?"

His voice is dry and precise, condescending. I don't remember him sounding so prissy when Maureen and I were in high school.

"I was just leaving," I say. "Thanks Wylie, have a great Fourth."

I pick up my satchel. As I move closer, Pritchard isn't stepping aside, he's not leaving me much room to get through the door.

His glacial blue eyes meet mine.

I steel myself, walk past him out to the parking lot. It's not until I take a deep thirsty drag of fresh air that I realize I've been holding my breath.

I haven't been that close up before, not since I was a student in his English class. Terrifying. His eyes drilled into me, his tight smile so menacing, nothing amiable about it.

The truth hits me: He's dangerous.

He has the eyes of a psychopath. He will stop at nothing to protect himself if he feels threatened.

Do I have any evidence of that? No. But still, I know it with absolute certainty. I could see it so clearly.

There will be no batting him around, no half-measures, no playing. I can't just wound him, enrage him, then expect to go about my life, tranquil and unburdened. If I decide to take him on, it's him or me.

I should either back off and leave him alone… or see it through to the end. So how important is justice for Maureen? Is it worth risking *everything*?

I'm walking quickly, trying to get as far away as possible. But then, as I start to turn down the street, I notice how light my satchel feels.

Shit. I look inside, and sure enough my purse isn't in there. I've left it behind. I have to go back.

He's still in there with Wylie, sounding loud and petulant, though I can't make out the words. I sit on a bench, partly obscured by landscaping, pretending to read our class syllabus until I finally see him leaving.

Fortunately he doesn't look directly at me as he strides furiously across the parking lot.

Just a tiff between work colleagues? I don't think so. This was personal.

Did she not step deferentially enough around his gigantic ego? Could he have caught her flirting with someone more age appropriate?

I give Wylie a couple minutes; she's probably upset. He's scary enough when he's *not* yelling.

I poke my head in the door.

"Sorry to bother you," I say. "It's just…"

"Shannon, oh good! Your purse. And your phone's in there too, so I wasn't sure how I'd get a hold of you."

She's trying to pretend nothing's going on, but she looks rattled.

"So… everything okay?"

I keep it light and casual, not syrupy.

"Famous writer dude looked pretty irate on his way out," I say.

She looks up at me. Hesitates.

"Totally none of my business. But my advice? As a cranky old broad who's been around the block a few times? Don't let a guy like that get away with giving you any shit. It'll only get worse."

She nods and gives me a weary half smile.

"Duly noted," she says. "And it's okay, I've got a pretty thick hide."

"Is he your boyfriend?"

She frowns. Now I've clearly overstepped.

"Sorry," I say. "Again, totally none of my business."

"Right."

Which, come to think of it, is not exactly a denial.

"Well, you know what they say." I pick up my purse. "Don't get mad… Get even."

CHAPTER NINE

SHANNON

Dark clouds have gathered, and thunder rumbles, still in the distance. Three more blocks until I get back to the cottage.

I hurry but soon the drops start falling, fat and far apart, almost like I could pass through untouched were I nimble enough. I'm not though, so I'm getting splattered. And there it is, that smell, so curiously specific: when rain first hits dusty pavement. I breathe it in, savor it.

I'm actually in the mood for a good rainstorm. I've reached a crucial fork in the road: I'm weighing the most momentous decision of my life. So I appreciate the drama in the atmosphere. I need the universe to acknowledge that yes, this choice I need to make is a big fucking deal. I just wish I didn't have a Fourth of July party to go to. I'd much rather hunker down by myself for the evening and think.

As I turn into the driveway, I can't quite believe what I'm seeing: Chloe, coming out of the front door to my cottage.

Did Allison give her a spare key? How dare she!

She sees me and stops. It's raining a bit harder now, we're both getting wet.

"Hi Shannon! Hope it's okay—your delivery? Just thought I'd put the boxes inside before they got totally soaked. Door was unlocked."

So the new sheets and blankets I ordered must have arrived. I guess it makes sense. But still, Chloe should have minded her own business.

Now I wonder: did I put away the bag of 'shrooms? Could I have left my antidepressant vial out on the counter? What if she snooped around a bit, maybe even discovered the Glock in my toolbox?

There were times in my life when I might have done that, prowled around. And no one who met me would have guessed it. You never know with people.

"Oh, thanks," I say, trying to sound like I don't care, like I've got nothing to hide.

But I feel violated. I'll double check that the door is locked from now on. I have this funny feeling I might need to be careful around her.

* * *

An hour or so later, I'm at Allison's, and rain is pouring down even more heavily. With each gust of wind, a fire-hose blast of water pummels the house. I'm getting the dramatic weather I was hoping for.

But instead of pondering what the universe intends for me, I'm stuck making small talk with, of course, Chloe. Allison abandoned her to go do something in the kitchen. Bobby is over talking to our two surprise guests, Alba and Martha. Octogenarians, by the look of them, from Allison's help-out-the-elderly volunteer gig.

I take a swallow of my beer.

I suppose I should try harder to like Chloe. On the surface, she even seems a little like Allison: conscientious, quiet, wholesome. But Chloe's more guarded. I'd be willing to bet that underneath her bland politeness, she's judgy. And honestly, I prefer people with more spark, more unpredictability. A hint of past trauma or damage, a dark sense of humor. One of the many reasons I drive most of my therapists crazy.

90

Allison was the exception. Fresh after losing Maureen, I just needed a friend who was loyal and uncomplicated, who would always be on my side and never judge. But it wasn't an experiment I've repeated very often.

"So Allison tells me you're taking a graphic novel workshop?" Chloe says. "My younger brother is totally into manga. Is that the sort of thing you're learning?"

"Kinda, yeah. Manga's just one type of graphic novel, from Japan. And comic books and graphic novels are technically a little different, but…"

As I yammer on to Chloe, explaining terminology I only just learned myself, I hear Bobby and the spunky senior citizens laughing and swapping tales about Provincetown's past. They're all a bit tipsy.

Chloe's concentrating hard, trying to think of good questions, even though she couldn't possibly care about the answers. It's like I'm having a conversation with ChatGPT. And, no judgment, but she's way less attractive than Allison thinks she is.

I get tired of talking about my workshop, so I pretend to be curious about Chloe's earnestly shitty little music group. I plaster a pleasant smile on my face as she tells me all about it. Meanwhile, from the other couch, I catch intriguing snippets about the former drug-runners behind some of Ptown's most celebrated restaurants; a serial killer, Tony "Chop-Chop" something or other. And an unhinged Norman Mailer on trial for getting drunk and confusing a police car with a taxi.

"Was that before or after he stabbed his wife?" asks Bobby, but I don't catch the answer. I'm missing a litany of entertaining scandals as Chloe explains the difference between a violin and a viola.

Finally, salvation arrives. Allison has left her post in the kitchen to address the group.

"Sorry guys, dinner's running a little behind, but I'm getting there. With the rain I knew barbecue wouldn't work, so, get this: I googled a recipe for lasagna!" She waves a spatula and gives a wild little laugh. "I guess I knew theoretically that cooking could come with instructions, but I've never really experimented before. So we'll see! *Something* will be coming out of the oven. In the meantime, relax, have another drink."

She's wearing an apron that's ridiculously small and dainty. Not only is it flowery, it even has ruffles on it. Clearly not designed for a woman of her brawn and butchness. It must have belonged to her mother. She's spilled red sauce all over the front of it, and she has a smear of something white on her forehead. She looks flushed and sweaty and a little harried.

But also… happy?

I turn to Chloe. I lean in, lower my voice.

"You put her up to this, right? Hosting a Fourth of July dinner?"

"What, me?"

"This couldn't have been Allison's idea."

"Well it sure wasn't mine. I thought maybe you suggested it?"

"Me? No!"

As Allison returns to the kitchen, I realize I could grab this chance to make the salad, and more importantly, escape from Chloe. I excuse myself from all things string quartet and follow Allison.

But Bobby intercepts me.

"Just heading out for a quick smoke on the porch, you wanna join me?"

"You smoke?" I ask him. Hardly anyone I know does anymore.

"Not *tobacco*, silly."

"Ooh, maybe later? I should peek in and see how things are going in there."

"Sure," he says, "but have you figured out who that plucky lady in the apron is? And could you ask her what she's done with Allison?"

"I know, right? What's up with that?"

"Must be the new girlfriend," he says.

"Probably. Although Chloe seems honestly kinda…"

"Tedious?"

I'm glad he said it and not me.

"As long as Allison likes her, though, that's the important part."

"Exactly. Who cares what we think?"

But he rolls his eyes and stifles a theatrical yawn.

When I get to the kitchen, Allison is standing at the oven, peering inside through the glass window.

"It's almost time, but I can't tell if it's done," she says.

"The top looks good; you don't want it much browner. Let's take a look."

I take it out; make an exploratory poke.

"You did good! Just cover it up with aluminum foil so you don't burn the cheese on top, and give it a little more time to cook down."

It's nice to be back in this kitchen again. Allison's mother and I used to make dinner together—even back then, Allison had no interest in anything domestic. Her mother taught me so much more about cooking than my own mother ever did, all the while chatting and laughing like I was just a regular teenage girl instead of a troublemaking, rule-breaking, wrecking ball.

I wonder if Allison knew how much I envied her? Her family inhabited a strange alternative world: a sweet bubble of appreciation and kindness, of random silliness, of jokes and nicknames and catchphrases that they'd always carefully explain so I wouldn't feel left out.

I suppose there were jokes in my family too. But once Maureen was gone, my humor grew darker. My father's stayed, as always, sarcastic, mocking. My brother had no sense of humor at all, as far as I could tell. But seeing my mother change, that was the worst. She used to be witty, joyful. We'd have real conversations. But then she shut down: lights out, shades drawn, doors locked. She'd never even mention Maureen. Did she blame me for not saving her? Did she wish it were me who'd died instead?

I go to the fridge to get the supplies I'd dropped off earlier: the lettuce, veggies, feta, and the makings for a balsamic dressing. When I told Allison I'd take on salad duty, she thanked me with such grateful relief you'd have thought I'd offered to donate an organ. I find a kitchen knife in the same drawer where they were thirty years ago.

I sharpen the knife. Eye the long blade.

Knives are quieter than guns…but you have to get awfully close to use them.

As I start cutting up bell peppers, I try to imagine myself as an actual murderer.

But it's too hard to make it feel real; it's more like deciding whether to take a part in a community theater production of *Arsenic and Old Lace*. In my imagination, I can only get murder-adjacent.

"Hey Shannon."

Something in Allison's tone, an earnest huskiness, makes me look up.

"Thank you," she says. "And I really mean it."

"For what?"

"For finding me after all these years. For, like, inspiring me."

"Inspiring you?"

"I guess I was feeling sort of stuck. Like a combination of inertia and just… I don't know, maybe depression? And then you came here, and you made things fun again. Challenged me a little, nudged me forward. Just like you did back in high school. And now look!"

I guess it's true—she *has* managed to make progress since I came. And Lord knows, no one on earth but Allison has ever seen me as a positive influence.

"Yeah, look at you—dating a woman you're crazy about, looking so sharp in your new clothes, cooking a lasagna from scratch, and hosting a holiday party!"

She's quiet a moment.

"So my parents always used to have a Fourth of July party. And I was feeling so sad remembering it. And okay, this is going to sound totally dumb, but… since you got here, I've been asking myself sometimes, 'What would Shannon do?'"

"Oh my God."

"What if *Shannon* missed having a Fourth of July party? Well, she'd just organize one herself!"

"That's… oh, Alley Cat. If you only knew how funny that is."

But I try to keep my expression gentle.

"I knew you'd think it was corny."

"No! It's very sweet. It's just…not giving a damn what other people think, it's empowering. But the results can be pretty unpredictable. I don't think you actually want to start being a Shannon."

And definitely not now.

"But you're so confident!" she says. "I want some of that. Signing up for a workshop for something when you've never even tried it before. Putting yourself out there, making friends so easily."

"Right! Also, dumping a whole pitcher of Sangria all over a guy for putting his hand on my ass in an Applebee's?"

"Shannon would do that?"

I nod. "Or, keying my ex's shiny new Wagoneer when I found out he was cheating on me? *While* they were busy boinking in the back of it?"

I love the look on her face.

"Blowing a security guard to get backstage at the Foo Fighters concert? Sending a gift-wrapped bag of dogshit to the manager who canned me for being ten minutes late during a snow storm?"

"Shannon would do all that?" She's laughing now.

"Totally. So you might not *always* want to ask yourself what Shannon would do."

"Okay then, point taken!"

"You didn't know me in my twenties or thirties."

"Jeez, my life would have seemed so boring to you. All I did was work, pretty much. Did you, um… ever end up in jail?"

I hesitate.

Back in high school, I loved to brag about my misdeeds to Allison. She was such a rapt audience. I'd feel like a pirate back from the high seas, showing off stolen treasure, recounting tales of sword fights and sunken ships.

I consider my rap sheet: Definitely not the drunk and disorderlies, those were embarrassing. Disturbing the peace, shoplifting, dealing in stolen goods? Also unflattering. Forgery? That was the most serious, but classier. With my fine motor skills, my talent for delicate drawings and calligraphy, I was really good at it. Back before everything went digital.

"I got arrested in a protest once," I say. Better safe than sorry. "But they let me out after a couple of hours."

"Good for you though! Standing up for what you believe in."

"Well, sometimes it just feels like you have to, right?"

* * *

"You're doing a workshop at the Fine Arts Center? I took one on poetry there myself, years ago," says Alba. "Turns out, I'm shit at poetry. Still, I don't regret doing it."

"Well I'm pretty good at poetry, at least when it comes to limericks," offers Bobby. "Let's see. There once was a well-endowed trucker, who…"

"Smartass," says Alba, waving him off. But she's laughing. She turns to me. "Boys and their penises, it's a never-ending love affair, isn't it?"

We've finished our lasagna. Allison is cutting up the cake Bobby brought, and Chloe is clearing the dinner dishes. After a couple of glasses of wine, I seem to have acquired a much greater tolerance for dinner party chat. Martha and Alba are a hoot, Bobby's been in fine form, and even Allison seems sort of sparkly tonight. Who would have guessed this would turn out to be fun?

Martha leans in from her seat across the table. She's got a big greenish gob from the lasagna stuck on her teeth.

"Wait, so did I just hear you're doing one of those writing workshops this week?" she asks me.

"Spinach, sweetie," says Alba, baring her own teeth and making a wiping motion.

Martha probes, picks it out with a fingernail. "Did I get it?" she asks.

Alba makes the thumbs up sign. "You're all pretty again."

I feel a brief moment of… what is it? Not yearning, exactly, but a gently piercing sense of aloneness. I don't have Brian anymore, to look out for me, to tell me I have spinach in my teeth.

But I can't quite picture him here, at this table with me. He wouldn't enjoy these people; he'd be sneaking peeks at his watch, wishing he could get back home to his video games.

Martha turns back to me. "I just hope you're not taking a class from, what's his name? The famous one, supposed to be a real jerk. Help me out here."

She looks towards Alba.

"Grant something. Richards? No, Pritchard," says Alba.

"Right!" says Martha. "Grant Pritchard. Why on earth did they invite him back again, I wonder?"

I try not to react too visibly.

"He writes best sellers," says Alba.

"But it's not literature," says Martha. "Provincetown is supposed to be an arts colony, not a Walmart. He's not exactly Mary Oliver or Michael Cunningham or Eugene O'Neill."

"His first couple were pretty literary, weren't they?" says Alba. "Before he found his winning formula? And he's apparently quite charming during his presentations and classes. Puts on quite a show."

"I'm in a different workshop," I say.

"Oh good. He's a real piece of work," says Martha.

"God, yes," adds Bobby, "a total prick."

It's all I can do to modulate my voice, pretend I'm only mildly curious.

"Really? So what's his deal?"

Martha rolls her eyes. "Where to start. I mean aside from his misogynistic novels, where all the women are quirky, beautiful, and completely useless, and all the men are endlessly patient and strong and capable…"

"Which for some reason, a ton of women keep buying and reading anyway," says Alba.

"I mean, what *is* it with straight women?" Martha asks. "Sorry, no offense intended," she says to me, shaking her head.

"Anyway," Martha continues, "it's not just his novels. There was a big thing on Community Space about him a few years ago, the last time he was here. Before the pandemic. But I doubt the people who arrange the workshops bother to go wading through that mess."

"Community Space?" I ask.

"The Ptown Facebook page," explains Alba. "It's incredibly toxic, but you do get a lot of the dirt on what's happening in town."

"Just don't ever mention certain subjects," says Bobby. "Like pickleball. Or piping plovers."

"Or dune shacks."

"Or anything about pedicabs or scooters…"

"Or coyotes, or cruise ships…"

I fear we're getting off track here.

"So what did they say about this Pritchard guy?" I ask.

"Oh, right," says Martha. "So he caused a ruckus in one of the bars, kept pestering some girl in a bachelorette party, propositioning her, saying all kinds of disgusting things."

"The bachelorettes. That's another theme to avoid on Facebook," says Alba.

"And by girl, I mean, literally, she was the little sister of the bride, like a young teenager!"

Another teenager?

"The waitress told him to back off and he got right up in her face. The bartender finally ended up decking him one. Then *Pritchard* decided to sue the restaurant, I think it was settled out of court. But you should have seen the comments coming in on the Facebook post. Because he'd done it before. He'd go out drinking he'd get handsy with the waitresses, hit on young girls, say rude things to everyone around him. All the while thinking he was too important to have to answer for it."

"Wow," I say, shaking my head. "What a horrible man!" I take another swallow of my wine. "I sure hope one day it all catches up with him."

* * *

By the time we start to say our good-byes, the rain has stopped. I hope Allison's pleased with herself; it was actually a pretty great party.

Although once dinner was served, I hardly got to talk to her at all. Chloe was latched onto her all night like a hungry deer tick. I've met her type before: insecure, hyper-vigilant. Now I wish I hadn't been so instrumental in getting them together! Knowing Allison, it will take her forever to get herself back out again. But how was I supposed to know?

Bobby and I head outside into the foggy night. The air is soft and the lights are blurry; there's a cozy humid dampness that feels both familiar and otherworldly.

But Bobby is looking wobbly. His phone starts buzzing and he drops it. He picks it up, looks down, types something. He's using a lot of backspaces. It buzzes again.

"Jesus, chill!" he says to the phone. "Damn it!"

"What's up?"

He sighs. "I forgot I was supposed to make a delivery tonight. Like an hour ago. When I set it up, I thought the party would end sooner. Then I got a little too wasted and just totally spaced."

"Catering?"

"No. The other."

"Oh."

"It's in Chatham."

He looks over at his driveway and his Jetta.

"No fucking way are you getting behind that wheel," I say.

"I'm not as bad off as you think."

It would be more convincing if he weren't swaying like he was riding on a lurching subway instead of standing on solid ground.

"Where are your keys?" I ask. "Are they in your pocket or inside your house?"

"I'm not gonna give you my keys."

"Yes, you are. Because either I'm going to drive you there, or I'm going to call the cops. I don't want you to kill anyone, including your own stupid self."

Chatham's not far away. And my wine wore off hours ago, I'm fine to drive.

He thinks about it. Digs into his front pocket, hands them over.

"Thank you," he says.

I guess we're going for a little ride.

* * *

It's late when I get back. I turn on the light in the cottage, but Niccolo isn't in his usual place on the sofa bed.

"Niccolo?"

He's here somewhere. No need to panic. I thought the trip to Chatham would be much quicker, mostly because I had it confused in my mind with Eastham. I don't really know the Cape that well.

"Where's my sweet baby boy?"

It's after one in the morning but I'm not sleepy. And it's not because of excess adrenaline from the impromptu drug run—that was all pretty

100

chill. We pulled into the driveway of an ordinary-looking house. Bobby rang the doorbell, handed over the bag to the guy who answered, took an envelope full of cash in return. Then we left. No biggie.

No, the reason I'm so much more energetic than usual is because of the uppers Bobby gave me, to stay awake during the drive. At first, I wasn't going to take them. I've avoided uppers since I went on anti-depressants.

But I was starting to get tired driving home, and it didn't seem that risky to try a couple. I've been in such a better headspace since I started micro-dosing. It's a real thing, I found out: even doctors are starting to prescribe psychedelics to treat mood disorders.

Of course "mood disorder" is just one of my diagnoses. If you have a personality that a shrink doesn't care for, then that's a disorder too. I have moods and personality in spades, plus a few other things. The particulars seem to vary, depending on what kind of insurance I'm on and what sort of degrees my therapists have.

I get it, that my brain isn't the standard model. But the way the doctors slap their ever-changing labels on me and hand out the requisite pills, it doesn't inspire confidence. I sometimes wonder if most of my medications are designed to make *them* feel more comfortable, not me.

"Niccolo?"

I climb the ladder and peek into the loft, but he's not there either. I climb back down, a little worried now.

"Niccolo?"

Then I see it. Why hadn't I noticed it before? The window screen above the kitchen sink—there's a rip on the side. Big enough for Niccolo to squeeze through? Hard to say.

I close the window.

I grab a can of cat food, pop open the pull tab. He's already had his dinner, but the familiar sounds and aroma might help lure him from wherever he's hiding.

Unless he's outside.

I get out his bowl, noisily, and tap blobs of food in there. Clunk down the dish.

"Niccolo, are you hungry?"

I try to sound normal, but I can hear the tremble of anxiety in my voice.

It can't be. He can't have escaped.

I take a deep breath, try to calm down, but I can't dampen it, can't stop the panic rising. I try not to think of him outside in the woods, lost, vulnerable. Easy prey for a coyote—he's not a savvy outdoor cat; he has no idea how to hide or fight.

I'm shaking. Niccolo had become so essential. It's simply not possible to think of how I'd manage without him.

Mrowww! *Here I am*!

He saunters into the kitchen. I feel so relieved. But also a little pissed off. Was he playing with me?

Shannon! You're home! My favorite person in the world.

He does an enthusiastic little roll-and-wiggle on the kitchen floor. Then he rights himself and I pet him.

I'm so glad you're back, Shannon, I've missed you so much! And what's this, an extra meal? That's so considerate of you!

"Niccolo, please don't hide from me like that anymore, it scares me."

My voice must sound a little sharper than usual; Niccolo looks taken aback.

But I wasn't hiding, Shannon, I was napping! I fell asleep under the couch. I followed a spider under there.

Then I realize my anger is misplaced. It's not his fault.

"I'm sorry baby, I just got scared. It's just… it's this stupid shithole cottage! Why doesn't Allison fix the screens, paint the walls, replace the furniture? It could be so much nicer in here!"

I take a few deep breaths, calm myself down. As Niccolo eats his late-night meal, I tell him all about class, and the drug run, and what I found out about Pritchard at Allison's party. I realize I'm hungry again, so I take out some cheese and grapes, pour myself a glass of wine, sit down at the kitchen table.

Taking on Pritchard, it's ridiculously risky. If I were smart, I'd just enjoy my workshop and forget all about that horrible man and what he's done.

But. He used Maureen so barbarically, and he's still at it, preying on women and teens! He needs to be stopped.

Niccolo jumps up on my lap, then onto the kitchen table. At home he's not allowed, but we're here, not there, and it's easier to chat this way.

"I don't know, Niccolo. Could I really kill him? Blow his head off, slit his throat, break open his skull with baseball bat? Because, you're right, I'm not a cat. I'm a person. I'm squeamish and skittish. All that blood!"

I don't even mention the moral question. He wouldn't understand. Though I actually think I've worked through that. It's like being a soldier during World War II, shooting at Nazis, or a SWAT team taking out a sniper. A veterinarian putting down a rabid dog. I can't say I think euthanizing a predator is "wrong." Just very illegal.

So you wouldn't enjoy the bloody part? Not like a cat would?

"No, I really don't think so."

He leans down to bite at an itch on his foreleg, then looks back up at me.

But Shannon, is that even necessary? In that show you like, the lady who solves murders every week—it seems like there are all sorts of ways humans can die! Even without blood.

Well duh. He's right, of course.

Bringing along my Glock, fantasizing about confronting Pritchard, seeing his wretched face, so deliciously terrified as I aim the gun at him…

it's been a distraction. If I can figure out a way to set things up properly, I don't actually have to *be* there when he dies. And I doubt the local police are anywhere near as brilliant as the fictional British detectives I watch, who can sort through a whole town full of people with obvious motives in order to find the least likely killer.

But is there time for all that? What would the plan be?

I'm still amped from the uppers. Rather than go to bed, I decide to put the extra energy to good use.

I get out a pad of paper to organize my thoughts. I'll have to remember to burn it or shred it when I'm done, just in case Chloe decides to prowl through my recycling.

1. I need to figure out how to stay in Provincetown longer.

2. I need a way to get closer to Pritchard, and into his condo.

3. I need a way to kill him and escape undetected.

4. If I stay longer, I'll have no job; I need income.

5. What comes next for "Colleen?" What's her superpower?

I almost cross the last one out because it doesn't really belong. But I don't want to. I have three days of class left, and I want to keep going with her story while I still have Wylie to help me.

But five questions seem like plenty for one night. I finish my snack and my wine. I create a page for each question.

Niccolo watches closely.

"Just jotting down some ideas," I explain. "Because you're right. I can't blow my one chance to nail Pritchard while I'm here. I need to be focused and ruthless, like you said. Like a cat. And this time... I'm going to finish things."

Niccolo reaches over and playfully bats my pen a couple of times, just to show he's excited.

I know you'll be so much happier when he's gone.

I pet him a couple of times, and he loses interest in the pen.

"And thank you, Niccolo. I don't think I could have gotten to this without your help."

Of course. I'm always here for you.

Yes. He always is. And so far, he's always been right! Steering me in the direction I need to go. Getting me off those horrible pills. Helping me be brave when I'm feeling unsure.

"Niccolo, can I ask you a strange question?"

Yes?

"How do you always know these things? Are you really just a cat? Or something… else?"

He looks up at me.

Am I <u>just</u> a cat, Shannon? <u>Just</u> a cat?

I have to laugh. "I didn't mean anything bad by that."

I'll say this: you'd do well to follow my advice. It does come from a special place. One that few humans have the capacity to hear, let alone understand.

And with that he turns, jumps gracefully off the table, and settles in his usual spot on the sofa bed.

I look back at my list: I realize that I already have an answer to number five!

"Niccolo, would you object to becoming a character in my graphic novel?"

Of course not Shannon, I'd be flattered!

By the time morning comes, I've made astonishing progress. I have at least partial answers to every single question.

I can't wait to get started.

CHAPTER TEN

ALLISON

Birds are squawking outside. I feel dazed and blurry, like I'm coming up from the wrong stage in my sleep cycle.

I roll over and Chloe is curled up in the bed next to me.

Chloe! I forgot about Chloe!

She spent the night again last night. Now I remember: we were bingeing *Ted Lasso* episodes because she doesn't have Apple TV and she's never seen it. And I don't mind watching it all over again just so I can see her laugh.

It's the third time in a week that Chloe's here in my bed, starting her day with me. Plus I've stayed at her place twice. We took a couple nights off because it seemed like something we should do on general principle.

So this is what people mean, when they talk about falling head-over-heels in love? No wonder there are so many silly songs about it. Totally new territory for me. Because aside from a few extremely short and mystifying relationships with women who were clearly wrong, wrong, wrong for me, it was always Courtney.

With Courtney, I was never head-over-heels. But I was impressed: a newly-minted corporate attorney full of energy and ambition. Courtney was so take-charge, so certain of herself! She seemed the perfect com-plement to someone like me: a bit indecisive, but good at compromise, able to let things go without causing a fuss.

It's just all those "things" I had to let go of kept piling up and piling up, eventually trapping me underneath a mountain of her wants and needs and moods.

With Chloe, it's all so different. She's kind. Generous. She listens.

Lying there, her face half covered with her dark silky hair, her delicate hands curled halfway into fists, she looks so innocent and precious. I just want to scoop her up and gently cuddle and kiss her awake.

I won't though, I'll let her sleep. I slip quietly out of bed and go start the coffee.

Half an hour later she's sitting next to me at the kitchen table and we're both drinking our coffee, looking at our phones and taking turns getting caught sneaking glances at each other. We're disgusting.

That's the weirdest part: she seems to be smitten too—it's not just me. I know this phase isn't supposed to last forever, but oh my God, I sure don't want it to ever end.

We're not doing a co-working day, because it's Saturday. Instead, we've decided we get to do touristy things, like we're on vacation. Living in a tourist town, you figure you'll always have time, that eventually you'll get to everything… and then you never do anything.

But which things? We can't decide.

"Whale watch?"

"Ooh, that sounds good. Or dune tour?"

"Or we could take the boat shuttle out to Long Point, have a picnic on the beach."

"Yeah! Or go out on the bike trails."

"Or rent kayaks?"

"Stand-up paddleboards?"

"Pontoon boat!"

"Trolley tour?"

"Drag brunch?"

"The Pilgrim Monument Museum, try out the funicular?"

And then we're back to staring at each other, grinning.

Chloe smiles at me, a little coyly. Picks up my hand, plays with it a little. I am buzzing.

"Or," she says, "we could just… go back to bed?"

"Or," I say, "we could just go back to bed."

* * *

"Want me to come back here so we can walk over together? Or should we just meet at the restaurant at six?" asks Chloe.

She's going home now to shower and change and make obligatory weekend phone calls to her mother and nosy older sister. Even though it's midafternoon, we still haven't managed to leave the house yet.

But we're definitely going to honor our dinner reservations. There's not much left in my kitchen besides Pringles, beer, and Honey Bunches of Oats.

"I guess meeting at the restaurant makes more sense," I say. "Coming all the way back here would be totally out of your way."

Though I love the idea of walking hand in hand through town with her on the way to dinner.

"Or I could come to your house," I suggest. "We could walk over from there."

"We're being ridiculous, aren't we," she says.

"Totally. We should probably be grown-ups and just meet there?"

We hug and wave goodbye to each other as though she's going off to war in the Middle East instead of to her condo less than a mile away. She walks backward blowing kisses and I stay planted outside the door blowing them back until she's gone around the curve of the driveway and is out of sight.

After I go back inside, it's only a couple of minutes until there's a knock on the door. I swing it open, thinking she's forgotten something, but it's not Chloe. It's Shannon and Bobby.

Shannon smiles at me in her special warm, amused way, like it kind of cracks her up that she's happy to see me.

I feel a little sad though. It was her last day of class today, she's leaving on Tuesday, and she's been so great to hang out with.

"Hi guys," I say, and I don't even have to invite them in because they're already walking past me into the living room. Shannon is carrying a big leather case, like a messenger bag. They both sit down on the couch, then wave me into my dad's old easy chair, like they're conducting a meeting.

"Shannon came up with a fantastic idea," says Bobby. "But don't say anything right away, just hear her out first."

"Sure," I say. They seem so serious.

"So I was looking at your Airbnb calendar for the cottage," says Shannon. "And you only have a couple of bookings before Labor Day, and they're both less than a week."

I nod. It's a little embarrassing.

"Are they friends of yours?" she asks.

"No, not friends, just people off the site."

"I don't want to hurt your feelings, Alley Cat," she says, "but I'm not sure the place is ready for the general public. It's pretty basic."

"And by basic, she means it's barely habitable," says Bobby. "I'm sorry, but it's time for some tough love. It's smelly and there's mold and bugs and drafts and leaks and the furniture's ugly and gross, and did I mention it's smelly? If you rent it out as is, believe me, those negative reviews are going to haunt you for years."

I sigh. "I know it needs some work. It's just, it's just that…"

"I know, right? We all get busy," says Shannon. "So here's what you should do. Make up some excuse and cancel the bookings. People do that all the time! And then let me stay there the rest of the summer. I'll turn that decrepit little cottage of yours into a gorgeous guesthouse, full of character and charm."

"She totally will, too," says Bobby. "She showed me some of her ideas. They're awesome."

It feels a little strange that they've been teaming up like this, having conversations about my cottage without me even being there. But then I've been AWOL, haven't I, spending almost every minute with Chloe?

"I'm really handy with paint and repairs and minor construction," Shannon says. "Plus I can do all kinds of other crafty stuff. I could spruce things up for really cheap. When I'm done, we do a photo shoot, and voila! You can charge at least three times as much when you rent out next year. And be booked solid the whole summer. It will way more than make up for the rent you won't be getting this year."

"And what Shannon can't handle—there's not much but, like, the roof work—I know a guy," adds Bobby. "He's pretty budget-friendly, you won't have to invest much. Plus you can write it off."

I look at Shannon. "Really? You want to stay here for the whole summer?"

"We'll have so much more time to hang out," she says.

How cool would that be? I wouldn't have to say goodbye so soon after all.

"That sounds so fun! I feel like we've only just started to get to know each other again. God, you make me laugh so hard."

I can't believe how much my life changed after Shannon got here, and all for the better. I love the idea of having a little "gang" to do things with: Shannon and Bobby and me and Chloe! And to end up with a spruced-up cottage to rent out, without having to do anything myself besides whip out my credit card?

"But can you get that much time off work?" I ask her.

"Not a problem! I've been thinking of moving on from the gallery anyway. Cynthia and I don't really click. When I get back home, I'm going to concentrate more on my own clothing designs, my art, and I'll market them on Etsy and take them to other galleries. But right now I need a creativity break. I'm totally into the graphic novel thing and I want to see where that goes. Did I tell you I'm going to be working with Wylie? She was my instructor, and she's going to be here all summer. She doesn't charge much, and she's going to give me coaching and feedback."

It sounds so Shannon. To just up and quit a job, and start a new project with no idea what might happen.

"I've got a great house-sitter, and she's agreed to stay on, to look after my other cats and take care of the place. And here's the best part," she says. "I've already lined up a part-time job here to tide me through, so all I need is a place to stay."

"You already have a job?" I'm amazed how fast she's moving.

"Yep," says Bobby. "Get this: she's going to be working for *me*!"

Aha. No wonder he's so involved in this whole cottage proposal. It makes sense, though. They're already good buddies.

"The catering business, it's been growing. My repeat customers are always asking for smaller things too. Like premade picnics, or desserts for a special occasion. I've been having to turn away so much business."

"I can help out in the kitchen," says Shannon, "and Bobby hates doing deliveries. For me it'll be fun, I'll get to learn my way around the Cape, meet new people."

"Wow," I say. "You guys have thought of everything."

"So does 'wow' mean yes?" asks Shannon.

I pretty much never make major decisions without weighing pros and cons, playing out worst-case scenarios, and generally tying myself into knots. But if saying yes is what I really want to do, why drag it out? Why not be more like Shannon?

"Wow means yes," I say. "It sounds like a great idea!"

* * *

I'd forgotten it was the first weekend of Bear Week. I thread my way to dinner along Commercial Street, and it's packed with throngs of people. And not just large hairy gay men—although there are a *ton* of them. But along with the bears, everyone else in the whole Northeast seems to have simultaneously decided to descend on Provincetown to party tonight. It's quite a scene.

When I get to Liz's Café, Chloe's waiting for me. She's wearing a tight pair of jeans that show off her perfect butt, and she's got on a black sexy tank top with a low neckline. I notice when I hug her hello that she's wearing some kind of perfume, something woodsy and wild, and it riles me up a little. It's all I can do to behave myself with her in public.

You'd think that having been together practically 24/7 the whole week, we'd run out of things to talk about. But all our stories about our lives are new stories, and we're finding out our likes and dislikes, sharing opinions about all kinds of things, which are fortunately amazingly similar. And honestly, I'd find the conversation enchanting even if she just sat there narrating every detail of washing her hair this afternoon. I love looking into her eyes and hearing the sound of her voice.

So it's not until we've finished eating dinner that I finally get around to mentioning my exciting news about Shannon and the cottage renovation project.

"Wow, that's a surprise," she says. "Were you expecting that?"

"No! I totally thought she was going home on Tuesday. But these last few days she and Bobby have been busy making all these plans, and I had no idea about it until a couple hours ago. Isn't that great news?"

"Yeah, totally. That'll be really nice for you, it seems like you really hit it off with her. Even after all this time."

She smiles.

But something's off.

"It'll be fun, right, for us to have more Ptown friends?" I say. "People to go do things with, go hear music, go out to the beach with?"

"Sure!" she says. "It's probably not healthy for us to spend so much time alone together. And you have such a good time when those guys are around."

"But…" I prompt, drawing out the word.

"There's no 'but,'" she says. "I think it's wonderful!"

I can see her trying to force a smile, pretend she's totally happy about this because she knows I'm happy about it and she doesn't want to rain on my parade. I'm pretty familiar with that maneuver.

Does she not like my friends?

The waiter comes to take away the plates, and by the time we get the check and pay it, it feels too awkward to try to revisit the conversation.

Later that evening, we're at her place, snuggled up on her black vinyl couch, watching a movie. When the evening started, I'd thought we'd end up going directly to bed after dinner, but ever since I mentioned Shannon staying, there's been something different between us. Words aren't flowing naturally anymore; it's like our feelings are coming out sideways and wrapped in cotton, all muffled and indistinct.

We'd wanted something lightweight to watch, and ended up with a silly romantic comedy from the '90s. It does have some funny slapstick moments and a lot of witty dialogue. But like most romantic comedies, the plot is stupid: the only thing keeping the lovers apart is a series of ridiculous misunderstandings they could have solved in twenty seconds if they'd ever bothered to talk to each other.

As the credits finally roll, it's hard to ignore what seems a little like a giant flashing message from the celluloid gods.

I decide to suck it up and go for it.

"So hey," I say, "the movie we just saw? I was kind of like that in my last relationship. I never really talked about things that were bothering me. And thinking back, I'm not sure that was the best idea?"

"Yeah. I hate having hard conversations too. But I guess you have to have them."

"So maybe we give it a shot?"

"Right. Um, so what's bothering you? Did I do something wrong?"

She looks so nervous!

"No, not at all. I just got the feeling that you weren't as happy as I was to hear Shannon's going to be around all summer."

She furrows her brows a little. And takes a long, long time to answer.

"Okay, yeah, so it worries me a little. But it's not really my place to say anything."

"But if you're worried about it, of course you should say something! What are you worried about?"

"Well, first off, Shannon doesn't like me. And neither does Bobby. They're not going to want to hang out with you much if I'm there."

I wasn't expecting that.

"Of course they like you! Of course they'd want you around. Why wouldn't they?"

"I guess because I'm kind of shy, and not very good at conversation? I didn't get into crazy situations when I was younger, I don't know how to do the teasing thing because I don't want to accidentally hurt anyone's feelings. But it's hard—they don't try very hard to hide how boring they think I am. And that makes me self-conscious, so then I get even more tongue-tied. At the Fourth of July party, when you weren't in the room? I saw them looking at me and laughing and yawning and rolling their eyes, commiserating about having to talk to me."

"No, they must have been joking about something else!"

I try to picture it, but I can't imagine either of them doing that. How could they not like Chloe? Let alone make fun of her?

I take her hand in mine. I feel terrible that she's been feeling so uneasy—and that I had no idea.

The whole thing seems so strange, because I have such a different impression of Shannon and Bobby. Sure, they like to kid around, but they're also kind and empathetic. Is Chloe maybe being oversensitive?

"Anyway," she says, "I think it's great that you have these fun friends you can do things with. I do sometimes wonder a little about Shannon, if she's okay and everything…"

Her voice fades and I wait, but it doesn't seem like she'd going to finish the thought.

"Like you think there's something wrong with her?"

"No! Not 'wrong' wrong, just, you know, different. She's pretty energetic, a little uninhibited, kind of, um, unconventional?"

"Yeah, which is why I like her?"

"Right, of course!" Chloe says.

All the things I admire about Shannon—they seem to scare Chloe. But then when I first met Shannon, I remember I felt pretty intimidated too.

"So are you saying…"

"Sorry, no, I'm not saying anything! I think it's great. Even though you guys are so different, somehow you get along so well. It just surprised me at first. And I'll do my best to just go with it. And just hope they get used to me. My job won't let me be here full-time anyway, I'll be gone plenty. This week has been amazing, but I need to get back to spending more time in Boston."

That's not actually comforting. I want Chloe here, not in Boston!

"Do you want me to talk to them?"

"Oh God no! Please don't. That would just make it worse."

"Okay."

She's probably right about that.

"But you should totally keep doing things with them. I'm so sorry," she says.

I put my arm around her.

"I'm the one who should be sorry. I was totally clueless! But I really appreciate that you were willing to talk to me about it. We'll figure it out."

As we head to bed for the night, I feel a mix of emotions. A little deflated, realizing my fantasy of the four of us having an adventure-filled summer together probably isn't realistic. But also a little proud of Chloe and me, for talking it through. I feel even closer to her now, hearing her be so vulnerable. When we finally do make love, it's less rowdy and crazed than before, more tender.

I feel bad for her, thinking Shannon and Bobby were making fun of her, even though I'm sure she must have misunderstood. But I'll bet once they all get to know each other better, it'll all work out just fine.

* * *

Pounding and ripping, booming sledgehammers and splintering wood. I'm in my office trying to get some work done, but I can't concentrate. I know I should be grateful that the roof guy had an unexpected opening, but the brutal sounds of destruction over at the cottage are putting me on edge.

Shannon's been working like a maniac, which I appreciate; I'd love to get this over with quickly. But it seems every five minutes she comes to interrupt me with an unexpected problem she's run into, but that she knows how to fix if I just spend more money. Plumbing, electrical, insulation, windows… we're going to be blowing through the original budget really quickly. I should have known: it happens on HGTV in almost every episode.

I'm both thrilled and terrified that things are moving so fast.

It's probably good that Chloe is back in Boston this week. And it's not just the noise. Why didn't it occur to me that renovating the cottage would make it uninhabitable a good part of the time? When Shannon said she needed a "place to stay," I was thinking she meant out in the cottage itself. But no, for now she's staying in the guest room. And while it's great to be able to hang out with her in the evenings, it's taking some getting used to. She's not as quiet as Chloe, and she stays up later than I do. Sometimes the sound of the TV makes it hard to get to sleep. And one morning when I was on a call, she reorganized all the kitchen drawers. She was just trying to be helpful, but now I can't find anything.

Then there's Niccolo. He doesn't like me. I scare him. And he scares me right back: I'm petrified I'll step on him, or let him escape and get run over by a car. He's always eyeing doors and windows, looking for opportunities. He's sneaky.

But I know it's all for a good cause. I'll have a renovated cottage, and Shannon really needed a place to stay. I can certainly deal with a few minor inconveniences!

I see Shannon's truck pulling up now, she's back from the hardware store. But it looks like she's also made a grocery store run.

"Hey Alley Cat," she shouts, "wanna help me unload?"

We schlep in bag after bag. She's bought a ton of healthy groceries; she's planning to make soups and chili and stir-fries. But she's also picked up my staples too: frozen pizzas and TV dinners, cereal and milk and peanut butter and jelly and bread and bananas, Pringles and Doritos and Cokes. It seems unfair: she's heavy and I'm skinny. Yet she's doing everything right, and I eat like a second grader who's managed to escape adult supervision her entire life.

As we're putting away the groceries, Shannon is talking a mile a minute about the cottage, and how great it's going to be. She wants to expand the kitchen, add a full-sized refrigerator and stove, upgrade the cabinetry and counters. She's probably right; it'll rent out for far more that way. I try to chill about the rising budget. I have some savings, and as Shannon points out, the reconstruction is not really an expense, it's an investment. But everything she's proposing will add not just more money but more time. I'm eager for her to get enough done so that she can move back into the cottage.

"And while I'm here this summer," she says, "I could also help you plan a renovation for this place too. Oh my god, there's so much potential here!"

And then she's off and running again, talking about knocking out walls and redoing practically every surface.

It's getting harder to ignore what I hadn't noticed before, which is what Chloe was probably trying to tell me a while back—yes, she does act a little hyper sometimes. She's always been energetic, but has she always talked so fast when she gets excited? Could she be taking diet pills or something?

But I'm also feeling a little irritated, both at myself for getting into this situation and at Shannon for being so presumptuous. This is *my* house, not hers.

"So yeah, Shannon," I say, when she finally pauses to ask what I think about turning the basement storage area into a combination media room and home gym, "all this sounds interesting, but I'm not planning on renting this out. I live here, right?"

"Of course, Alley Cat! I mean, for *you*! You're forty-five, all grown up now. You work hard, you deserve to live in a house just for you, a really nice house, not a dumpy old place from the '80s."

Wow.

I can't believe she just said that.

The fact that it's true doesn't make it hurt any less.

"Oh shit, I'm sorry," she says. "I didn't mean it like that. You know, all houses, over time, even nice ones like this, they could use some refreshing at some point."

"Yeah, whatever," I say. "Anyway, I like it here. So let's just save your efforts for the cottage, okay?"

"Sure, of course," she says, chastened.

"That's okay."

"No," she says. "It's really not."

We both look at each other but I'm not sure what to say.

She pulls out one of the kitchen chairs for me, and I sit down, and she sits down in the other one.

"I was being an idiot, okay?" she says. "Just being flip and insensitive. Saying something so clueless, to *you* of all people! I just adore you Allison, you know that, right?"

I shrug. Then I nod, reluctantly. But I'm having trouble letting it go.

"And I was wrong. This house," she says, looking around again, "is perfectly fine just the way it is. It's cozy and quirky and it has character. It's not an interior design project, it's a life! It all just screams how much you loved your mom, and how happy your family was here. So why would you want to toss the chairs she used to sit in, take away all the mementos, knock down walls that have pictures of her on them, or clear out a basement full of memories that she and your dad collected? I was being stupid and thoughtless and you have every right to be pissed at me."

And yet, I don't feel so mad anymore.

"We're good," I say. "I mean you're right. About both. The house is dumpy, but I'm comfortable with it. At least for now."

"It's not dumpy!"

Should I be even more honest? I bet if the shoe were on the other foot, Shannon would speak up.

"And so is everything… okay?" I ask. "Lately you seem a little, I don't know. Extra."

What a clumsy way to put it! But I don't know the technical terms.

"Oh. I seem weird to you?"

Her face: she's stung. Embarrassed. And so *this* is why I don't go around doing the whole "frank and honest" thing. I already wish I could take it back.

"Not weird at all! But… maybe faster? Like you've got a lot of energy?"

As I let the sentence dangle Shannon nods, like she knows what I mean.

"So okay. I've been trying out some new medications, and they warned me it might take a while for them to balance out. I didn't realize it was so noticeable."

"It's not noticeable, really!" Erase, erase, erase.

"I'd just been a little depressed and anxious. I mean, in this crazy world, who isn't? But then my doctor went and put me on something way too heavy-duty. So I went to someone new recently, and changed them around. And it's working, I'm feeling so much better! But yeah, until my body gets used to them, they could make me seem… a little, like you said, 'too much.'"

"Extra! I didn't say 'too much.' And it's barely noticeable. I'm so sorry I said anything."

"No, I'm the one who's sorry," she says. "And please don't worry about me. I've always been pretty 'out there,' remember?"

She does have a point.

"I throw myself into things. I have no filter; I sometimes say stupid things. I doubt I'll ever be completely appropriate. This crazy lady you're looking at? That's me, all my life. Worry if I'm *not* being at least a little bit of an asshole. If I'm spending too many hours in bed, if nothing gets me excited or angry or makes me laugh anymore. *That's* when you need to worry."

It actually makes sense. And I'm so relieved to hear there's a simple explanation, that doctors are involved, and that she has things in hand.

We go back to putting away groceries, and I relax a bit.

Because come to think of it, she's always been volatile and provocative. But also authentic, heartfelt, and sincerely regretful when she messes up.

So she's not a perfect human being. But who is?

CHAPTER ELEVEN

SHANNON

"Niccolo! Breakfast time."

Where has he gotten to? I'm not really supposed to be letting him out of my room anymore. Little fucker charged the front door last week and almost managed to escape.

Actually, it was Chloe's fault; she opened the door way too wide on her way in. At least she's quick: she grabbed him before he got more than a foot away. But he fought her fiercely, ripped up her arms with his back claws. Chloe then spent a half-hour dramatically dabbing herself with Neosporin and putting Band-Aids all over, totally paranoid she'd get infected.

Dinner that night was awkward. And I'd gone all out too, cooking them a nice Mexican casserole, making a salad with cilantro dressing. I'd even bought a bottle of nice wine.

It's like that a lot, actually. I was looking forward to spending time with Allison, but lately whenever she's here, so is Chloe, which always ruins everything. I feel like she's watching me, taking everything in. I'd be willing to bet it was actually *Chloe* who thinks I'm "too much," and poor Allison was just the messenger.

"Come on, Niccolo! Allison will be home any minute!"

She spent last night at Chloe's again, which at least gave me a chance to let Niccolo roam around the house a little. He hates to be cooped up.

As I walk down the hall, I can see Allison's bedroom door is open. I swore I closed it. Maybe not all the way?

Uh oh.

He's not on her bed, leaving hairy evidence of our transgression, so that's good. The closet door is cracked open, maybe he's in there? I go in and turn on the light.

It's huge, and full of old clothes. Clearly not all of them are Allison's. This would have been her parents' bedroom, and it looks like she's cleared out only enough of their stuff to fit her own clothes in.

"There you are!" He's way in the back, probably enjoying all the musty vintage smells. "C'mon, baby, you can't be hanging out in Allison's room."

I pick him up and start to carry him out of the closet.

But what's that other, fresher, more disgusting smell?

"Holy fuck, Niccolo. You didn't…"

I look down into Allison's laundry basket.

"Oh my God."

He's taken a big dump and peed all over Allison's Red Sox hoodie.

I pick up Niccolo, shut him back into the guest room, then take the sweatshirt into the bathroom to flush away the poop. I rinse it off in the sink the best I can. It's the Red Sox hoodie Allison wears all the time, the one that used to belong to her mother. A man-sized sweatshirt, probably the only thing of her mother's Allison could fit into. I remember they were all such big fans, loved going to the games. Poor Allison would be devastated if it got ruined.

Most of the shit didn't penetrate, just a few smears, but I can't even begin to get all the urine out. I hope it doesn't leave a stain. I've got to get it into the washing machine ASAP.

But how would I explain that to Allison? What was I doing in her room and why did I throw her sweatshirt in the washer? Better to find a laundromat. Then slip it back into her laundry basket when it's clean.

I wring the hoodie out and stuff it in a plastic bag.

Now there's no time for Niccolo's breakfast, which he should have thought about before he took a dump in the laundry basket. I give him a few cat treats and put him into his carrier. We're off to Wylie's this morning.

I'm so sorry Shannon! It was an accident!

I'm so mad, I don't feel like talking to him right now. I sling my satchel over my shoulder, pick up the bag in one hand, the carrier in the other.

After I close the front door, I don't get far before I see Bobby approaching.

"Where are you off to?" he asks. "You're looking rather random, like you're on one of those scavenger hunts they have on cruises. 'Let's see, I've got the big leather bag, the live mammal, and something drippy in a plastic bag. Now I just need a deck of tarot cards, a Bundt cake, a toilet plunger, and I win!'"

Bobby can always make me smile.

"Oh God, don't get me started. His royal highness here has not been on his best behavior. I won't go into details. But now we're off for my graphic novel tutorial."

"Another session already?" asks Bobby.

"I'm going over twice a week. I'm really into creating this graphic novel thing, and she's hardly charging me anything. And Wylie actually wanted to meet the little stinker, since I've made him an important character."

"So, are you game for some more deliveries later this afternoon?"

"Sure, the more I'm out of the house, the better."

"You mean Chloe?"

My arm is getting tired so I set down the carrier.

"Not just her. Although yeah, it's tiresome. Now she's being all fake-friendly, you know, forced perky. Even after Niccolo practically shredded her to pieces. Which is somehow even *more* annoying than just being real about it, you know, appropriately pissed off?"

But it wasn't my fault; she was strangling me!

Not now, Niccolo.

"I'm just totally over not having my own space. But I'm still waiting on furniture and appliances and cabinetry."

"You up for two drop-offs in Ptown, one in East Harwich, and one in Barnstable?"

"No problem! I'll stop by after I'm done with Wylie. Oh hey, a quick question about your, um, inventory?"

"Yeah?"

"A roommate of one of your clients was there when I was dropping off an order, a really sweet lady, and the poor thing is so sick. She's got bone cancer. And her doctor is being stingy with the opiates. Which is so unfair! Because by now she's got a high tolerance and she's really suffering. The cancer's pretty advanced, so she's not too worried about long-term side effects, if you know what I mean."

"She thinking fentanyl, something like that? I don't usually do opiates."

"She didn't say what flavor of painkiller. Whatever's really strong."

"And you're sure she's legit? Junkies can be awfully creative when they want their fix."

"Right? I ran with a pretty rough crowd back the day. But she didn't strike me that way at all. In fact, she was worried I might think that, so she showed me her medicine cabinet, and sure enough, it was full of chemo drugs with her name on the labels. I might have even taken a picture, let me get my phone. Let's see, I wonder what folder I would have put the photo in…"

I bend down and open my satchel, start rustling around.

"No worries," he says, "she sounds on the up and up."

Just what I was hoping; otherwise I'd have to pretend I accidentally deleted them.

"So yeah, let me see what I can do. Probably by the end of the week?"

"Great, she'll be so relieved!"

It seems the pieces are finally starting to fall into place.

* * *

We pull up outside of Wylie's building, but we still have a minute.

"Niccolo," I say, trying to keep at least some of the exasperation out of my voice. "This has to stop."

What has to stop?

"You know what. You've been an absolute dick lately. Biting, scratching, peeing, shitting, going into rooms where you're not supposed to be. You're making everything so much harder for me with Allison and Chloe."

I didn't realize you cared that much what they thought.

"Of course I do! And here you'd almost had me convinced to take you seriously. Like there was something mystical about our connection. That you had access to some higher form of knowledge. But the kind of crap you're pulling lately—I should listen to *you*?"

He's quiet a moment.

I apologize, Shannon. I forget that we express ourselves so differently. Humans rely solely on words, don't they. We just have a misunderstanding! My fault entirely.

"A misunderstanding?"

What I have been saying is that we need to get out of that house. You're not happy there. You've been tiptoeing around, trying not to be in the way, repressing your true feelings, getting frustrated and irritable.

"But the cottage isn't ready! There's not even any furniture anymore, I had it all hauled away. Allison is being really nice to us, letting us stay in her place."

I can't advise you on the logistics, Shannon. I just know you need to get us out of there.

There's no more time to argue, and I'm not sure I'm getting anywhere with him anyway. I grab the carrier and head for Wylie's condo.

The building is old, and surprisingly ramshackle, considering what real estate on the water must cost. There are probably seven or eight units, and she's in the small studio on the bottom floor below the unit Pritchard's renting.

It's frustrating: Wylie hasn't mentioned any details about their arrangement, neither pretending their proximity is a coincidence nor confirming that she's sleeping with him. I don't know if she always spends her summers with him during his seaside getaways? Does she hide out somewhere on those rare occasions when Pritchard's wife visits?

There's a brisk wind today, and it's high tide. The surf roars as it breaks, sending spray over the seawall. It's so exhilarating!

But as we get closer, the carrier starts swinging wildly. Niccolo's kicking up a fuss in there, clawing at the door, hurling himself around.

Let me out, Shannon! I have to get away from here!

"For Christ's sake, Niccolo, chill! I can't even walk when you jump around like that."

I set the carrier down, lower myself to look at him.

"What are you going on about now? I thought you wanted to come here?"

I'm so sorry, Shannon, please don't kill me. I promise I'll never relieve myself in Allison's laundry basket ever again!

"Kill you?"

The water, the water, it's coming to get me and it's so angry! So many piles and piles of it. Please don't throw me in there, I'm so sorry about the hoodie!

Poor thing. I try not to laugh at him.

"You've never seen the ocean before, have you?"

It's technically a large bay, not an ocean. But almost the same difference. High tide on the East End can be pretty intense.

"Don't worry, sweetheart. I'm not trying to kill you. And I won't let that scary water get you. We're just going around the corner and into the building, not all the way out to the waves. People pay a lot of money to live in buildings like this, right next to the water."

I find that rather hard to believe, Shannon.

* * *

"Ah there he is, the famous Niccolo!" Wylie looks happy to see us when we get inside. "Feel free to let him wander if you'd like."

"He could be feeling shy today, the high tide freaked him out a little."

"Take your time, little man," she says.

I set down the carrier and open it while Wylie goes to the kitchen to make us coffee. Her apartment is about the size of our cottage, simple and rustic.

I feel surprisingly comfortable here. Wylie's getting a lot more friendly. She's told me about her creative highs and lows, her time in an all-girl rock band, the Boston roommates she's currently taking a break from. She's hinted at a troubled childhood and adolescence, but avoids any details. I've told her about my breakup with Brian, about the strained temporary living situation I'm in now, my clothing designs and the big house with all the cats I have waiting for me when summer's over. We've both mentioned previous therapists, though not the specifics of what led to us to need them.

But whenever I try to push a little further to get to anything useful about Pritchard, she's evasive. Like when I first asked: "So how did you end up working for Grant Pritchard, is he a good boss?"

She said, "Oh, I can't remember exactly, but it's a job, you know? And how about you, are you working while you're here, or taking a break?"

"Just picking up a few things here and there," I said. Like drug dealing.

Meanwhile I try to figure out if she has a key to his place, and if so, where it is. I listen for any clues about where he goes and what he does, or what her job for him entails, or when they might be going to events together, but she's not dropping any hints. And I'm equally evasive about my reasons for hanging around Provincetown. Neither of us shows our cards. Probably because she doesn't want me to know she's sleeping with a man more than twice her age. While I don't want her to know that I'm trying to kill him.

So mostly we just end up talking about the reason we're supposed to be here: my graphic novel. Which I keep working on, despite how busy I am with everything else. I guess because it brings me so much closer to Maureen?

But it's intense. Sketching and writing my way through "Colleen's" freshman year, panel by panel, it brings it all to life: how torn Maureen must have felt. She must have known Pritchard's interest in her was inappropriate, out of bounds. But that charming snake: he singled her out, made her feel special. So smart, so pretty. The flattery, the attention, it all must have seemed irresistible.

Our own father was never there, never interested. Did that make her especially vulnerable?

Wylie's back with my coffee, some gourmet blend from Brazil that she grinds fresh each time. As we settle at the kitchen table, Niccolo finally leaves his carrier and starts to explore. Wylie seems curious, almost like she's seeing a cat for the first time. She cocks her head, watches him sniff and circle, smiles to herself when he suddenly stops to gnaw at an itchy spot on the base of his tail. It occurs to me that she's probably seeing him through artist's eyes, imagining how to capture his expressions, his movements.

Wylie turns to my latest pages, spreads them out, looks each one over carefully. Niccolo comes over to see what we're up to.

"You can come up on my lap, sweetheart, but not on the drawings," I tell him.

"We can clear some space for him up here if you'd like," says Wylie.

She even puts a folded beach towel down on the table to make it more comfortable for him. I plop him on it and he looks back and forth at us, finally settling his gaze on Wylie.

"You've got such an intelligent face, Niccolo," she says. "I can see why you might inspire Shannon to give you such an important role in her story."

Niccolo meows at her and she laughs happily.

"And of course you're quite handsome too," she says.

He meows again.

"Jesus," she says. "It's almost like he responds to what I'm saying!"

"Right? He's much more attuned to humans than any other cat I've ever known. It's how I got the idea to make him a character."

"Do you ever find yourself chatting with him? I'd be doing that all day long."

I pause for a second, but decide to answer honestly. After all, I was talking to him long before he started holding up his end of the conversation.

"I mean, how can I not?"

Wylie moves a little closer, slowly extends her hand toward him, but stops a few inches from his head. Niccolo wrinkles his nose, trying to catch her scent.

Finally he can't seem to help it. He moves toward her hand, practically begging her to pet him. Which she does.

She seems very polite, Shannon. I like her. Even if she's sleeping with the enemy.

I know. I feel the same way.

Wylie finishes petting Niccolo, turns her attention back to the drawings. She smiles and nods at some of the panels, but then her expression shifts, more thoughtful.

"So actually, I have a few questions about Niccolo. The character, not the actual cat. Just some food for thought."

Niccolo the actual cat takes this as his cue to relax and lie down on the towel. I pet him a few times before I turn my attention to Wylie.

"Okay, go ahead, shoot."

"So, after Colleen rescues Niccolo from the dog that was after him, they discover they can have conversations that no one else can hear."

"Right."

"So they're essentially reading each other's minds?"

"Exactly."

"And Niccolo can't talk with anyone else?"

"No, only Colleen. She's, like, special to him, because she saved his life."

"But can he hear anyone else? Can he read other human minds?"

"No, just Colleen's."

She nods like she understands, but like that's not the answer she wanted.

"So he mainly serves to clarify her own intentions."

"Well, no, not quite. He advises her. I mean, she's a teenager, she doesn't always know what to do. He's got a higher sort of awareness; he knows things she doesn't. And when she doesn't listen to him, things don't go very well for her. That's coming later in the story."

"So Niccolo's always right?"

"Well, it wouldn't be much of an advantage to her if he was just random about it."

Where is she going with this?

"Is he going to do anything else that's superpowered? Shape-shift, create force fields, incinerate things with laser beams coming out of his eyes, anything showy?"

"No, nothing like that!" I can't help laughing, thinking of Niccolo having laser beam eyes. "He just has conversations."

"So I'm wondering… if you're going to make the leap to fantasy, might you not want a more *powerful* magical cat? What if Niccolo could read other people's minds too? That might spice it up a little. This poor girl who's getting harassed and preyed upon, what if he can give her insights into what *other* people are thinking?"

"You mean, like Niccolo could tell her more about her enemies? Their weaknesses, their fears, their secret hopes?"

"Right! And maybe not just her enemies? What if there are allies out there in her world, and he helps her realize it?"

It makes sense, I suppose, but I don't like it.

"But his ability to understand her thoughts…I see that as having to do with their emotional connection, and how special they are to each other. If he had that same power with other people… I don't know."

"Like I said, just a thought," she says. "I'll be so curious to see where you go with all this."

She picks up the sketch on the top of the pile.

"Now, on to some technical aspects. Let's look at the background here, these buildings…"

Wylie goes on to share some pointers on technique. Very helpful, and I'm enjoying our session, but I keep finding myself distracted by the heavy footsteps above us.

He's up there right now. Just a few feet away.

When we're starting to wind down, I decide to tell Wylie about Niccolo and the laundry basket.

"Oh no, he didn't!" she says, laughing.

"And it wasn't just any hoodie," I explain. "I told you how hung-up Allison still is about her mom dying, right? This is the Red Sox hoodie her mom used to wear."

Wylie shakes her head. "Wow, Niccolo, you do have a way of expressing yourself."

"Do you happen to know if there's a laundromat in town?" I ask her.

"Well, there must be one… but if it would help, Grant lets me use his washer and dryer. I could throw it in today, actually. Maybe with a couple of old beach towels the last renters left here. I keep meaning to wash them."

"Really? That would be such a huge favor!"

"He usually heads off pretty soon," says Wylie. "Mondays he's got his personal trainer at noon, then kickboxing, and then he goes out to lunch afterward. The leisurely kind, with several cocktails. So it's at least a three-hour window; that's when I usually use the machine. He prefers it that way. He's not crazy about any disturbance when he's trying to write."

Finally. This is exactly the kind of information I've been looking for.

"Does he ever show you what he's working on? Seems like your perspective would be really useful."

It's the sort of question she usually deflects, but I give it a shot. I'm sensing a slight easing of her usual guardedness. Maybe something to do with my bringing along Niccolo, trusting her with that part of my life?

"At first—sure, he'd ask me what I thought. Because he's like that, right? He flatters you. 'You're so perceptive. Wise beyond your years.' Now he doesn't give a crap what I think. I'm not his target audience. Too feminist, too woke, whatever."

Hmm. If they *are* sleeping together, it sure doesn't sound like she's that into him.

"He's struggling a bit on his latest though. Says he's blocked. Publisher's getting antsy, because he's way behind. And his sales… they haven't been great on the last couple of releases. Maybe because he keeps writing the same book over and over?"

The footsteps above resume, this time at a more purposeful pace. A door opens and closes.

"There, he's heading down the stairs. Let's get that hoodie washed. And you can come too, if you want. See that amazing view I was telling you about."

Jackpot!

"That'd be cool," I say.

After I retrieve the plastic bag from the truck, Wylie and I walk up the stairs to Pritchard's condo. I'm trying to stay sharp, hyper-focused. I've got one quick opportunity to gather information, and it's going to be like one of Brian's video games: a series of unpredictable challenges with a limited time to collect as many tokens and trophies as I can.

The first and most important: how to get inside.

So there's a keypad on the door, and Wylie's not being particularly careful to shield my view as she punches in the numbers. And talk about lazy: it's 1234. Even with my middle-aged brain I can remember that!

No security camera at the entrance either. So far, so good.

We enter and… Wow. What a contrast.

Wylie's unit is small and dark. A screened-in porch and the deck outside obstruct most of the view of the water from the lower unit. But this place is two or three times bigger, bright and renovated, with cathedral ceilings. A wall of windows in the living room faces the bay, and looking out, it feels almost like you're adrift in the water, on a high deck of a large and luxurious ship.

It's so exposed though. People on the deck and beach below can look right in; it's hard not to be aware of them. If I had to choose, I actually might pick the cozy studio down below, wandering the shore only when other people were scarce. It's probably why I love my secluded house in the woods.

I make a mental note to be careful to avoid standing too close to the windows when I return to do my prowling.

"I'll go start the laundry," says Wylie, and I give her the garbage bag.

It won't take her long to load two towels and a sweatshirt, so I don't dare venture too far. All I can see within safe snooping distance is a lengthy grocery list he's got on a magnet on the refrigerator. I take a picture of it with my phone.

I'm innocently staring at the ocean view again by the time Wylie gets back.

"Oh, don't be shy," she says. "Want to see the very room where Grant is writing—or actually, where he's mostly *not* writing—his next masterpiece? I gotta show you something."

There's a small office off the kitchen.

"Check this out," says Wylie, turning to his desk.

Above it is a large bulletin board, filled with photos and newspaper clippings. Grant is the subject of all the clippings, and he's in every one of the pictures. As a young boy next to a man who must be his father—tall and dark-haired like he is. In a high school football uniform, in a cap and gown graduating from Harvard, on a sailboat, Kennedy-style, with his pretty new wife. There are surprisingly few of his family, though. Only one with his two sons in their Little League uniforms. Then starting in middle age, he's often shown in the company of celebrities, or attractive jet-setters, or showing off some exotic background, like the Taj Mahal or Machu Picchu.

Throughout the years there are a few shots in academic settings, but Maureen isn't in any of them. But there's one where he's standing in front of a blackboard, looking just like he did back then. I look at it more closely. I think I even remember that plaid flannel shirt. I certainly recognize the amused, self-satisfied smile.

I feel a growing sense of revulsion, almost like the beginnings of nausea.

"So he brought this with him?"

Wylie laughs. "Yep! He takes it with him whenever he's gone for more than a week or so. For 'inspiration.'"

"What a total fucking narcissist," I say.

I try to backtrack. "I mean, sorry. You guys are…"

I start over.

"That wasn't nice of me to say. I don't know the man at all."

"Don't apologize! That's why I showed it to you. It's comical, right? Almost Trumpian, the naked ego of it. Like, 'Look what a big important man I am.'"

It feels like time to ask her again.

"So you're *not* sleeping with him then?"

She considers.

"And if I say I'm not, would you believe me?"

"Sure! I mean, why would you lie?"

But as the sentence hangs there, the absurdity of it hits me, and she can see it in my face.

"Okay. Yeah, so if you *were* sleeping with him, you'd probably still say you weren't."

She shrugs. "Wouldn't you?"

She's got me there. But either way, at least it doesn't sound like she's in love with him.

"Let's just say we have a complicated relationship. Somewhat mercenary, to tell you the truth. A tale for another time," she says. "Maybe over a few cocktails."

"I'd love that."

I wonder if she's serious? I hope so.

"Speaking of cocktails, that's an impressive collection of alcohol," I say, as we pass a stand-alone cabinet in the living room serving as a liquor cabinet. But it's mostly filled with identical bottles of single malt scotch. It must be his favorite.

It's a long shot, but I read in the news a couple of years ago about a woman who killed her husband by putting fentanyl in his nightly cocktail. But I can't picture being here to prepare Pritchard a drink, so it would have to be waiting for him. Would the fentanyl stay lethal over time in a bottle of scotch? I'd have to research.

"His muse," Wylie says. "Though she seems to be failing him lately."

"I've never much liked Scotch," I say. "Do you drink it?"

"Not normally. But he asks me to join him occasionally, and it's easier just to say yes. But once he really gets going, he's so full of himself. So I'm always out of here after one drink."

So much for that idea. I don't want to poison Wylie; I've gotten to like her quite a bit. I realize she reminds me a little of myself at her age. I sense turbulence beneath the surface—struggle and darkness, but also passion and intensity.

"I mean I get it, what he's trying to do," she says, "I'm not against using chemicals for creative inspiration. But personally, alcohol just doesn't do it for me."

"Exactly," I say. "It's great for relaxing, but it doesn't expand your mind. You need different chemicals for that."

She tilts her head a little, like she's assessing. I've given her a pretty good opening. She said she's not against chemical inspiration… did she mean caffeine? Or is she more adventurous?

"You ever tried ayahuasca?" she asks.

"No," I say, "never had the chance."

"I did a retreat in Peru once. Talk about expanding your mind! You really start to see how everything is connected."

"I wonder if it's similar to 'shrooms? I've had great experiences with psilocybin. And you don't need to go all the way to Peru."

"Yeah, I've always wanted to do 'shrooms," she says. "But I'm not sure how to get any. And I think you need a guide for your first trip, right?"

I smile. "I think maybe I can help you with that."

CHAPTER TWELVE

SHANNON

Something's wrong.

I'm gripping the steering wheel so hard my hands ache. I feel jagged, jangly. Like somewhere inside me a huge disturbance is churning, gathering force, about to explode itself wide open.

I focus on the mechanics of driving. Bobby warned me how aggressively the cops go after even minor speeders during high season. I've got drugs in my truck, two deliveries to go. I can't risk getting pulled over.

It's been years since I've had a had a full-blown panic attack. I picture myself losing control, impulsively steering my car into oncoming traffic. That's never happened. It won't happen. I tell myself this over and over.

I try concentrating on five things I can see, then four things I can hear, counting all the blue cars on the road, singing a familiar song.

Something dark, troubling, eddies toward the surface. But then it sinks back down again too rapidly to identify.

Should I try to distract myself from it? Or try to snag it, bring it all the way to the surface, confront it squarely?

But this one feels like something big. A gravitational force I shouldn't venture too close to, or risk spiraling into a vortex that could obliterate me. It has something to do with losing Maureen, I'm sure of it. Something important but forgotten. Something devastating.

Could it be something I *wanted* to forget?

It's coming back, the tug, the terror. Years of getting too close, then fleeing. Heavy drugs, chaotic acting out. Eventually I learned to avoid the roads that led anywhere near there; I chose different routes, more practical destinations. I've so memorized the detours I'd forgotten there were older pathways, narrowed now to trails, mostly obscured by the overgrowth of time. Where do they lead?

Look away, look away. Keep going straight ahead.

But I can't talk myself down. I can't stop thinking I'm going to drive the car off the road or do something crazy. Finally I see a gas station coming up and I pull in.

When the car stops and I take my hands off the wheel, I feel a bit better. I can't kill anyone while I'm parked here. I try to slow everything down, exhale properly, stop gulping for air. I decide to just sit awhile. My parking spot is the farthest one from the convenience store entrance, so I don't feel too conspicuous as I close my eyes and concentrate on my breathing. In and out. In and out.

A red plaid flannel shirt. Rage. Accelerating, faster and faster. So much pain.

I open my eyes, my heart galloping. Where did all that come from?

Like dream fragments, they make no sense. The doctors said head trauma, that's why I don't remember much about the hospital. But did Pritchard come visit? Did he feel guilty for what he'd done? Or was he just making sure I didn't say anything about where Maureen had been going?

I can't keep poking and probing; I need to settle down. I feel another big wave coming. How am I supposed to get back on the road feeling like this?

But I have to. I still have two more deliveries to make.

I reach for the Kleenex box sitting on the floor on the passenger side. Under an inch or so of tissues are the three vials. There's ecstasy and Adderall for East Harwich, but I'm not interested in those. It's the Barnstable vial that has a tranquilizer in it, although it doesn't look like the one I used to take.

Thirty gelcaps.

It's tricky work, twisting pills apart, tapping a bit of the powder inside into a gum wrapper, then twisting the two halves of the capsules back together again. I keep going until I have what looks like enough powder to quell my panic. Each of the pills I've opened still has most of the powder left, so hopefully the client won't even notice the difference.

I chase most of the bitter taste of the powder away with a few gulps from my water bottle, but some lingers, and I appreciate this. It's a reminder that relief is on the way.

Do I need to make another medication adjustment? I've been way more careful around Allison since my slip-up about the dumpy house. And I've been vigilant about slowing my voice and movements. It's working too, I can see she's stopped worrying. But I couldn't bring my-self to go back to the old meds, the antipsychotic, the mood stabilizer, and the tranquilizer.

My psychiatrist would say that because I'm taking my antidepres-sants but not the others, the only way to go is up, up, up. Maybe I should increase my 'shroom dosage to compensate? I certainly don't want to go back to the shrink and deal with her nosy questions and lectures. She'd turn me back into a zombie. And worst of all, I wouldn't be able to talk with Niccolo anymore.

He knows me better than anyone. He knows what I need to do.

And here's what he'd say to me right now: The real problem is not what drugs I'm taking or not taking. The real problem is Grant Pritchard. His continued existence on this earth is what's setting me off. I just need to get the fentanyl from Bobby, get a big fat fatal dose of it into him, and remove the trigger entirely. Then I won't need any drugs at all.

After more time passes, the tranquilizer starts to do the job, and it feels safe to get back on the highway.

Barnstable is a middle-aged guy; his living room wall is lined with bookcases, and he has the look of a history professor. East Harwich is a twenty-something hipster couple; I have to ring the bell a couple of times because they've been trying out their new espresso machine and couldn't hear me at first. They apologize and offer me a decaf cappuccino. All smooth sailing.

When I get back to Provincetown, I still have one more errand to do. The delay at the gas station has me running later than I was hoping. I know Niccolo will be getting restless. But this won't take long.

When I approach Wylie's condo unit, I can hear her talking to someone through the window. Through the screen door I can see she's got a visitor on the living room couch. A little younger than Wylie, maybe mid-twenties. She's a cute blond with a wholesome face, almost as tall as Allison. Her hair is cut in a fade with a few blue streaks, and she's wearing a Boston Dyke March T-shirt.

I rap on the screen door, and the woman looks over at me, squinting into the sun behind me.

"Hey babe," she shouts toward the kitchen, "someone at the door!"

I can see Wylie coming from the kitchen. She hands a pint of ice cream with a spoon in it to the woman on the couch. She's got her own pint of ice cream as well. She smells pretty heavily of weed.

"Sorry to interrupt, just here for the sweatshirt," I say. "Thank you so much for washing it."

"No worries," she says. "Be right back."

As I wait, the woman on the couch gives me the blissful, checked-out smile of someone who is very happily and thoroughly stoned.

"Are you the woman with the comic-book cat?" she asks. "Wylie says it's almost like he talks in real life too."

"Yep, that's me," I say.

"Cool," she says, then turns her attention to her ice cream.

Are they girlfriends? Maybe Wylie isn't sleeping with Pritchard after all. Although she could be bisexual, polyamorous? So many more options these days.

Does calling someone "babe" necessarily mean you're together?

I know it really doesn't matter if Wylie's gay or not. It's just that I hate to think of her having sex with that man.

Wylie comes back with Allison's Red Sox hoodie. It's completely clean, thank God—no trace left of Niccolo's misbehavior.

"So," she says, "would Friday work for the 'shroom thing? If you can get them that soon. It's perfect because he'll be in Boston all day. He has a doctor's appointment and a meeting with his agent."

"Sure, that works," I say.

"And hey," she adds, "bring Niccolo along too! I like the little guy."

I leave her to her ice cream social with Boston Dyke March. When I turn to go, I hear a car pulling into the gravel parking area in front of the building.

No.

It's the white Jaguar.

His long strides take him to the building's front gate before I can get down the walkway to pass through it.

"Hello," he says, making the greeting sound like an accusation.

He's blocking the walkway, so I have no choice but to stop, not unless I want to run right into him. This is the second time he's forced me to come uncomfortably close to him in order to get where I need to go.

"I've seen you before, haven't I?" he asks.

There's no point in lying.

"Yeah. You're the author guy, right? I was in a workshop at the art center a few weeks back, I think I saw you there."

"But somewhere else too. Maybe more than once."

"Don't think so!" I say. "I don't live around here."

"I definitely recognize you. From *before?*"

His voice is so poisonous.

"I wasn't sure at first. You weren't as… big." He looks me up and down. "I'm not trying to be cruel, but you should maybe talk to a doctor about that? Carrying extra weight, it can negatively impact your health."

My body is screaming, alarms and sirens blaring from all quarters.

"And your hair, it's gotten quite a bit grayer, stress can do that. So you see, it's not good for you, what you're doing to yourself."

What *I'm* doing to myself?

"It's not the first time you've followed me. Do you think you're invisible? Women sometimes have these fantasies about me; they start to confuse me with characters in my books. And then they start to believe their own stories. They feel I've promised them something, that I owe them somehow. I feel sorry for you, truly. It must be a hard way to live. But you're not getting any money from me, just be clear on that."

"I think you've confused me with someone else."

"No. I haven't. And just so you know… I have excellent attorneys. And they do love to file lawsuits—defamation, harassment. I suppose it's their job, to be ruthless. I don't try to second-guess their legal strategies. But be careful, is all I'm saying. Litigation is expensive; it can bankrupt most people. And often the women who pursue me… well they have issues. They have pasts. It all tends to come out."

He leans in closer. Puts his hand on my upper arm. It's even worse that he does it so gently. But I'm frozen now, unable to move away, or say anything. I can barely breathe.

"I can tell you feel hurt, and I'm sorry about that." His voice is so much softer now. "But this—this isn't the answer. Whatever you think happened, it didn't. You need to go back to your life, try to make it a peaceful and happy one. And I wish you luck with that."

He lifts off his hand, and I charge past him, shaking, and get in the truck.

He stares at me as I leave like he's thinking, hard. But I have no idea what's in his head.

* * *

By the time I pull into Allison's driveway, I'm even more shaken by what's just happened. I don't have any more tranquilizers, but there's wine and beer in the fridge and vodka in the kitchen cabinet. I have gummies as well, with a hefty amount of indica and CBD. I know not to add too much booze to the tranquilizer I already took, but I need more calming substances in my system than are currently circulating.

When I open the door, I see Chloe sitting primly at the dining room table, working on her computer. Even the back of her head radiates hostile vibes. She hears me close the front door and turns to look my way, gives a weak smile and a half-hearted wave. I manage a polite smile and a "hey there."

As tempting as it is to get the booze and cannabis going ASAP, I need to try to drop off the sweatshirt, then go check on Niccolo. I've been gone for a good part of the day.

I'm in luck: Allison is in her office with the door closed; I can hear she's on a Zoom call for work. And with Chloe busy on her laptop in the dining room, I have no problem slipping the sweatshirt back in the hamper.

When I open the door to my room, Niccolo isn't on the bed where I usually find him napping. He's on the floor, pacing back and forth.

There you are, Shannon! You've been gone so long!

"I know, baby. I'm so sorry!"

You're shaking! Are you okay?

"I hope so. Jesus."

I pick him up and rock with him back and forth, he's rubbing his forehead against my chin, purring intensely, like he knows how distraught I am and wants to heal me with as many calming vibrations as he can muster.

We sit on the bed together, and I tell him about my day. But going back over my encounter with Pritchard gets me even more agitated than before.

I stand up, go over to look in the mirror hanging over the dresser. Staring back is a fat ugly woman, a fat ugly *old* woman with so many gray hairs, how have I been kidding myself that it's only a sprinkling?

A hideous old hag.

It starts to echo in my head. *I am hideous. Hideous. Hideous. Hideous. Shannon! Stop that!*

Niccolo's voice is sharp, more emphatic than I've ever heard it.

You are not hideous. You are beautiful! You are a good person. Repeat that instead.

He's a cat. But I do what he says. I even start saying it softly out loud, like a mantra. "I am beautiful. I am a good person. I am beautiful. I am a good person."

It's helping. I take a deep breath.

"Thank you, Niccolo," I say. "I'll be right back."

I pick up his empty food and water bowls. Go out to the kitchen to refill them, then make a second trip for a large glass of vodka and cranberry juice.

I sit on the bed, chewing on a gummy, drinking my cocktail, while Niccolo eats his dinner. I try not to think of anything. When I start to remember Pritchard standing there, insulting me, threatening me, I push it away for now. I just keep repeating my mantra, *I am beautiful, I am a good person.*

I toss aside any distorted memory images that try to intrude. They don't make sense; I don't have to pay attention to them.

I am beautiful, I am a good person.

What would I do without Niccolo? Even though we have our disagreements, he is by far the best thing in my life.

My drink goes down easy, like a soda. I'd like about three more but that would be stupid. What I need is food. I get off the bed to go make some dinner. Poor Niccolo looks up at me. I hate to leave him locked in here, but I have no choice.

I can't wait to get out of this house.

As I walk toward the door, I catch my reflection in the mirror. There she is again. Fat. Ugly. Old. Hideous, hideous, hideous.

I see a pair of scissors in the pencil jar on the desk. When I step into the hallway Chloe walks by, nonchalant, like she just needed something from Allison's bedroom and happened to be passing by.

Nosy bitch.

I go into the guest bathroom and close the door.

There are a couple of big white streaks that starts at my temples, so I snip at them. A lot of white on the left, near my ear.

Big hunks of white hair, and plenty of red too, it's hard to separate them, they're falling into the sink, onto the counter, down to the floor, I don't care where they land. In the mirror there are tears coming from my eyes, but it's like my eyes are doing it on their own, it has nothing to do with me.

Snip, snip, snip, I didn't plan it this way but off it all comes. It's horrifying and satisfying at the same time. I am cutting out the old, cutting off the hideous, snipping away the shame, hoping my real self can somehow shine through.

There's a knock at the bathroom door.

"Hey Shannon, are you okay? Everything all right in there?"

It's Chloe's voice.

"Go away," I say.

Finally I've gotten all the hair off that I can with the scissors. It's quite a look I've got going. Tufts of red and white, all different lengths, depending on how close I could get to my head.

I take out my razor from my toiletry bag. I don't have shaving cream, so I do the best I can with lotion and a bar of soap. It's harder than I thought to shave your head. I'm halfway through when more banging on the door startles me.

"Go away!" I shout again. "Fuck, you made me cut myself!"

The cut doesn't hurt, but head cuts always make a show of bleeding like crazy. I look straight out of a horror movie, bald on one side, jagged tufts of red and white hair on the other, and a stream of blood spilling from the top of my scalp onto my forehead and face. The scar on my left side, normally covered up by hair, adds a bit of Frankenstein flair.

But there's no use trying to clean up yet. I won't bleed to death. I just let the drips keep coming. When they stop I'll wash up and see if I can find a Band-Aid.

But I don't get too much further towards shaving the rest of my scalp before there's another knock.

"Look Shannon, I know you'd rather talk to Allison, but she's still on her call. You're not thinking of hurting yourself, are you? I… I saw the scissors."

Great. I'd forgotten she worked for a hospital. She's playing amateur shrink: doing a suicide check like I'm some sort of mental patient.

Why won't she just go away?

I unlock the door to explain I'm not planning on offing myself, and I swing it wide open.

"I'm fine all right? I don't need your help, Chloe."

She looks at me and makes an absurd sound, a cry of alarm somewhere between a moan and a scream.

"I am just cutting my hair!"

I'm just so tired of her lurking presence, her relentless, constipated disapproval.

"So could you please just mind your own goddamn business, you nosy cunt? I've seen you spying on me, I know you want to get rid of me, you're trying to turn Allison against me. I get it, you don't like me, and that's fine, I honestly don't give a rat's ass what you think!"

There's a movement to my left. And there's Allison, standing off to the side. She's heard the whole thing. She must have come running as soon as Chloe made her weird yelping sound.

Part of me can see how comical this all is, how horribly crazy I must look, a screeching, bleeding, hacked-up zombie woman, and I want to laugh. But instead the tears are falling harder now. And I know how badly I've just fucked up.

Again.

The weight of the last few hours comes crashing down on me and I feel like I can barely stand up.

"I'll go now," I say. "I know you guys don't want me here. I just need to go get Niccolo and…"

"No," says Chloe. "You stay here. I'll leave. You have nowhere to go, especially not like that."

Her voice is unusually direct and forceful.

"And I don't think you should be driving," she says. "I'll go back to my condo tonight. No big deal."

Allison looks totally at a loss. "Chloe, wait, you can stay. You don't have to…"

"It's okay," says Chloe. "Have you got everything you need for her cut? I don't think it's serious, it's mostly stopped bleeding. Disinfectant, bandages? And if you need shaving cream or clippers to finish the job with her hair, I can make a quick run to CVS, drop the stuff off outside. I really don't think you should leave her alone right now."

Allison is just nodding, too shaken to speak.

"And another thing," says Chloe. "Make sure she gets professional help, okay?"

Chloe is talking to Allison as though I'm not standing right here in front of her. But in a way, I'm not. It all feels very far away.

CHAPTER THIRTEEN

ALLISON

The house is so still. But the silence isn't restful like I thought it would be. It feels heavy, almost like I can hear the blankness, the emptiness.

Maybe a grocery store run? I'm about due. I need to get out of here. And I should check in on Shannon. I haven't seen her in a couple of days.

It took me a while to get over the shock, the ugliness. She called Chloe the "C" word! So shouty and nasty and out of control. But then right after, so regretful, just crying and crying and crying. I got her to agree to get in touch with her doctors, and she was totally on board with that. I just hope her new medications work better than the last ones did. Her psychiatrist called them in the next morning, and she's doubled up on her therapy video calls too. The last time we talked she said she was feeling much better.

But I couldn't just abandon her and tell her to leave. Not after all she's done for me. She's rescued me twice now; she's turned my life around! What kind of friend would I be if I just shut her out when it was her turn to need help?

But still, I'm feeling a bit nervous as I walk over to the cottage.

When she opens the door: oh my God.

It still throws me, that she's got no hair anymore. It's not so notice-able when she's wearing a headscarf, or the fedora, or the shaggy blond Rod Stewart wig Bobby lent her from his costume collection. But now, up close, her naked head is distracting and it's hard to maintain eye contact like normal.

"Hey Shannon. Just off to Stop and Shop. You need anything?"

"No, I'm good, stocked up yesterday. But thanks! Oh, and guess what just arrived?"

She opens the door a bit wider.

"The dining room table!"

Finally, she's got one real piece of furniture in there. Niccolo is sitting on top of it, I guess so he can look out the window. He looks over at me briefly, then turns away. Starts cleaning his paw.

"Nice, right? Clean lines. You like the cherry finish? You'd never know I got it for practically nothing off Wayfair."

Shannon steps back a bit, waves me forward.

"Come on in! I don't want to tempt Niccolo with the door open."

"Oh right!" That's the last thing we need. "So, wow. Everything looks great!"

I try to sound enthusiastic. I can definitely see the potential—the wood floors look so nice now that they've been refinished, and the fresh paint brightens everything up.

But with her camping out in here, it's not exactly a showplace. She's got a couple of beach chairs and an air mattress she borrowed from me, and Bobby lent her his sleeping bag. Instead of a fridge, she has her cooler. And she made a run to the thrift shop to pick up an ancient microwave, a hot plate, and a dingy orange corduroy beanbag chair. As well as my parents' old green lamp. The one I thought was so ugly that I gave it away.

She sees me looking at it.

"Isn't that awesome? So retro. Classic '60s. And it's back in style! It'll be perfect for the Airbnb."

"Totally," I say, not offering up its origin story. Does she need further evidence of how clueless I can be?

But the cottage is all still such a mess: her clothes heaped in piles because there's no dresser, cat toys everywhere. And almost half the living room is taken up with paint cans, pails, tiles, tarps, a ladder, and various tools.

It seems silly now, Shannon sleeping on the floor out here in the middle of a construction site, when Chloe's been spending almost all her time in Boston anyway. We're texting more than talking—still friendly, but not as goofy and gushy as before. She's using far fewer exclamation points.

"So are you doing okay out here?" I ask Shannon. "I mean, really?"

"I'm doing great! *Really*. And I'm still so sorry about my blowing up like that. I'd had such a bad day, and I didn't realize the last prescriptions just weren't kicking in the right way. And Niccolo. He was so unhappy. Anyway, I should have come out here earlier, instead of taking everything out on poor Chloe."

She's apologized over and over, and explained what happened: how one of Bobby's clients made a joking reference to gray hair—he wasn't trying to be mean; he was including himself in the joke as well—but it struck a nerve, which made her freak out about looking older. And being single again, and feeling ugly and undesirable. I guess a lot of straight women take the aging thing super hard.

Shannon goes over to her cooler, opens it up. "Want a beer or anything?"

It's a little early for me. I notice there's not much else in there besides the beer bottles and a sweaty block of ice. A couple of yogurts, half a cantaloupe. But I guess without a real stove or an oven, she has to do a lot more takeout.

"No thanks, I'm good."

Shannon reaches in for a beer, opens it.

"You know, I hadn't really thought about it before. How my being around this summer would be awfully hard on Chloe."

She's right. It *has* been hard on her. From the very beginning, Chloe convinced herself Shannon didn't like her. At first, without much evidence. Then it became a self-fulfilling prophecy, because Shannon picked up on Chloe's uneasiness and took it personally.

What is it with the two of them? And how do I make it stop?

"So how come you think it's been hard?"

Since Chloe never talks about it, I'm curious what Shannon thinks.

She reaches into the cooler, opens another beer and hands it to me. She pulls out the two chairs and we sit down. It feels a little surreal, drinking beer in beach chairs before noon. Like we should at least be outside, staring at some water.

I take a sip of the beer to be polite.

"Well, Alley Cat. It's just... we go so far back. There's a kind of connection you make when you're young. It's intense, even if it's not really logical. Totally crazy sometimes. Like, we couldn't have been more different."

"Practically polar opposites."

"I'm not usually like that. I don't let people in. You caught me at a strange time in my life, after Maureen died. I mean, sure, since then I've had boyfriends. Roommates. Drinking buddies. Business partners. But best friends? That was a one-off. And so long ago. So it surprised the hell out of me, coming here, just how natural it still felt between us. After all this time!"

"Totally the same for me! It's like seeing you again, all of a sudden we went straight back to being besties," I say.

But wait, isn't Chloe my 'bestie?'

"You probably act a little different around me than most people?" Shannon says. "More comfortable, more open?"

It's true. I feel so close to them both, just in different ways. Shannon knew me back when I was at my most awkward, vulnerable, and miserable. Yet she acted like I was totally normal. Completely acceptable. Even fun! Only my mother ever had that same magical power: to change how I felt about myself.

And Shannon's still got it. I wouldn't even be with Chloe now if Shannon hadn't assumed it was possible.

"So yeah," Shannon says. "I'm sure Chloe senses how you feel. And for a lot of people, it would be no big deal—our history, this bizarre bond we have. But some people, if they're maybe a little insecure? It hits different. But you know her better than I do."

When I first met Chloe, I thought she was so self-assured. I thought *I* was the insecure one. Is Shannon implying that Chloe's been jealous?

Chloe knows I've never been attracted to Shannon; it's not a sex thing. But as innocent as it feels to me, could she feel threatened?

But Chloe's always encouraging me to spend time with Shannon. That's not how jealous, possessive girlfriends work.

"Anyway, tell Chloe again that I'm really sorry," Shannon says.

"She's already forgotten all about it," I lie.

"Right." Shannon smiles like I've just made a joke.

She rises from her beach chair.

"So hey, while you're here, can I show you something? I wanted to see if you're cool with it."

Above the bathroom door in the hallway, she's painted some ivy— like a vine is growing on top of the doorframe. There's a mouse peeking over the edge, looking out toward the rest of the cottage.

"I was just playing around. I thought, maybe a touch of whimsy…"

"That's so cool—I totally love it!"

It's adorable. So detailed, and the clever way it's shaded: it almost looks three-dimensional.

"It's like something you'd see in a picture book for kids, one of the classics," I say. "Wait, which one am I thinking of…"

"*Wind in the Willows*? That's what I was riffing on."

"Yes, exactly!"

"So you don't mind? I can totally paint over it; you'll never know it was there."

"No, don't do that. The Airbnb people will love it. You're so talented, Shannon. Seriously!"

She grins.

"That's what I love about you, Alley Cat. You've always been my biggest fan."

* * *

Left foot. Right foot. Left foot. Right foot.

The dune is much higher and steeper than I expected, and my feet sink helplessly with each step. Sand leaks into my shoes, they're getting heavy and squishy. I'm already short of breath and we've only climbed a quarter of the way up the first hill.

When Shannon proposed we go on a dune hike, and said she wanted us to get up at four in the morning to avoid the heat and the crowds, of course I wanted to say no. But she's been spending a lot more time holed up in the cottage lately. Which is actually partly my fault. Because I've been inviting Chloe to stay over a *lot* lately, and Shannon reacts by hiding out.

But I'm so glad Chloe's back! I love our endless conversations about nothing. Or the way she snuggles herself against me before we get out of bed in the morning, wrapping me in her arms. Even sharing a sink when we brush our teeth—the way we take turns spitting. Every silly second of being together feels like a gift.

It's such a frustrating teeter-totter: when things are "up" with Chloe, they seem to go "down" with Shannon. I hoped that by dragging my butt out of bed in the middle of the night to go on a hike with her, I could level things out a little more.

Shannon notices me slowing down, so we stop for a moment to rest. There's no real view yet, but the sun is just coming up. The light is golden, the shadows long and evocative. The air is still and cool.

We continue up the hill; it gets even steeper. Left. Right. Left. Right. But when we reach the top, my aching legs seem like a small price to pay.

How could anything be this beautiful?

We're standing at the top of a huge bowl of sand, so pristine, swept clean of footprints by last night's winds. And beyond the farthest edge you can see another rise, with more gorgeous lunar landscape to come. Farther still, the sea and sky and clouds. It's like getting off a ski lift with a whole mountain of virgin white powder waiting. Our own private wonderland.

As I start down the other side, Shannon says, "No, not like that!"

"What?"

I stop. She's never been out here before either, what is she on about?

"You can't just walk down, plonk plonk plonk. You have to run and jump a little! Take big steps!"

And with that, she's off, bounding down the hill, shouting "Whoooooooo!"

Theoretically, the sand should be pretty forgiving if I fall. But still. It's so steep!

But I go for it. And each step is a thrilling leap, my landings softly cushioned as though I'm bouncing through fluffy clouds, and I'm laughing, and it almost feels like the sand is laughing with me as I spring from one foot to the other all the way down into the sugar bowl.

"See?" says Shannon, grinning.

At the bottom, the trail curves upwards again, but I feel stronger now, more energized, and the next hill isn't quite as daunting.

When we reach the top, we take a narrow trail that cuts across the edge of another steeper, more angular face of the mammoth dune. It's so slanted that it's almost, but not quite, scary. It feels like rock climbing but without the bad part about rocks: the hard edges, the danger.

We reach the other side. No more up. Below are trees and a creek and underbrush in various heathered colors, and in the distance I can see a couple of the dune shacks. Eventually, the ocean. So much ocean.

"Should we just sit a minute and soak it all in?" Shannon asks.

"Sure."

A large bird flies overhead, maybe some kind of hawk. After all our slogging, it's funny to see it swooping so high, so effortlessly, not even moving its wings.

"I can't believe you've never been out here before," Shannon says.

"Courtney and I got as far as the trailhead once," I say, watching the bird settle into one of the trees below. "But we had this huge fight. I still remember it. I'd sounded too "half-hearted" when I thanked her for packing our lunches. I mean, it was probably true. I've always hated tuna fish sandwiches."

"And she made them anyway?"

"I guess that day she just decided I should try a little harder to like them? Then, when I apologized for not apologizing right, she thought I was making fun of her. Of course I wasn't; I never dared. Anyway, she canceled the hike and dumped me off back at the rental and went off by herself to the beach. Took her a few more days to stop pouting."

"Wait. The rental?"

"We never got to stay with my parents. Courtney wasn't comfortable around them."

"Holy fuck, Alley Cat."

"Yeah. Holy Fuck, right?"

For some reason, that makes me laugh, swearing like Shannon does.

"It was just tuna fish, but it was pretty typical. Eighteen years. Everything was always about her and her feelings. Like I wasn't a person too. Like I didn't count."

"It's too bad we lost touch, the two of us," Shannon says.

I'm thinking the same thing.

"I bet I wouldn't have stayed. If I'd had you to talk to. I mean, my mom tried. She hinted. But she didn't want to interfere."

"I would have *so* interfered. I mean, not by wiping the floor with her. Though I wouldn't rule that out. But I would have made you see it."

"Yeah."

We go quiet again, just looking at the view.

"Should we keep going, all the way to the water?"

What's gotten into me? Proposing we hike all the way out to a distant beach, when it takes all of ten minutes to drive to Herring Cove, which has nice clean bathrooms and a snack bar?

"Another time, maybe," says Shannon. "I haven't been sleeping so great; I'm a little wiped out."

She does look a little drawn, now that she mentions it.

"We could at least move the guest room bed into the cottage for you. You might sleep better on that, until the real bed arrives."

"Nah, it's not the air mattress. Maybe it's perimenopause? So many nightmares lately, I don't even *want* to go to sleep."

"I hate that. Like you're taking a final exam in a class you never went to? Or you're out in public and you realize you're only wearing your underwear?"

She laughs. "Alley Cat, those are so *you*! No, mine are, um… darker. A lot darker."

"Like…?"

She takes a moment or two to answer. "Car wrecks, mainly. I've been driving off the road almost every night. I wake up right before I'm about to go off a cliff, or plow into oncoming traffic, or slam into a building."

There's something pent up in her voice.

"That sounds so creepy!"

"Well, I know exactly why I keep dreaming it. That horrible day when I cut off my hair? Earlier I had a panic attack while I was driving. I kept thinking I'd lose control, just swerve out of my lane into oncoming traffic for no reason. It was…"

She drifts for a moment, pulled into the memory. Then abruptly shakes herself, like a wet dog flinging off bathwater.

"Anyway," she continues, "I can't even explain it. It was awful. But fortunately with the new meds, I haven't had another one. Now I just keep dreaming I'm crashing, over and over."

Shannon, a panic attack? I can easily picture her angry, or drunk, or weepy. But scared?

"No wonder you don't want to go back to sleep!"

"Last night, though, I had a dream that was even worse."

She pauses and looks at me, like, do you really want to know?

I nod for her to keep going.

"So I was a doctor. Standing in an operating room, lots of bright lights, machines beeping. I was about to perform surgery. I can still see that tray with all the scalpels, and needles, and scissors, and a huge saw. I was supposed to be doing an amputation, taking off a leg, but no one was sure which leg it was. I look down at the patient, and it's Maureen! And she says 'no Shannon, don't!' But somehow I have to do it anyway. And then the sound of screaming, horrible screams, over and over."

"Oh my God!"

Poor Shannon. I'm no psychiatrist, but it sounds like even after all this time, she still feels guilty for not somehow saving Maureen. Now *she's* the one driving. *She's* the one in the dream who's cutting off her sister's leg. What's that called… survivor's guilt?

I wonder how good Shannon's therapist could be, if she's still struggling so much?

"You still miss Maureen, it sounds like."

"Yeah," she says, staring intently out to the horizon. As though her dead sister might be out there somewhere. "I still do."

Then she turns to me.

"But for me it's been decades. With your mom… it hasn't been so long. You must still feel pretty wrecked?"

Wait. We were talking about Shannon, about her nightmares, her trauma. I don't even talk about my mom's death with Chloe. Maybe because I don't want to admit to her that I'm a bit broken? That she's stuck with damaged goods.

I just sit with it for a while.

"So I must not be doing it right? This grieving thing. Three years, and I'm still so messed up! I think about her all the time. I know it's real, that she's gone, but at the same time, it can't possibly be true."

Shannon nods. Doesn't say anything for a bit.

"But Allison. Your mom, she was amazing! And you guys were so tight. Of course you're a mess. There's no right or wrong when it comes to grief. But I promise, eventually it'll get easier. Less like you're being stabbed through the heart every few hours, and more like you're just being slapped silly in the face every now and then."

"Wow, that's so reassuring!" I say, but I can't help smiling a little.

We sit in silence, looking out at the water. Just watching a couple of fishing boats leaving ephemeral white wakes behind them as they make their way through the vast ocean.

CHAPTER FOURTEEN

SHANNON

Low tide is spectacular on the beach outside Wylie's condo. We're taking a watery walk along the shore, waiting for her mushrooms to kick in. I'm in a sundress and Wylie's wearing shorts, so we're not shy about splashing around.

The soles of our feet sample the soft sand, the slimy seaweed, the sharp edges of shells. Currents here arrive from different directions; they've sculpted the sand into peninsulas, islands, tumbling streams and murky swamps. Industrious crabs scuttle below, tiny fish dart in perfect synchrony. How do they all know to change directions in the very same millisecond? An occasional jellyfish lies there trying to look innocuous, but we are wise to them. We step carefully around their tentacles.

"Snakes!" Wylie points and laughs. The terrain now includes a stretch of fat, undulating ripples of sand. They do look a lot like giant serpents.

"Is it just me or are they moving?" she asks. "Like slithering, slowly. Slowly slithering snakes. That's hard to say!" She giggles again.

And we're off.

"How are you feeling?" I ask. "So far so good?"

"Wow. Nice. Very nice. And getting nicer. Oh my God, just look at those two dogs! They act like they're just innocently playing fetch, but they're so transparent. They're obviously superior beings, alien angels sent from another planet, to help humans learn how to behave."

"I think you're onto something."

We walk a little further. I'm so glad the mushrooms agree with her; when it comes to drugs, brains are tricky.

And thank God my brain chemistry finally seems to be titrated exactly right. The balance between edgy energy and expansive-but-disorienting spaciousness is at perfect equilibrium. I'm not using a "real" doctor, though it's better Allison thinks I am. Poor thing worries about me, but she doesn't need to. Between the micro-doses of mushrooms, strategic use of alcohol, THC, my anti-depressant refill, and a double order of tranqs I attributed to one of Bobby's clients but paid for myself, I think I've finally got it nailed.

"So hey," I say to Wylie, who's smiling quite blissfully. "Are you okay if we start to head back now? I don't want to leave Niccolo alone too long without checking on him."

I'm sure Niccolo's fine, but I can't get done what I need to from out on the beach.

"Niccolo! Yes, let's go see how he's doing. Talk about a superior being!"

When we get back to her condo, the superior being is sitting on Wylie's couch, back legs splayed, licking his butthole.

"I'd say he looks pretty comfortable here. I think he likes you, Wylie."

I do like her! Niccolo reassures me.

Wylie looks quite pleased.

"You think? Well, the feeling is mutual. There's something about him I find very compelling."

"Okay if I put on some music?" I ask. "I have a pretty good trip playlist on my phone, if you don't mind me pairing it with your speaker."

"That sounds perfect."

As we listen to the music, I realize how nice it feels to be back here again. I've missed talking to Wylie, but I haven't dared return for fear of seeing Pritchard. And I'm not sure I can even keep going with the graphic novel. I'm at the point where I have to decide whether "Colleen" is going to sleep with her teacher or not. To be seduced, and then to endure the shame and regret, in order for her ultimate victory and self-acceptance to be meaningful. For the sake of the story, it probably needs to happen. But I don't know that I can face putting it on the page.

I notice Wylie swaying; she's starting to sink into the rhythms, her eyes closed, going inward.

It's time. I can't leave her alone too long, but she seems to be doing exceptionally well so far.

Can you keep her entertained while I'm gone? I ask Niccolo. *If she gets antsy, just pay lots of attention to her. Be your usual adorable self.*

Of course, he says.

"So Wylie, are you okay here for a few minutes? I left some stuff in the truck that I think will be fun, really good for tripping. Niccolo can take care of you while I'm gone."

She grins.

"I'll be right here, inside the music!"

I go outside and take the stairs to the upper floor, treading softly. I put on a pair of elastic surgical gloves like they do in the movies to avoid leaving fingerprints, and I punch in the code, 1234. I don't know if there's much of any insulation between the floor and Wylie's ceiling, so once I'm inside I slip off my sandals and move slowly. The music I picked to play for her has a lot of percussion, a thrumming bass and lots of drums, so I'm hoping any sound from my footsteps will just wash into the mix.

The vial of twenty fentanyl tablets was expensive, but they should do the trick. I'm just hoping to find something in the condo, quickly, that I can slip a bunch of pills in. Something that already tastes bitter, but not anything he'd conceivably share with anyone else.

I've written and addressed his suicide note, using the grocery list I took a photo of as a handwriting sample. It took quite a few tries. I haven't forged anything in a couple of decades, for starters. But I got better and better with each draft.

What was harder was to capture the right tone.

My first attempts rang false somehow, until I realized they were far too apologetic. Grant Pritchard is not a man who would face his end feeling remorse. Resentment is more his style. So while I left his justifications vague, I hinted at "unfair" accusations against him, his conduct misunderstood, his peace of mind and creative energy shattered by small minds and puritanical attitudes.

But first things first: I need to find a way to get these pills into him. I've ruled out the refrigerator, because anything edible or drinkable could be offered to Wylie or another guest. What I'm hoping for is something in his medicine cabinet.

There are some possibilities here… a bottle of Pepto Bismol—would the tablets dissolve in that? Some allergy pills that are gelcaps, but they look too small and the recommended dose is one every twenty-four hours. And could I be absolutely sure a guest of his wouldn't borrow one, or need the Pepto for an upset stomach?

I close the medicine cabinet and start pulling open drawers under the bathroom sink. In the second one are supplements of various kinds.

Bingo: a large bottle of Testo Blast, a "proprietary blend of ingredients crafted to naturally boost testosterone." Ha! The pills are nice and large, they're white gelcaps. Best of all, the bottle suggests taking three to five of them twice a day. I could carefully crush the opioid pills and probably fit four or five in every gelcap!

But damn it, I don't have time today. I don't have a mortar and pestle, and I've got to be precise so nothing looks suspicious. I'll need to order another bottle of his pills online, plus some identical white capsules, and fill them up at home. Then get back in here at least one more time to swap the bottles out. But I'll only need a minute or two the next time.

I take a picture of the bottle, and slip one of the pills in my pocket to be sure I get everything exactly right.

I could probably sneak back in when he's off with his personal trainer, but it seems too risky. A session could easily be canceled, or he could forget something and come back for it. Plus, Wylie's usually home then. I don't want her to see or hear me. Will Pritchard be out of town again, like today? That would be perfect. It would give me a long enough window to make sure Wylie's out of the house too.

I go into his office. He's a boomer, so I'm hoping he's old-fashioned enough to have some sort of calendar or datebook. Boomers I've known rarely rely solely on their phones.

And there, right in the top desk drawer: a big leather-bound day planner, with workout goals, medical and legal appointments, meetings with publishing people. Some of these meetings might be virtual, but he's got a four-day trip to Los Angeles coming up. It's during Carnival, which is not for almost two weeks, so I should have time to get the fake supplement pills ready. And Wylie will likely go watch the big parade. Even if she doesn't, she loves to go on long walks, and three days will give me plenty of chance to stake out the place and sneak in when she's gone.

I slip my sandals back on, close the door, remove the gloves, and hurry out to my truck.

When I return, Wylie's at the kitchen table facing Niccolo, who is perched on his beach towel, returning her gaze.

"Oh good, you're finally back!" she says.

I put all my playthings onto the kitchen counter: bongo drums I found at the thrift shop, a big pink bottle of soapy solution for making bubbles with wands of different sizes, a kaleidoscope, a large candle and some matches, a mandala coloring book.

"Time seems funny on 'shrooms, right? Like I've been gone for hours or something instead of just a couple of minutes?"

"Exactly!" she agrees.

"What have you two been up to?" I ask her.

"So I was just trying to have a conversation with Niccolo. I think the 'shrooms are helping, like I'm almost there. But I can't quite hear him yet. I need your help."

Oh.

I'm not sure how I feel about this.

"You do realize that this is the real Niccolo, an actual cat? Not the Niccolo who's a character in a book? Because that's the Niccolo who knows how to talk."

"Oh, a candle, that's perfect!" says Wylie, undeterred. "Staring at a flame is one of my favorite induction methods. My therapist says I'm quite suggestible, but I'm really not very good at self-hypnosis. I need a voice to guide me."

"You want me to hypnotize you?"

"Oh, could you please? I'll tell you how, I'm pretty easy. Guided imagery, basically. Going down staircases, walking slowly through a forest, more and more relaxed, until things start to feel all floaty and magical. God, it's been so long since I got to have a deep conversation with the spiritual world. I knew that the mushrooms would help, and I know Niccolo will be the perfect totem guide. He already seems so tuned in, right?"

I'm so conflicted.

What would it mean if Wylie could hypnotize herself into hearing Niccolo talk to her? Would it be the *real* Niccolo? And if so, how jealous will I feel if I have to share him?

On the other hand, it would be so nice to have someone open-minded like Wylie to talk to about Niccolo. It's been hard, having to keep this huge, exciting part of my life a secret. Who knows where he comes from. But if he's a special being from the spiritual world, maybe he has a soul that's large and generous enough to commune with two humans at the same time?

"What do you think, Niccolo? Is that something you'd like to try?"

Only if you'd feel comfortable with it, Shannon. After all, you are my person.

"That's sweet of you, taking care of my feelings like that. But I think I'm okay with it. So if you're good, let's give it a try."

"Oh my God, I knew it!" says Wylie. "I knew you could really hear him!"

Shit. I've just been talking to Niccolo out loud, not in my head.

"I suppose I'm pretty suggestible too," I say.

"I'm not surprised. You give off this aura. Like you see things most people can't? When I first met you, I sensed something, like you're a kindred spirit."

I wonder, does the headscarf I'm wearing make me look like a fortune teller from an old B movie? But still, I feel flattered. The feeling is mutual. I do feel a confusing sense of connection with her.

I put the big chunky purple candle on a saucer and light it; it smells unsurprisingly like lavender. I place it in the center of the table.

You still okay with this? I ask Niccolo.

I am if you are, he says.

"I'm good."

I look over, but Wylie doesn't seem to hear him. At least not yet.

About half an hour into our session, after Wylie has stared into the candle flame until her eyes fluttered closed, and I've led her through a long walk through a magical forest full of friendly elves and talking trees, we arrive at the moment we've been waiting for.

"And now, Wylie," I say, using the calm, lulling tones of the countless meditation and visualization audios I've listened to over the years, "you may open your eyes. Is there anything you'd like to talk with Niccolo about?"

She opens her eyes, moves her head to face Niccolo, but her stare seems vacant, her face slack.

"Niccolo. Hello there."

There is only silence. I hear nothing.

"Oh God," she says, "me too!"

She hears him! I'm not sure how I feel. Excited? Afraid? Both, I think, braided tightly together.

"Do you like being a cat? I mean, if you could choose, would you be something else?"

After a moment, Wylie laughs.

"But a lion, that's just a bigger version of a cat, right?"

Poor little guy: the soul of an apex predator, trapped in the fluffy body of a domestic housecat.

She asks a few more chatty preliminary questions, nothing momentous, sort of like she's warming him up.

Then she asks, "so can you predict the future?"

A very long pause. So not a simple yes or no answer.

"Sure, that makes sense. Probabilities. But from a different perspective, that's cool."

She takes a moment to think of her next question.

"So do you think I should just call it? Is there any reason to keep hanging around?"

It sure sounds like she's talking about her relationship with Pritchard. I hope Niccolo tells her to cut him loose!

"I guess that makes sense, maybe just a little longer. And so do you think she knows?"

Who is *she*? It couldn't be me, could it? It's probably Dyke March: if the two of them are getting together, Wylie must be hoping she doesn't know what she's been up to with Pritchard.

"Oh, okay," says Wylie. "That's kinda what I thought."

I so wish I could eavesdrop! But Niccolo's sending his voice to Wylie, not me.

"Your turn now, Niccolo. Is there anything you want to ask me about?"

Wylie waits attentively. Then laughs.

"Oh, that big box, I can't explain it. Electronics, radio waves, even most humans don't understand how it works. But no, the miniature people and animals don't actually live in there, even though it sure seems like they do, right?"

And with that Wylie falls silent. Her head starts to nod a bit.

"Are you ready to come out of trance now?" I ask.

"Yes. All ready."

I walk her back through the forest and up her special spiral staircase, getting more alert with each step, until she's present again, back at the kitchen table. She looks peaceful. But still very sleepy. Happens to a lot of people with 'shrooms. I help her over to the couch, where she opts for a nap. I bring a pillow from her bedroom, cover her with a throw. She thanks me sweetly and conks out almost immediately.

I sit in the nearby armchair, and Niccolo jumps into my lap.

Did that go okay for you? I ask.

Yes, it was very interesting! Thank you, Shannon. But you look worried—there's no need. You are still my person. You will always be my person.

I feel a rush of relief—I hadn't even realized how afraid I'd been that she might steal him away. But he sensed it. I love that about him.

Thank you, Niccolo.

I shouldn't ask. I want to respect Wylie's privacy. But I'm so curious…

Niccolo, can you tell me anything about what you two were talking about?

He takes a moment to answer.

I'm sorry, Shannon. I can't. It doesn't work that way.

I'm disappointed. But I think a part of me already suspected that.

As I watch Wylie sleeping, I feel strangely protective. I can't let Grant Pritchard ruin her, even if she's managed to convince herself that she's using him just as much as he's using her.

When she wakes up, it seems neither of us feels like talking about her conversation with Niccolo. It's so different from how I imagined it—no comparing notes about the shared miraculous experience of talking to a member of another species. But there's still a calm sense of togetherness, of a shared understanding. Or at least I feel it. We don't need to hash it all out.

Before I leave for the evening, I do finally get a chance to ask her about her plans over Carnival. And it's perfect: she's been commandeered to drive Pritchard to and from Logan Airport. He hates taking the tiny plane from Provincetown to Boston, and he refuses to board a crowded and possibly barf-inducing ferry, rubbing elbows with all the common summer revelers.

So. The date is now set for me to eliminate that nasty, manipulative, predatory pile of excrement from this earth. Finally setting myself free.

Chapter Fifteen

ALLISON

Two fat photo albums, one brown, one green. I tried to dust them off, but they're still giving off that musty basement smell, which I've been breathing in like a penance for neglecting them so long.

Smiling faces, laughter, outings and occasions, outfits and haircuts from long ago—each frozen slice of time greets me, invites me in, then shatters me. I'm holding a big wad of damp Kleenex—so much for the idea that I'm not a person who cries.

I feel bad for luxuriating in my grief like this. I also feel bad for not doing it more often. Both avoidance and wallowing, they seem like wrong answers. Why can't I get it right? The albums' pages often stick together, and when I peel them apart a photo or two will come loose, which adds a fresh sting and another layer of culpability. Because I'm destroying the house where all these precious memories live, even as I try to revive them.

I guess my mother was what they're now calling a "trad wife." But not because she was conservative, or churchy. She was genuinely happy—and I don't think I imagined it—making our home her world, with my father and me at its center.

I can see it everywhere in the photos: the fanciful cakes that sometimes won her prizes. The hand-crafted Christmas decorations on virtually every surface during the holidays. The garden, lush and colorful, where she spent so many hours, planting, pruning, weeding. And the countless pictures of me she took at every school play, recital, softball game, or field hockey match I ever went to. She made cookies for bake sales, sold books at book fairs, she was the first neighbor to bring a casserole or do errands for any nearby family dealing with a crisis.

Times were different. My dad's job gave us enough for a comfortable life, and the Ptown house we inherited was a wonderful bonus. As much as my mom admired women who had careers, she wasn't particularly interested. She told me only a few years ago that she'd hoped to have more children but couldn't. Something that never even occurred to me, because she made it seem like me and my dad were enough, all she ever wanted.

I do remember though, feeling that it was Shannon who had the "cool" mom: someone who went out in the world. And that my mom, as much as I loved her, was somehow something less.

Because I was an idiot.

If she'd been "cooler" and had a career, we couldn't have spent so many summers together in Provincetown: playing, laughing, talking, exploring. My dad would join us on weekends, but my memories of this place are so much more about my mother.

Could that have been the real reason I moved here? Was I looking to return to that enchanted world we created, just the two of us?

In any event, it didn't work. Because she's not here anymore. What I still can't accept is that she's not *somewhere*. That she's just... *not*.

A knock at the door, and when I open it I'm relieved to see that it's Chloe. Of course it is, she's right on time. But I'd been half-afraid it might be Shannon or Bobby, innocently stopping by at the wrong hour on the wrong morning. I don't want to have to explain where we're going or what we're doing or why they're not invited along too.

Chloe takes one look at my face, and even though I feel like I'm faking a normal smile pretty well, her expression shifts. She sees right through it.

"Aw Allison," she says, giving me a big hug, holding me, stroking my hair.

We're pretty much back to normal now. Relaxed, easy, and best of all, getting more cuddly and giggly and goofy, just like in the very beginning.

It helps so much that Shannon isn't in the house. She's getting more active again, not holing up, so that's good. She's busy installing the kitchen cabinets, plus she's doing catering deliveries and probably her comic book too, so I don't see her that often. Bobby's been scarce too, probably because he figures I've got Chloe now.

I miss Bobby and Shannon. When Chloe and I are a little more solid, I'm hoping I can figure all that out better. But if I have to choose: today it's Chloe that I want with me on the jetty.

* * *

The sun blazes hot and the air is thick and dank with humidity. I want to go almost to the end of the jetty, but it's over a mile each way and it's not like walking on a sidewalk. While most of the huge granite slabs are at least roughly rectangular, they tilt every which way. There are big gaps between them, steep inclines and slippery surfaces. Every year you hear about the tourists who underestimate them, spraining ankles, breaking bones, gashing themselves on the sharp edges.

After a while I get thirsty, so I stop for a moment, take my water bottle out of my backpack, offer some to Chloe. To our left is the sprawling Provincetown Inn and views of the harbor; to the right are the marshy grasslands and dunes. The tide is fairly high but receding. Enough water for dispersing ashes, but no danger of us getting stranded out there.

And now I'm noticing how beautiful it all is, how spectacular the light, how amazing the sky, as though an oil painter had carefully brushed

175

the cirrus clouds into the bold blue sky. Almost too perfect. Aside from an energetic trio of teen girls who passed us early on, we have the place to ourselves. Which is good, because what we're planning to do is illegal. And for probably the first time in my life, I don't care what the law says.

As we resume walking, the sound of the water flowing through the rocks below starts to calm me. Timing my footsteps and gauging where to land on the uneven surfaces feels meditative. It's just difficult enough to take up attention, but not with the thinking part of my brain. My muscles have to figure it out themselves, and it's interesting to feel my body moving, shifting, pushing, bracing. It's really quite remarkable what bodies can do. I feel floaty, observant in a different way than normal. I'm letting the jetty walk me, with its own rhythm, taking me to where I need to go.

I feel Chloe's quiet, solid presence right behind me, even though we don't speak.

When we arrive at a slightly pinkish slab, I'm sure it's the right one. My mom's favorite swimming spot was just a couple of rocks down, closer to the water. I move carefully, it's steep, and look back to make sure Chloe is managing it okay. She is. She's nimble. We sit down together, still saying nothing. We just look out beyond at the water, the boats, the lighthouse, the gulls. The water has been receding, but it's still a busy, bustling presence. It's hard to believe that in a few hours most of it will be gone, revealing a huge expanse of sand below.

I reach into my backpack, open the canister. The ashes are inside a plastic bag. Fortunately the breeze is at our backs.

I should have prepared something. I thought I'd have a lot to say, but the words aren't coming. It's just too big, an enormous tangle of memories, of love, of grief, of gratitude, it's all so dense and interwoven I can't find a simple, graspable thread.

"Bye, Mom," I say at last. "You'll always be with me."

I empty the plastic bag into the water, helpless tears slipping down my cheeks. Again. I'd really like to go back to being a person who doesn't cry.

Chloe hands me Kleenex, holds my hand, and we stand on the rocks together for a long time. Watching little pieces of my mother float away.

* * *

We're eating dinner at Fanizzi's, it was always my parents' favorite restaurant. It's right on the water, the food's good, and it's homey, not pretentious. Very popular with the older crowd—we've already said hello to Martha and Alba, who are here with another senior couple.

I'm relaxing into the bright buzzy social energy: glasses clinking, shouted greetings, laughter, voices rising as people start to let go of their daytime worries.

Such a hard day. But I'm glad I went through with it. My mom's ashes will be much happier swirling around in the ocean currents than they were on a shelf, imprisoned inside a cheap aluminum canister.

"More wine?" asks the waitress, and Chloe shakes her head.

"Sure, I'll have another glass," I say.

It's my third, but tonight, all bets are off. I'm down to my last few bites of an expensive steak, and I'm planning on ordering chocolate cake for dessert. Because my mom, the best mother on the planet, is dead. And it doesn't matter that it happened three years ago. Today is the day I finally had to let her go, for real.

"I know it must have been super difficult," says Chloe, who can tell when I'm back there again.

"But having you there? That made it so much better. It was really important to me."

"I'm so glad you asked me to go with you! It felt like …well, an honor."

There's a crash a few tables over, then the sound of laughter. A busboy hurries over. Someone has knocked their martini glass off the table.

"So we won't mention any of this to Shannon, if that's okay? The year we were friends, she really bonded with my mom. I guess because she was never very close to her own mother."

"Oh! I didn't know that."

"It surprised me, actually. Shannon was so cynical and badass. And my mom was so, I don't know, apple pie."

Chloe squints a little, like something's bothering her.

"So then, how come you didn't ask Shannon to come along?"

"Well, you know."

The waitress comes back with my wine, and I take a big swallow.

"I know what?" asks Chloe.

"Would you like to see dessert menus?" asks the waitress.

"Sure, we'll take a look." I wait for her to leave.

"It's just, I know you're not comfortable around Shannon. And I get it, Shannon's a handful! So today, I chose you, over her. Because it was a really important day."

But it doesn't look like Chloe is taking it as the compliment I intended.

"So you thought you couldn't invite Shannon too? But I don't have a problem with her. She's the one who has a problem with me, remember?"

"Sorry. I just didn't know what else to do. For whatever reason, you two don't get along, and I really couldn't cope with that kind of energy today. So I didn't invite her. Because you're more important."

Chloe looks like she wants to say something more, but the waitress returns with the dessert menus. I realize I don't want chocolate cake anymore.

As we're walking home, I try to make conversation. How good my steak was, how fast the summer has gone. I check in about her string quartet. But Chloe barely replies to anything I say.

What did I do wrong?

When we get back to the house, she goes straight to the couch. I don't know how someone sits down angrily, but that's what she does. I sit down next to her.

"You always act like we're the same," she says. "Shannon doesn't like me, so therefore I don't like Shannon. Shannon's openly hostile to me, so I must be acting the same way. We're equally responsible. Even though from the very beginning, I've gone out of my way to be nice to her. I swallow every insult, tiptoe around her feelings, smile even when she's glaring at me, try to stay out of her way, encourage you to spend as much time with her as you want. And still, she keeps treating me like shit! But the worst part? You think that's totally okay. Because she's Shannon."

I'm stunned. Where is this coming from? And on a really hard day. I keep picturing little burnt bits of my mother, drifting away, lost to me forever. I'm scraped up, peeled out, shredded. She's had all summer, why spring this on me now?

So I'm just going to be blunt.

"Does it really matter though, how nice you think you're acting on the surface? You don't like Shannon. I can tell. She can tell. And it hurts her feelings."

Chloe looks at me, maybe a little surprised. But still pretty pissed off.

"I don't know. Maybe I like Shannon? Maybe I don't. She's certainly entertaining. But the truth is, I don't even *know* Shannon. Not the real Shannon. The Shannon I see is a woman with serious mental health problems who's obviously gone off her medication. Who's not getting the treatment she needs."

So that's what Chloe thinks? I thought I already explained, but maybe I wasn't clear about it.

"No, she hasn't gone off her medications. Her old pills weren't working very well, so she had her doctor call in new prescriptions. She's feeling better now. And she still talks to her therapist every week! They do video sessions."

"And you know this because… that's what she told you? Have you seen her pick up her meds? Have you seen the bottles? Has she mentioned when these therapy calls are supposedly happening?"

So suspicious, so mistrustful. It's a side of Chloe I'm not used to, and I can't say that I'm crazy about it.

Chloe doesn't know Shannon like I do. With me, Shannon's always been honest. Uncensored, never ashamed to spill whatever she's up to, however illegal or outrageous it might be. If she thought she was better off stopping her treatment? She'd tell me! She wouldn't outright lie about it.

"So you think I should be following Shannon to the drugstore, and snooping around trying to find pill bottles? Listening in on her therapy sessions? That would be creepy! She's my friend, she wouldn't lie to me."

Chloe looks exasperated. Then she takes a deep breath, composes herself.

"So I have a cousin, Yoshi. Pretty much the same deal."

Now she leans forward, her elbows on her knees as she meets my eyes. Like I'm a lineman and she's the quarterback, about to call a crucial play.

"Yoshi's bipolar. He's got at least one personality disorder, has occasional psychotic breaks. I may not be a doctor, but with my job, you can't help learning your way around the DSM-5. That's how psychiatrists define mental disorders."

At least she sounds less testy now.

"So every now and then, Yoshi decides he doesn't want to take his medications anymore. He doesn't like how they make him feel. He ditches them, lies about it to all the people who care about him. And then what happens? There's a crisis. He's almost died a couple of times."

But she's talking about her cousin. A completely different person.

"Don't you see it, Allison?"

She leans back again, but she's still looking at me so intently.

"Shannon just keeps getting worse. And I feel like I can't say anything, can't point out the obvious signs. You take anything I might say as though I'm trying to criticize her. But she needs professional help, and instead of steering her in that direction, you do the opposite! You make excuses for her behavior, try to normalize it. And then you project the whole problem onto *me*, you make it *my* fault that she finds me so threatening."

"I know Shannon's had her problems," I say. "But you're exaggerating. What are all these 'obvious signs?'"

"You mean besides hacking off all her hair on a whim and screaming obscenities at me? Well, there's the hyper way she talks and paces and fidgets. The fact that she's barely eating anything? You don't notice she never goes to the grocery store? Never even gets ice for her cooler? Her clothes are getting looser and she's looking, well, crappy, all tired and pale."

"But maybe she's just on a diet. Or she could have started Ozempic or something."

"You don't hear her banging around in the middle of the night, up at all hours?"

"No. Since I don't get up to pee three times a night like you do. But so what if she's a night owl?"

"Or the way she talks to her cat?"

"Oh come on! Everyone does that. I've talked to her cat too."

"But does he answer you? She has these extended conversations with him. Like she hears him answering her back. And have you checked out the wall in the cottage? I don't think Airbnb folks are going to find *that* to be much of a selling point."

So all those things, when you put them all together, they do sound a little worrisome. I still don't think Shannon's lying, but maybe her medications need another adjustment? And what does Chloe mean about the wall in the cottage?

But wait. Why is Chloe poking around over there in the first place?

"So you've been hanging around the cottage, listening to her when she thinks she's alone? You've been going inside to see what's on the walls? How would you like it if she just waltzed in and went snooping around inside your condo?"

"Oh sure, make this about me. I haven't gone inside. I walk by and hear and see weird things going on, and I'm supposed to pretend I don't notice? I'm not supposed to poke my head in through an open window and have any kind of reaction to what I see there? And you probably haven't figured out she and Bobby are dealing drugs, either. You think all they're delivering are freaking cupcakes."

I'm floored. What has gotten into her?

"Now you're saying Bobby is a criminal. Bobby, who also happens to be my only other good friend in Provincetown. Based on what evidence?"

"Just open your eyes and you'll see it, Allison! I don't have to prove anything to you."

I've been patient. But I'm getting angry now.

"But you *are* proving something, Chloe: that Shannon was right. She tried to warn me. That you were jealous of our friendship. And now here you are, doing exactly what she was afraid of! Sneaking around, trying to dig up dirt, turning me against her. And now Bobby! It's like you want me all to yourself. But I need to have other friends too!"

I can't believe I'm actually shouting at Chloe, the person who means so much to me. But I feel like I can't even find the real Chloe through the wall of paranoia and resentment she's built up.

"So no problem then! I'll get out of the way of you and your friends. I'm done here."

She stands up.

"Chloe! Don't be so dramatic. We're both just a little pissed off right now, but we'll figure it out."

But she walks out of the room. Letting me stew for a few minutes. I'm really not in the mood for all of this. She comes back, carrying her overnight bag.

I'm pretty sure she's not really serious. Courtney used to threaten to leave me almost every time we fought.

"Oh, and one more thing," Chloe says. "So yeah, I guess I'm a horrible, terrible person. Because watching Shannon escalate like this? I got worried she might have a history. So call it spying if you want. But I did some basic internet research. Which I guess you never did yourself?"

So to her, it's weird *not* to google-stalk your friends?

"Actually, I did, a little. It's just she has such a common name. So many pages of people who weren't her. And she's not on Facebook or Instagram. I didn't find anything. But you did?"

"Last night. I wasn't going to go in to any of this until tomorrow. Given… the plans for today."

I appreciate that, at least.

"So there were a few arrests that ended up in local newspapers. But none of that was recent. It was the whole thing about her sister Maureen."

Chloe has such an I-told-you-so expression. I know she's going to say something that, on the surface, looks bad for Shannon. I already feel defensive about it. Then I realize what it must be.

"I hope you're not implying Maureen's death was somehow Shannon's fault? She was only there in the car because she was trying to help!"

"No, not at all. It's just…Shannon never *had* a sister."

"What?"

That's ridiculous. Yet Chloe looks so smugly sure of herself.

"Of course she had a sister. Maureen!"

It's a fact, the existence of a person. Not an opinion you can choose to believe or not.

Chloe puts her overnight bag down, sits on the couch. She's not making sense, but she's still here at least.

"I found her grandfather's obituary. It mentions Shannon and her brother and their parents, but nothing about a sister. And her grandfather died when Shannon was twelve. So unless her parents ran right out immediately afterwards and adopted a thirteen-year-old girl? Shannon made up the whole story."

But Shannon didn't just make it up. I remember it even now, how choked up she got telling me about it. How close the two of them were growing up. How having Maureen by her side made up for the distant relationship she had with her parents. She wasn't faking anything, I'm sure of it.

"So whoever wrote the obituary just got it wrong, didn't realize there were two daughters."

"Shannon's *mother* wrote it. She was writing about her own father's death. I think she'd remember how many daughters she had."

But it still makes no sense.

"If Shannon made up a dead sister just to get attention, then why didn't she go around telling everyone else? I think I was the only one outside her family she told. And she only mentioned it to me that one time. What would be the point of lying?"

"My guess? Maybe she was dealing with something difficult, something she couldn't face. She invented a sister who died as a way of thinking about it, because that's what it felt like to her, a huge loss. Maybe her own mental illness? Maybe not feeling loved? I have no idea. But then eventually, she came to believe her own story. And it sounds like she still does."

I'm trying to picture it, Shannon making up such a huge lie, then pretending to herself all these years it was the truth. It's pretty hard to swallow.

"Just be careful, okay?" Chloe says. "I wouldn't rush in and confront her. If she's been thinking for thirty years that she used to have a sister she totally adored … I don't think she's in a good place to deal with a whole different reality."

"But… why didn't… I mean, how could…"

Chloe stands up again, picks up her bag. She's heading for the door, and she looks purposeful, and I'm realizing that it's not at all what I want.

We need to talk this through some more. I'm so confused.

"But Chloe, wait. Just because an obituary doesn't mention someone, does that really mean they never existed? That seems like a big leap."

But even as I'm saying it, I realize I've taken a wrong turn. An argument over an obituary? Is that really how I want to end our relationship?

"Maybe you're right! You could probably find out? Or you can just keep believing whatever Shannon tells you. It doesn't matter anymore what I think."

"Hang on, you're not…

But she is. She's leaving.

Chloe's not the kind to slam a door. She just closes it, calmly, deliberately. The latch makes the usual tidy click when it's secure.

I sit on the couch, staring at the TV even though it isn't on. What just happened?

I look up at the portraits on the mantel. There's my mother, smiling, watching over me. I so wish I could talk to her again, ask her what I should do now. My father: so kind and patient, but I can't imagine trying to explain this whole mess to him. We don't really talk "feelings;" that was always my mom's department.

I can't go ask Shannon. Or Chloe. Or even Bobby, who may have been lying to me about everything ever since I first met him.

I feel so alone.

CHAPTER SIXTEEN

ALLISON

When I woke up this morning, reached for Chloe, and found the bed empty beside me, I felt like I was falling off the top of a skyscraper. Of course I just wanted to pretend she and I never would have worked out anyway, so, no big loss. And that Shannon's doing fine, she's just a bit eccentric.

But I realized: this time I can't just go into hiding, wishing things were different, waiting for some confident, more grown-up person to come along and tell me what to do. *I* need to be the grown up. And start putting one foot in front of the other, like I'm back on that enormous sand dune, climbing to the top.

I stayed up so late last night, searching, scrolling. When I woke up and found myself alone, I sent Chloe a text right from bed, still feeling wretched, asking if we could talk. Next, I called her, but she didn't answer. A few minutes later I sent an email. Then two more texts.

But I haven't heard anything back. There's a good chance a long, rambling voicemail is in my future too. I just wish I could unsay a few things.

A lot of things, actually.

So it's starting to look like Chloe might be right about Maureen. I found the obituary she mentioned, plus I did a trial membership on an ancestry site. If you're just snooping, you can't find the names of anyone who's alive unless they're part of your own family. But I found Shannon's father: his listing showed him with two children, not three. Then I ponied up twenty bucks to a shady-looking website to get a phone number for Shannon's mother.

I must have changed my mind a dozen times before I finally dialed her this morning. I was so nervous I could barely say "hello."

She remembered who I was. And at first, she seemed pleased to talk to me. But then I told her why I was calling, explained what was going on with Shannon, and she got flustered. She said she couldn't talk about it over the phone. Was I willing to fly down to Florida and meet with her in person? She'd be happy to book me a flight and a hotel and pay for my trip.

Who does something like that? Acts like telephones and video calls were never invented, offers to pay for someone they barely know to fly in from another state? I guess rich people really *are* different.

But I don't think I can help Shannon without knowing what I'm dealing with. Was Maureen real? Or if not, why does Shannon think she is? What's going on with her?

So I went ahead and gave Nora Callaghan all my information, and she booked me a flight.

Next up: Seeing for myself what's going on with Shannon over in that cottage.

Left foot, right foot.

* * *

Shannon has a paintbrush in her hand when she comes to the door, but she puts it into a jar of water, wipes her hands off with a towel, gives me a big smile.

And… Jesus.

The living room wall. If Chloe caught a glimpse of it when she was walking by an open window? Now I can't say I blame her for leaning in for a better view.

The sweet little vine Shannon painted above the bathroom door in the hall, she just kept going with it, snaking it around the corner into the living room. Where it exploded into a massive jungle full of colorful animals and plants and birds and flowers.

But they're not normal animals. The giant boa constrictor has wings, the hippopotamus has fangs, the zebra has the head of an alligator, and the parrot walks on eight furry legs like a tarantula, only they're yellow.

And at the center of it all, there's a giant… is that supposed to be a lion? But it looks just like Niccolo. With a fluffy mane. It's a Siamese lion. He's got a limp dead animal hanging from his jaws, maybe a gazelle or an antelope, with bright red blood spilling everywhere.

"Hey, Alley Cat! What's up?"

I try not to look at the wall.

"I just wanted to let you know that this weekend I'm…" But I can't even finish. "Wow. That's quite a painting."

"Isn't it cool?" says Shannon. "Niccolo keeps inspiring me, it was his idea that it could all just keep growing and evolving naturally. Like a real jungle!"

"Yeah, I see that!"

She looks over at Niccolo and laughs.

"Sure, the portrait was my idea," she says. "But you thought of the gazelle, right?"

"I'm not quite following," I say. "I didn't say anything about a gazelle."

"Sorry, not you. I meant Niccolo. *He* thought of the gazelle."

The bloody gazelle is definitely a creative touch I wouldn't have come up with.

"You sure have put in a lot of work here. The cabinets, the counters, the couch, the dining room chairs, everything looks great."

"Just a few more details to nail down."

My heart is sinking as I'm realizing how right Chloe was. Shannon does look different. Paler, thinner. Her cat is telling her what to paint on the walls.

"Such a huge job," I say. "How on earth are you finding time for everything? I mean, this mural, that looks like a really big project."

"It's my new medication routine. So much better than before. I have so much energy, I hardly need to sleep! Or to eat, for that matter. It's like I'm running on sunbeams, naturally powered."

She grins and churns her arms enthusiastically, showing off her new solar-fueled metabolism.

"That's so interesting! But I thought everyone needed food and sleep?"

"Not nearly as much as people think."

"Right. And so, like, all those pills over there, are they your new medications?"

There are white capsules all over the kitchen, on the counters, the table, the floor.

"No, they're for making your own supplements, with natural ingredients, like spices and herbs. Not full of chemicals like the drugstore kind! But the drop-down menu on the website was confusing. I accidentally ordered five hundred instead of fifty. I don't need five hundred! Turns out though, Niccolo loves to bat them around. So for a new a cat toy, they were a bargain."

"Makes sense!" I say, absurdly.

My own house is only a few feet away, so I can't really ask to use her bathroom, but I don't think I need to check her medicine cabinet. I'm pretty sure I won't find any of the new prescriptions she was talking about.

I brush an accumulation of capsules off the nearest dining room chair and sit down. Niccolo chases after one of the fallen pills, pounces on it, then bats it across the floor. Shannon laughs happily, then sits down in the other chair.

"I just wanted to let you know I'm going to go visit my dad this weekend," I tell her. "Just a quick trip. I didn't want to you to worry."

I'm a little nervous; I'm not very good at lying. Normally I only visit my dad over Christmas.

"I hope he's okay?"

"He's good! Been a long time since I've seen him is all."

"That'll be nice then! Is Chloe taking you to the airport? If she can't, I'd be happy to."

"No worries, I'm flying out of Ptown, not Logan, so I can just take a cab."

"Absolutely not, I'm driving you!"

She looks like she's not going to take no as an answer.

"Well sure, thanks!"

Then she tilts her head, peers into my face. Like she's just noticed a suspicious mole on my cheek that I better tell the dermatologist about.

"What's going on, Allison? You seem, like, not your regular self."

Wow. The irony.

"It's just…Chloe and I, we broke up. Had a big fight last night, and she left me."

"Oh, honey no! Jesus, I'm so sorry. Alley Cat, you poor thing."

She looks at me so tenderly, puts a comforting hand on my shoulder, then squeezes my hand. She was no fan of Chloe, and the breakup is at least partly her fault. But still, I can see she's genuinely sad for me.

I'm pretty sad for me too.

Just keep moving, Allison. Keep moving.

* * *

Bobby is out on his porch, wielding a big old-fashioned watering can. Headphones on, he's in his own universe, dancing a little as he douses one after another of his many pots and planters. He startles when he sees me, spills water on his shoes.

He sees my expression, takes out his earbuds.

"Can I talk to you a minute?" I ask. "About your 'catering' deliveries?"

He can't hide his reflexive "oh shit" look, though he recovers fairly quickly.

"Chloe seems to think you're selling more than just bakery items."

"She does?"

Yep. I can see it in his face.

"Have a seat," he says, putting down the watering can. "I hardly ever see you anymore! So, what's up?"

As I sit down, I feel stretched in such different directions. I really miss him. A lot. But I'm worried about what he's up to. There's still so much I don't know. Is he just dabbling in recreational psychedelics for a few friends? Or is he out there peddling hardcore drugs, seducing vulnerable addicts, ruining lives?

"So Bobby, do you want to keep lying to me? Or would you rather tell me what's really going on, explain things so I understand it better? Either way, there's something you have to promise me."

He looks at me curiously.

"What's that?"

"You have to keep Shannon out of it. She's not in a good place right now. She can't be dealing with risky situations, and she especially can't be handling dangerous drugs. Drugs that could be tempting to misuse."

He nods a couple times, slowly.

"Yeah. She's been acting pretty strange lately, right? Strange even for Shannon. I guess it kind of snuck up on me."

He thinks for a moment.

"She's not here much longer. I don't want to 'fire' her and freak her out even more. I'll just tell her I need more help with the cooking side of things, get her out of the other business."

"That would be great."

But Bobby's not denying anything, or making up convoluted cover stories.

"And I'm going out of town over the weekend," I tell him. "You mind keeping an eye on her?"

"Sure thing," he says.

We both fall into an awkward silence.

"So I know what you're probably thinking," he says finally. "And yeah, it's obviously illegal. But not unethical, not the way I do it. I'm way more careful than your average doctor about making sure the right products go to the right people. And sure, some of my clients are just partying, taking drugs that aren't any more harmful than alcohol. Some are exploring, expanding their minds. But there are also folks who aren't getting what they need from their doctors. If they didn't have me? They'd probably go somewhere else way more dangerous."

It's surreal, having this conversation on Bobby's porch, surrounded by well-tended greenery and flowers, with his carefully chosen patio furniture and nautically themed decorations. It's not at all how I'd pictured a drug dealer's porch.

"But I'm not Mother Teresa or Brownie Mary. I also do it because I need the money. My rent has tripled since I first moved here! I didn't inherit a house like you did. Sure, I work two or three jobs during the summer, run myself ragged, but how do you think I get through the winter? All the rich people coming in, they've driven up prices so bad that everyone else, all the people like me who keep this town going, we're being driven out."

I'm not sure what to say. It's funny that in all this time, we haven't had a conversation like this. I feel a bit sheepish that I knew so little about his situation. That I never asked.

"But you didn't even try to explain," I say. "And you've known me for almost three years. Yet within about five minutes, you trusted Shannon more than me?"

There it is.

There are bigger issues at stake. Yet that's actually what hurts. Shannon and Bobby creating their own exclusive little world together, full of secrets and schemes. I feel like I'm reliving my school days: left out. Never a member of the club, never invited to the parties, never able to understand the in-jokes.

"Allison, Jesus, that's not it at all." His face softens. "I would have told you a long time ago, but I figured it would stress you out. That you'd be better off not knowing. Shannon's a different story. God love her, but she's even sketchier than I am, which I don't mean in a bad way, but not in a good way either? Anyway, she's the one who came to me. She caught what I was doing at the Boatslip and wanted to score some magic mushrooms."

It's not good news that Shannon's been self-medicating with psychedelics. But Bobby's explanation helps.

"But here's the thing," he says. "Do you feel better, now that you know?"

Damn. I'm looking at Bobby, but I'm seeing a slightly different person across from me than the one I thought I knew.

No, I don't feel better.

I'm not sure that what he's doing is as harmless as he thinks it is. Plus now I'm going to feel constantly worried about him getting arrested, or something bad happening to one of his clients, and I'm going to feel complicit for not reporting him to the police. Because there's no way I would turn him in. I'm just not built that way.

"We can talk more," he says. "Ask me any questions you want. But first… you have to tell me. What the hell is going on with Shannon?"

Where to even start?

"That's a really, really good question."

Chapter Seventeen

Shannon

This day has been *so* shitty. I'm hoping a picnic at the beach will be just the thing to cheer me up. I'm supposed to meet Wylie at Herring Cove for lunch.

Horrible nightmares again all last night. The hospital dreams are increasingly gruesome; more blood and pain and terror. Sometimes I'm the doctor; sometimes the patient. Usually Maureen is the one I'm supposed to mutilate, but last night it was a nun. Like, what the hell?

Then a couple of hours later, when I was finally feeling a bit more myself, Emily called. Crying. Three animal control officers showed up first thing in the morning. Not the friendly kind. They took all the outdoor cats away.

At first I thought Brian must have had something to do with it, to get back at me. But Emily said no, it was all her fault. A new cat had started coming by and she'd assumed it was feral. Turned out it had an owner down the road, some asshole who didn't just collect his cat but reported me as a "hoarder." I told her that of course it wasn't her fault.

But what's going to happen to those poor cats now? How is the underfunded local shelter going to find better homes for seven at once? They won't. It's too horrible to think about.

When I told Niccolo, he tried to sound sympathetic, because he could see I was upset. But I realize he's probably pretty happy about it. They were mean to him. It didn't take him long to ask me if this meant now he might be able to go outside again.

Then Bobby showed up. Acting friendly, but in a nervous, snoopy way. Eventually he got around to telling me he didn't trust me to make deliveries anymore.

He didn't say it like that. He just suddenly needs a lot of extra help in the kitchen. Is he worried that I'm skimming product? But with all the orders I've handled for him, I've been completely scrupulous. Except for just those two times: the fentanyl, and the extra tranquilizers. And I'm pretty sure he didn't notice either of those or he would have said something sooner.

I pack my tote bag for the beach—a towel and a sweatshirt in case it gets breezy, some sunscreen, and a big floppy beach hat.

Niccolo wanders over.

Shannon. I know you're sad about the other cats, but I think what happened may be a sign.

"A sign? Of what?"

That we should go soon. That you should hurry things up here. You've already got the pills ready to go. You just need to figure out a way to get in there sooner.

"I don't follow. We only have to stay until the Carnival parade on Thursday. It's already Saturday, so that's less than a week away. Why would I want to risk rushing things?"

You know how animals are sometimes better at sensing hidden vibrations in the universe? Like earthquakes. We feel those coming way before you humans do. This feels urgent, like bad things will happen unless we leave as soon as we can.

"Like someone's on to us?"

Are you sure you can't feel the vibrations?

Could he be right? Things have definitely been off lately. All the nightmares. Bobby acting so strangely. Even Allison seemed different than before. And now the outside cats.

"But the day of the parade, that's the only time I can be sure both Wylie and Pritchard won't be home."

Is that even necessary? You already know that he goes to the gym at the same time every Monday. Slip in then! Just be very quiet. Like a cat.

I don't actually need much time to swap out a bottle of pills. And the building is ancient; it creaks and shudders when it's windy, or often for no reason at all. Even if Wylie were home, it's unlikely she'd come running at the slightest noise in the upstairs unit.

"But it's only a few days different," I remind Niccolo.

Just consider it, he says. *Listen for the vibrations.*

I put the pita chips and peanut butter pretzels in the tote bag. I bought fresh ice for the cooler and inside are some apples, Manchego cheese, hummus, salami, seltzer, some cans of craft beer and wine. Wine in a can! How convenient!

I don't know what Wylie might like, so I wanted to be prepared.

I was so thrilled when she invited me. I'd been feeling bad about stopping our sessions, but I can't risk running into Pritchard. And I've stalled on the book. Trying to force Colleen to go through the horrible darkness her story requires—it was too much.

Niccolo comes back over, peeks into the tote bag, paws a little at the bag of pita chips.

Why can't I come with you?" he asks. *"I haven't seen Wylie in forever. I'd really like to chat with her again.*

"I know, baby. But I told you before, we're meeting at Herring Cove this time. Remember how frightened you were when you got near the harbor? The ocean is *so* much bigger and scarier."

But I'll be braver this time! I'm so tired of being stuck inside, so far away from you.

"I'm sorry sweetheart. You can't be with me every minute, you know. But I'll be back really soon."

Niccolo narrows his eyes, but he lets it drop. I'm sure he'll be happily napping soon enough.

* * *

The parking lot is packed. Wylie texted me her approximate location, but with all the other beachgoers, it's tough trying to weave my way through their sandy encampments with my tote bag and heavy cooler, looking for her.

Bright colors everywhere, my sunglasses can't mute them. Beach umbrellas and towels and folding chairs and kites and tents and inflatable toys, all the colors are screaming at me, SUMMER! SUMMER! GET IT? IT'S SUMMER! So much louder than they are in other seasons.

I finally spot Wylie. She's set out a big beach umbrella and two folding chairs. She looks up when she sees me and gives me a beautiful smile—uncomplicated and warm, just like the toasty sun.

"So sorry I'm a little late," I say.

"No worries! I'm just happy sitting here. You'd think with all the people everywhere it wouldn't feel so peaceful. But when I'm just watching the waves, feeling the breeze… everything else just kind of disappears, you know?"

I envy her. To me the other people seem *very* present. Shouting when they could just talk, running when they could walk, reeking of fake coconut scents from their pharmaceutical sunscreens, blasting crappy music from their Bluetooth speakers.

As I settle into my chair, I wonder: Not long ago, I upped my 'shroom dosage again, I thought they might help with the nightmares. But they're actually getting worse. Before, the 'shrooms were helping to calm me down. But I wonder if taking too many can make it go the other way?

"Are you hungry? Want something to drink?" I ask. "I brought a few things."

"Yeah, me too," says Wylie. "Maybe just a drink right now?"

"Sounds good." I'm hardly ever hungry anymore.

Wylie opts for a beer, and I give the canned rosé a shot. Doesn't suck, actually.

"So different from the beach on the harbor. A whole different vibe."

"Is it the ocean you think? All the people?"

We talk for a bit about the beach. This one in particular, and the way the demographics have changed over the years, all the tribes blending together more. Then we get on to other beaches we've loved. And "the beach" as a cultural icon, as a mood, as a metaphor. Wylie's so bright, I love to listen to her. She's open-minded, thoughtful, curious. Not show-offy. The wine loosens me up, blurs the sharp edges, and the chaotic energy of people nearby starts to diffuse like a bad smell, replaced by the fresh ocean breeze.

Then I feel something bump me from the side, something wet and awful.

"Ahh! Get away!"

It's an unleashed German shepherd, wet from the surf, sniffing, slurping, inspecting me and my tote bag, probably looking for food. I shoo it away. I see its irresponsible owner approaching; she's shouting, "Here, Lucky, here, Lucky! Be a good boy, please? Over here, Lucky!" and I instantly hate both of them, dog and human.

Lucky looks up at me. *Just kill him and get home, Shannon,* he says. *You don't have much time.*

Then Lucky runs away.

Fuck.

Fuck fuck fuck fuck.

But I have to keep my composure.

"You okay?" asks Wylie.

"Just a little rattled. The dog took me by surprise."

"It's not supposed to be here, let alone without a leash," she says.

"I'm good. He didn't bite or anything. Just slimed me."

"Yechh." She frowns sympathetically.

We both decide it seems like time for lunch. We have way too much food; Wylie brought even more than I did, but the time we spend digging it all out and arranging it gives me a chance to think. I'm proud of myself for keeping calm, not visibly freaking out.

So. The dog sounded just like Niccolo; it was his voice. And Niccolo is the one who wants me to hurry up. The dog doesn't even know me! I didn't let Niccolo come along, so now he's figured out how to talk to me, even when he's not here. I didn't know he was so powerful.

Wylie fills her plate; she's sampling a bit of everything. I put one of the sandwiches she brought on my plate to be polite, some grapes and carrots. I take a bite of the sandwich, it's turkey and cranberry and cheddar, lots of mayo. One bite feels like an entire meal. I drink more wine; I still feel on edge from the slobbery dog talking to me like that.

Niccolo is getting so bossy. But maybe he's right? Monday might be as good a day as any to take care of Pritchard and get back home. I'll be super quiet when I go in, Wylie won't even know I'm up there.

But that would mean my Provincetown summer is about to end. Who knows when I'll ever be back here?

"You look pensive," says Wylie.

"I was just thinking about how I'll miss Ptown when I get back home. It's a pretty special place."

"Sure is. You need to head off soon?"

"Yeah. I've got stuff I need to get back to."

"Me too. But living in Boston, I can come back here easily enough when I have enough cash again. I think I'm about tapped out here. Can't get blood from a stone, so they say."

So she's ready to come clean?

"That stone you can't get any more blood from, that wouldn't happen to be Grant Pritchard? Are you finally going to tell me what the deal is with you and him?"

She laughs. "I think I can trust you, right? We know each other pretty well by now."

Do we? I certainly like her. But I can't say I know her at all.

Wylie pops a couple of peanut butter pretzel bites, takes another swallow of her beer.

"Wow, you wouldn't think that would be such a good combo."

She puts a wedge of cheese on a slice of salami and balances two grapes on top, puts the whole thing in her mouth.

"Another winner," she says, after a lot of chewing. "I don't know why food always tastes so incredibly good at the beach."

It's fun to see her enjoy her lunch so much. It's hard to remember feeling hungry like that.

"So yeah," she says, "to answer your question from many weeks back—I'm definitely not sleeping with Grant."

That's a relief. Though I note the present tense: she didn't say she never had, just that she isn't now.

"It's just that… I've been blackmailing him for the last few years."

I laugh with surprise. It sounds like quite a story!

"I mean, at first I didn't even realize that's what I was doing. One thing sort of led to another. He got me admitted to the MFA program the year he was chair of it, even though I went to a shit college and didn't have any connections. And that award I got? He was the one who persuaded the nominating committee to take a look at *Nom de Guerre*. And he hired me to be his assistant. But at the beginning, we never talked quid pro quo. He never asked me to keep anything secret, not in so many words. But want to know how naïve I was? I thought he actually *cared* about me. Like he's capable of that."

There's a bitter bite to her voice.

"Now, our arrangement is more straightforward. I keep my mouth shut, stay in my place, and he knows he has to compensate me. But that's all coming to an end soon. He's made some risky investments, and there's no new novel on the horizon. He blew through the advance a long time ago. Now he's living off credit cards, mortgaged up to the eyebrows."

I notice she still hasn't told me yet what she's been blackmailing him over. Sleeping with your grad student wouldn't be nearly enough, would it?

"So he's run out of money, but he still drives a vintage Jag?"

"Right? Because he'd rather cut off his dick than sell that car. Anyway, I should have moved on a long time ago. I'll be happy to see the last of him."

She goes quiet, looks out at the water for a moment or two.

"I mean, *you* know. What kind of guy he is."

"I know?"

She looks at me pointedly.

"Grant told me he recognized you. Said you'd followed him before. So I already figured you must be one of the women he's taken advantage of. That's why you came here for the workshop, right? When you'd never even read a graphic novel before? Surprised the hell out of me that you were actually good at it."

I know there are much more important things to focus on, but I can't help but feel pleased she said that.

"He didn't take advantage of me," I say.

"No?" she asks. "Except then It's funny, because once you found out I was connected to him somehow, and staying in the same building, you decided to hire me, to start working with me on your graphic novel. You're not the first woman from his past to come looking for him. But week after week, you'd show up, meanwhile doing all these cool things with your book. I've never understood the plan, exactly, what it is you've been after. An apology? Money? Some kind of revenge? I've been trying to figure it out. But you're cagey. Just like I am."

I feel so stupid. She was on to me, all this time! Although she still doesn't know my reasons, or what I want, or how it's all going to end.

"When I took you upstairs that day, I wanted to see your reaction to the bulletin board. And sure enough, you zeroed in on one photo in particular. I saw the look on your face. It was back when he was teaching high school. He only did that a couple of years, early '90s. And you're what, mid-forties? You would have been in high school right about then, right?"

I take another sip of my wine. Then I put the cool can against my face for a moment. The midday heat, Wylie's sudden flipping of the script, the questions. I'm feeling flushed, unsteady.

"And it's okay," she says. "I understand why you'd do it. And even though I knew you were playing me? I also felt like we genuinely hit it off."

"We did!" I say, and it feels terribly important that she believe me. "I wasn't just pretending. I felt a real connection. I mean, no one else but you knows about Niccolo. That he talks to me. And now to you! You're the only person I've ever shared him with."

She smiles at that.

"I know that's a big deal. It feels special to me too. So. Don't you think it's time we dropped the pretense? Started being more honest with each other? There are things I've been wanting to tell you, but I don't think I can if you can't even admit why you're really here."

I need to think. I dig my bare feet in the sand, wriggle them a bit, feel the roughness. Like it will somehow ground me.

"But Wylie, I wasn't one of Pritchard's 'conquests.' I know that's what you want me to say, but he never touched me!"

She doesn't look convinced.

"He told you to keep quiet about it, or that he'd retaliate, right? He does that. And he tries to convince women not to trust their own memories, not to believe what they know to be true."

"No, not me."

"You would have been so young. He would have seemed so powerful. What choice did you have?"

She looks at me more closely.

"Eat something," she says. "You've had one bite of your sandwich. Don't just drink wine. Have some water."

She takes a pita chip, dips it in hummus, and hands it to me. Like an obedient child I put it in my mouth, chew, swallow. I reach in the cooler, take out a lime-flavored seltzer water.

"But you've got it wrong," I tell her. "He didn't abuse me. He abused someone who was important to me. My older sister. He got her pregnant, she'd just turned fifteen."

"Your sister?"

She looks at me, perplexed.

"When Maureen told him she was pregnant, she was so sure he would help her. That he'd leave his wife, that they'd raise the child together. Instead, he abandoned her. He wanted to kill the little baby!"

My eyes start to water, tears fall and I wipe them away. Poor Maureen, abandoned, grief-stricken, so desperate.

"She took my mom's car. She was going to his house that night, going to make him change his mind. But she'd been drinking, the car ran off the road, and she died."

"Maureen died? Oh my God," says Wylie.

"I was there with her, in the car. I almost died too."

She looks at me with such compassion, but I can see she's confused, recalibrating. She had it so firmly in her head that it was *me* who'd been seduced by Pritchard, not Maureen.

"That must have been… I can't imagine. So traumatic. I'm so sorry."

We fall silent for a while, sip our drinks. I'm so rattled, a little dizzy. I keep feeling like I'm back in that car, it's going so fast, it's going to crash.

I have to move my mind in another direction.

"So," I ask her, "he went after you too? Like my sister? Did you feel like you *had* to sleep with him?"

She takes her time. She's still looking at me so curiously.

"No. We've never had that sort of relationship."

I hadn't realized I'd been holding my breath until I let it out.

"Turns out, he's my father. It was my birth mother he went after."

It takes me a few seconds to even process this.

It makes sense, he's certainly old enough. But it also doesn't make sense. He's a monster. Yet he fathered Wylie?

"My God," I say.

"I always knew I was adopted, but I couldn't find out who my biological parents were. The original birth records are still sealed. A lot of states have opened those up, but I was born in Florida, some hospital down in the Keys. There you can't get access without the birth parents' permission."

She pauses, looks at me. And it's bad timing because I'm having another intense rush of heat and panic, it might as well *be* Florida, I remember how horribly hot it got there. I don't know what's going on with me today. I take another drink of water, take a deep breath in. I need to steady myself, act normal, pay attention to what Wylie's saying.

"So once day I overheard my mom saying something to one of her friends, about my birth mom being a 'wayward girl.' That's what churchy ladies like my mom used to call them."

"Your birth mother was another young girl he preyed on then," I say. "Just like Maureen."

She cocks her head. "Uh, yeah. Just like Maureen."

Disgust, rage, the blazing sun, the wine, it's all converging. The tart seltzer, it's not soothing, the bubbles are too busy, they sting my mouth and throat. I put the can back down.

"You okay?" asks Wylie.

"Yeah. It's just… losing Maureen was a big deal for me, when I get too close to it, I sometimes feel a little shaky."

"I should stop."

"No, I want to know everything. Please! Go on."

She takes a couple of napkins, opens the cooler. Dips the napkins into the icy water at the bottom.

"Here," she says, reaching over to wipe my forehead. "You're burning up. And it's not all that hot out, could you be coming down with something? Put some water on your neck too, your wrists. And keep drinking more water. We should get you home soon."

The coolness feels so good. But the napkins are getting soggy. I take my sweatshirt out of my bag, dunk it in the ice water, drape it over my shoulders.

"Ah, that's better."

"I'll keep going. But I'm keeping an eye on you."

"No, I'm good."

I try my best to look normal, pleasantly alert, to just focus on her face, her words, not get pulled into the panic that seems to be circling, looking for an opening.

"Anyway, so my adoptive parents were born-agains, narrow-minded, and just generally shitty people. So I was always pretty desperate to find my 'real' parents. And eventually they invent consumer DNA tests! Suddenly everyone wants to know who their ancestors are. You pay your money, spit in a tube, and go online to see if any relatives pop up. I was already grown up, in college before I found out."

"Pritchard has an account?"

"No, but both of his brothers do. It was enough though; there was no doubt Grant was my father. So finally I had a name. And I just wanted to meet him, right?"

"Sure." It must be difficult, not knowing, always wondering.

"And so at first, well, it was amazing. He was so curious about me. And he was a writer! I'd always wanted to be one too. He was smart and sophisticated and rich, everything my adoptive parents weren't. He took me under his wing, helped me out, seemed so pleased that I'd found him."

"That doesn't sound like blackmail to me," I say. "Accepting help from the man who fathered you?"

"But it was clear he hadn't told his wife, or anyone else, who I was. And that I shouldn't either. I had to be happy with the role of 'promising student.' His protégé. But I was so naïve. I kept waiting, not saying anything, feeling like I was auditioning, wondering when he'd finally acknowledge who I really was. Even if that meant admitting he'd made mistakes in the past. The sad thing? I thought the problem was *me*. My parents raised me in a little town in Alabama, a godawful backwards racist shithole. I couldn't wait to get out. But once I escaped, I had to keep working on my accent, catching up on all the books and movies I'd missed, trying to copy how the other students dressed, so I'd fit in better. I thought once I made myself into the daughter he thought I should be, then I'd be part of the family too! But he always seemed slightly disappointed, like he had someone else in mind."

She sighs, takes a long swallow of her beer. I can see the hurt.

"So I finally wised up. And I started noticing what I'd tried not to see before: that he hadn't changed. That was he still using women, pressuring them. I'd had enough. That's when I made it official. A couple years ago I asked him to fork over enough to pay off all my student loans, and double my salary."

"Or you'd tell his wife?"

"And everyone else. I'm not sure his wife was ever really the issue? By now she must know the kind of man he is. It's his readers, the public, his precious reputation. If it all came out he'd been having sex with young teenagers? It's not a good look. And for him, image is everything. Like the Jaguar he drives. He needs the validation from outside, because inside, there's just a soulless fucking void."

She looks over at me; frowns.

"Water," she says. "Drink more water, Shannon. You're so flushed."

I take another half sip, but the bubbles are really too prickly.

"Any idea who your mother is?" I ask. "She might be out there looking for you."

Wylie looks at me strangely yet again, like I've asked an absurd question. But it seems logical to wonder about it.

"Actually, yes. I just found out, very recently. It's so tricky, though. Birth parents sometimes don't want to be found. I imagine she has good reasons."

I'm feeling dizzy again.

"Shannon, you're shaking, let's get you out of the sun."

A seagull approaches. At first I think it's just looking for crumbs. *Kill him, and go home,* it says.

Another gull joins it and now they're both shrieking at me, *Kill him! Go home!* And then a third, and a fourth.

I don't know what to do. I have to get away. Our food is spread out everywhere, towels, people all around, noisy waves, Wylie, looking so alarmed—I can't deal with it all so I stand up and start running away from the horrible shouting birds. I hear Wylie calling after me but I keep going, weaving through the people and the bright colors and the noise, running, just running and running and running.

CHAPTER EIGHTEEN

ALLISON

I check my messages yet again as my Uber driver pulls over to the curb. Still nothing from Chloe. I try to change gears. We've arrived. Nora Callaghan lives in the historic northeast district of Saint Petersburg, just one block off the water.

"Must be nice," the driver says, before pulling away.

The street is straight from a movie: grand homes on huge lots, stately trees and carefully trimmed hedges. But Nora's has an unusual design: low slung, with lots of brick and wooden beams, massive eaves jutting out extravagantly, windows divided up into tidy grids. The whole exterior seems somehow sliced into horizontal lines. So contradictory: both old and modern; forbidding, yet inviting.

I feel so nervous, waiting at the entrance. No one answers right away. Did I press the doorbell hard enough?

I hear movement inside, and then Nora opens the door. She peers into my face for a few tense seconds.

"Allison!"

She seems to truly recognize me now, and such an affectionate, spontaneous smile lights up her face that I feel truly welcomed.

Meanwhile, I've been doing the same thing: reorienting, trying to find Shannon's mom in the face of this much older woman. My smile is just as genuine when she comes into focus.

Nora takes me into the living room, and a quiet middle-aged woman brings in a serving tray with coffee—Nora's maid, I guess. Do they still call them that?

"Thank you, Luisa," Nora says as the woman retreats into the kitchen.

I feel self-conscious as I pour in an abundance of cream and sugar. Nora drinks hers black.

Though Nora lives in luxury, there's still something spartan about her. She's trim and muscular. She wears minimal makeup, doesn't dye her hair. It's a beautiful shade of white that makes her face look that much more vibrant. While her pale green linen dress is probably expensive, it's simple, not showy. She moves deliberately, gracefully, like a ballet dancer.

She puts down her coffee cup, leans forward a bit.

"Thank you again for coming all the way down here. It's so nice to see you! I just wish it were under happier circumstances. You must have thought I was ridiculous, insisting we talk in person."

"No, not at all."

Actually, yes, totally. But I'm here, and I have to say, it's nice to see her again. It brings the past back in a different way, to be with someone you once knew, rather than just listening to cold facts over a telephone. I'm remembering how Nora seemed so different from other mothers, the way she'd talk about politics, joke about her haphazard cooking. If it was after five, sometimes she'd make herself a martini, and pour our Cokes into fancy highball glasses.

I look around the room. "Your home is so lovely."

The furnishings are old, but in a hip, vintage way, not in a dreary antique-store way. Clean geometrical patterns, warm woods, stained glass, clever art—but not too much. Plenty of tranquil open space. Just enough upholstery on the sleek furniture to soften it, unlike the beige Naugahyde whale of a sectional that sits in my own living room.

"Thank you," she says. "I was so lucky to find it. Something about these Prairie style houses, I've always been drawn to them. So peculiar, yet confident, like they couldn't care less if they happen to be in fashion."

We spend a few minutes catching up. She's curious about my job, asks about my parents. She'd only met my mother a few times, but she says all the right things. Nora tells me a little about the nonprofit she volunteers for, focusing on women who are facing religious or political persecution overseas. She doesn't mention that she founded it, or that she managed to build it up from nothing into an organization that's already making a difference in several countries. If I hadn't searched the internet looking for her, and seen the write-up in an online magazine, I might have thought she just spent a few afternoons a week stuffing envelopes. I guess she likes to keep a low profile.

We both know why we're here though, so it doesn't take us long to wind down. We look at each other a moment. I decide to go first.

"So, I'm getting really worried about Shannon. She's hardly eating or sleeping, she thinks her cat is talking to her, and I'm afraid she's gone off her medications. I want to convince her to get some help. But before I even get started, I feel like I need to understand something better."

"Her delusion about Maureen, you mean?"

"Yes! She told me about her back in high school—I always thought she was real."

Nora sighs.

"I'd hoped she'd made more progress on that by now. It's the reason she totally withdrew from me. Well, she could give you plenty of other reasons too—we've had a tough time, the two of us. But when she talks about Maureen, I never seem to handle it right. She thinks I'm in 'denial.' That I'm this cold, heartless person for not grieving enough.

Believe me, I've done plenty of grieving. Just not about the death of a girl who never existed."

Nora's expression, it's so pained. I give her a moment, looking over toward the massive fireplace. Rough but intricate, like the rest of the house. It's built from an assortment of irregularly shaped stones so cleverly fitted together that I can't help picturing some long-dead craftsman spending thousands of hours toiling over it.

"So," Nora says, leaning into a long pause, like she's preparing me for quite a tale, one that won't be short or simple, "Maureen was Shannon's imaginary friend. Her pretend older sister, back when she was a little girl. At the time we didn't think anything of it—I'd had an imaginary friend myself. A sweet little boy named Franklin. He liked to dress entirely in yellow, for some reason."

She smiles as though remembering a real person.

"It was actually quite adorable, the way 'they' would play together. When I'd listen in, I could almost imagine what Maureen was saying from Shannon's side of the conversations. And when Shannon would misbehave, she'd often tell us it was all Maureen's doing! But once she got to be seven or eight, Maureen disappeared. It wasn't until after Shannon had her baby that Maureen came back."

What?

Shannon had a baby?

"Shannon decided it must have been 'Maureen,' who'd been having sex with her English teacher, not her 'Maureen' who'd crashed the car."

She was having sex with her English teacher?

Nora smiles gently at me; she can see the confusion on my face.

"She never gave you any hint about any of that, then? I always wondered what she told you."

"No! She just said Maureen had died in the car accident. She did say Maureen had just gotten pregnant though."

So the car crash had been real, as well as the pregnancy. But it was Shannon who was pregnant, Shannon who drove off the road. It's hard to get my mind around.

"We'd had no idea that she was being abused by her teacher," says Nora. "What sort of man does that? And she was just fourteen when it started. She was a child! Teachers are supposed to guide, to encourage, to help children grow and thrive, and instead he destroyed her. I could barely function, I was so blind with fury."

Nora's voice is shaking. Her rage still simmers, and not far beneath the surface. It makes me wonder what it would look like if she ever let it completely escape.

But she must hear the same thing, because she stops. She picks up the coffee pot, carefully refills both our cups. I imagine she's not someone used to losing her composure.

And I'm having a moment myself.

You hear of this sort of thing happening all the time, but it's different when it's someone you know. I try not to picture it, and yet horrible images come to mind anyway. I'm suddenly seeing the Shannon I knew back then in a whole new way, and I don't want to.

"We did see that she was struggling," says Nora, calmer now. "She was falling behind in her classes. But we thought she was just having trouble making the transition to high school. We didn't suspect the real reason. Shannon was always different. So creative, but sometimes moody. One of her teachers warned us she thought she might have emotional problems. But we chose to see her as unique and unconventional—just very much her own person."

"I've always admired Shannon for that," I say. "She never worries that much what anyone else thinks. She's just herself!"

Nora smiles.

"She is! But that should have been our first clue, when suddenly she wasn't. When she started withdrawing, acting so insecure. Completely infatuated with a man who cared nothing for her, who was just using her. But we didn't know that. And then she started getting in trouble. Minor things at first—skipping school, staying out too late. We thought she was just testing limits, normal teenage misbehavior."

Normal for everyone but me, I guess—that is, until I met Shannon.

"But I have to admit," Nora says, "her father and I, we were distracted. We argued constantly, though we tried to do it behind closed doors. Children can sense it though. And our son had a severe learning disability; he wasn't coping very well and we were probably focusing more on his issues right then. It wasn't a happy home."

She shakes her head, looks so regretful.

"We should have questioned her stories more carefully. Even before this all happened, Shannon was always so convincing when she wanted to deceive us. Probably because when she'd invent something, half the time she'd come to believe it herself! And the other half, well, she'd feel justified. She always felt she had her reasons."

I can't help thinking about my fight with Chloe, and my absolute certainty that Shannon would never be anything but honest with me.

Focus, Allison.

"So was that why she went away to Florida to live with her grandmother?" I ask. "To have the baby?"

Nora nods.

"She'd made it sound like it was because you two weren't getting along."

"Well, she was right about that part," Nora says, "we weren't. She'd gotten even wilder—shoplifting, drinking, vandalism, taking drugs, staying out until all hours. I'd raise my voice; she'd yell back even louder. I'd ground her; she'd sneak out. I'd take away her allowance; she'd steal from my purse. The more I intervened, the less good it did. Her father was hardly ever home. I felt so overwhelmed, so defeated."

There's a sudden roaring sound, a blender or a food processor, and it's loud, but Nora doesn't startle like I do, doesn't even seem to hear it. Because she's not here, is she? She's back in that house in Newton, help-lessly watching her daughter turn into someone she no longer recognized.

"But you were still working full-time yourself, right?" I remember showing my mom and dad her name on the masthead of that magazine. "I was so impressed. You were a mom, but you also had this important job. You were a role model!"

"A role model?" She laughs. "That's sweet of you, Allison, but honestly. I was barely keeping up at work. And at home, I felt like I was the world's shittiest mother. Excuse my French."

But I have to smile. I'm glad she still swears.

"Going to Florida was actually Shannon's idea," she says. "She loved the thought of her grandmother taking care of her during her pregnancy; they'd always been crazy about each other. My mother was the bohemian type, a beatnik back in the day. An anarchist for a time. So it didn't faze her, all the trouble Shannon was getting into. I was more judgmental. And I couldn't help it, I kept trying to talk Shannon out of keeping the baby. Which only made her even more adamant about wanting to raise the child herself. When she found out it would be a girl, she was going to name her Maureen. Which gave me an uneasy feeling; it was like Shannon was back living in her fantasy world. With no idea what a real baby would require of her."

I try to imagine the Shannon I knew my senior year, but an even younger and wilder version, coping with the round-the-clock demands of an infant.

"My mother convinced me that Shannon would be more likely to make a rational decision if I weren't there pressuring her. And sure enough, she gave Shannon the space to work it out for herself, helped her realize the best thing for both her and the child would be adoption. So I thought I'd made the right decision, staying out of it. But I had no way of predicting my mother would do what she did. I so wish I'd been there."

My phone starts ringing. The interruption couldn't come at a worse time.

"I'm so sorry, I should have silenced it."

"No problem," she says, as I dig into my bag.

It's a call from Chloe. I can see I have several text messages as well. It's all I can do to swipe it away, decline to answer, silence the phone.

"Do you want to take that?" Nora asks.

Yes, oh my God, yes!

"No, that's okay, I'll call back later."

It takes a moment for us to settle back in.

"So your mother talked Shannon into putting the baby up for adoption," I prompt.

She nods. "Just a couple of weeks before she was due. And then Shannon went into labor. It was traumatic, almost thirty hours in terrible pain; the doctors didn't manage it well at all. The baby was in the wrong position; there was concern about whether she would even survive. And then Shannon started getting disoriented. She kept thinking she was back in the other hospital, recovering from the car accident. She started mixing up the two Maureen's: her baby, and the imaginary sister she used to have. She was asking if Maureen was all right, did she survive the accident? My mother was with her, and very worried, but finally, Shannon gave birth, and thank goodness, the baby seemed fine. Shannon signed the adoption papers, and went back to my grandmother's house to recuperate. It looked like everything had worked out as well as it could have."

But it's obvious from Nora's face that it didn't.

"But then two days later, my mother called me. She said the baby hadn't been as healthy as they'd thought; the difficult birth had deprived her of oxygen. She'd died before she even left the hospital. And she said

Shannon was so devastated, she didn't want to talk to me. In her mind, I was 'against' the baby, so I was somehow to blame for her loss."

It doesn't make sense, Shannon blaming her mother. But since when do emotions follow logical rules?

What a sad story. When Nora said Shannon had "had her baby," I'd assumed she'd survived. I'd even started to let myself wonder about the little girl, what sort of woman she'd grown up into.

"At first I was a bit in shock," says Nora. "Even though I knew I'd never get to meet little Maureen, she was my granddaughter! My Shannon's little girl. And now she was dead. It took me several days before I started realizing that it didn't add up. How did my mother even know the baby died? And why did she tell Shannon? Why give her such horrible news when she was still traumatized from giving birth, from giving up her baby?"

I realize my coffee cup is still in my hands—full, untouched, forgotten. I put it very slowly back down on the table.

Nora takes a deep breath, then continues.

"And my mother stuck to her story, at least for a couple more weeks—pretending the hospital had called her, pretending Shannon had overheard. Then I finally got the truth out of her. The baby hadn't died after all."

"Oh good!"

I know all this was happening decades ago, but it feels so pressing and present.

"So then why did your mother say she had?"

"Because the day after she gave birth, Shannon changed her mind again. She wanted to raise the baby herself. But she'd already signed the papers. The law was clear: in Florida, minors couldn't revoke their consent. And when my mother told her that, Shannon became hysterical. Crying, screaming, threatening to kill herself, hitting her head against the wall, pulling out her hair. Telling my mother she had to get the baby back. And my mother panicked. She was picturing Shannon endlessly pursuing 'her' little girl, derailing her entire life trying to get the child back. So she told Shannon she'd see what she could do. Then she told her the baby had taken a turn for the worse and never made it out of intensive care."

"But how could she do that?"

"That was my mother. Rip off the band-aid, yank out the loose tooth. She thought she was sparing Shannon a lifetime of suffering by letting her grieve the loss all at once, get on with her life."

Luisa walks in from the kitchen, catches Nora's eye.

"Whenever you're ready."

"Thank you Luisa."

"And so… to be continued," she says to me. "I suppose we should eat something?"

Nora stands up, but then seems to reconsider.

"Oh, but there's no hurry, do you need to return your call?"

I still have so many questions, and I can tell there's a lot more to the story. Still, it's Chloe. I have to talk to her.

"Actually, if you don't mind… and maybe I'll stretch my legs a bit? Just a few minutes."

It's true I've been sitting down almost constantly since I left, aside from the brief back and forth through the lobby of the very swanky hotel Nora paid for. But this isn't about exercise, it's about privacy. There may well be some tears and groveling as I return Chloe's call.

"Of course," she says. "Take your time."

* * *

As I close the front door I'm walloped by the hot humid air. Nora's house is only a block from the walkway along the Coffee Pot Bayou, but by the time I get to the waterfront I'm sweating and soggy. I take a seat on a park bench to return Chloe's call.

Then I see she's left a voice message. I notice there are also four texts, all from Bobby within the last forty-five minutes. But Chloe first.

I feel so nervous playing it back, but also hopeful. She's gotten all my messages, and she's finally responding!

"Allison? Where are you?" she says. Impatient. "Bobby says he keeps texting you. He thought maybe I'd have more luck getting through. He wants you to call him as soon as you can. Something about Shannon. It sounded really urgent."

And that's it.

No mention of all my apologetic texts, emails, and calls. No response to my pleas that we try to talk things through.

I read Bobby's texts; they're all variations on "call me ASAP."

So I dial his number.

"When are you coming back?" he asks, with no preamble.

"My flight gets in tomorrow afternoon."

"So can you change it? Come back today?"

"Seriously?"

"We have a bit of a situation."

* * *

The frittata is fluffy and fragrant; the home fries have just the right amount of caramelized onion, and there's also a fancy fruit salad, fresh squeezed orange juice, and even cinnamon rolls. I feel self-conscious about gobbling everything up, given the seriousness of the current situation. But the food is really good and I'm starving.

It took Nora all of fifteen minutes to rebook my flight. I told her everything Bobby had told me: that Shannon had gone missing; she spent last night outdoors somewhere in the woods. She came back, but has been agitated all morning, pacing around, shouting things, most often "Shut up! Shut up!" because Niccolo won't stop yelling at her. But she absolutely doesn't want to go to a hospital to get help. She's terrified of being locked up. She keeps threatening to head off to the woods again, to get away from the voice, and Bobby's trying to babysit. But he hasn't called the paramedics or the police because he's afraid Shannon will blame him if she ends up locked up somewhere. Implying it would be better if I got home fast so she could blame *me* instead.

Nora and I both agree that it's probably better if she doesn't make a surprise appearance herself. But she says she'll book the next flight out if Shannon is willing to see her.

Nora spears a strawberry with her fork, frowns as she eats it. And then returns to her story.

"So I had to wait two more months before Shannon came home from Florida. She was quiet and moody, but coping. No more head-banging or hair-pulling, she was eating again, showering, going for little walks, reading, coming out of her room to watch television. Even starting to talk about going back to school, where and when that might be. Given where she'd been, it all felt like major progress."

Then Nora stops, puts her fork down. She looks at me with such exasperation I start to wonder what I could have done wrong.

"But Allison, do you know what? I couldn't do it! I was just too damned afraid to tell Shannon the truth."

"That the baby was still alive?"

She nods. "I thought it might start a whole new cycle of crisis, of rage, of suicide threats and self-harm. That she'd obsess about getting her baby back again. So I decided to wait until she was calmer, to tell her. When it wasn't all so fresh."

It's funny how things that seem like such simple questions of right and wrong can get so complicated.

"Shannon was seeing a psychiatrist, and I'd told him the whole story. One of those smug Freudian types with an ostentatious beard, not my choice, but he was a friend of my mother's and was well-regarded. So I stepped back. I didn't want to make things worse; I thought I'd let him handle it. I kept things light, encouraging, neutral. Because every time I'd tried to intervene with Shannon before, I'd botched it."

"It doesn't seem like an unreasonable decision," I say, "to wait."

"But for how long?"

Nora gives me a sad smile.

"As Shannon finally started opening up again, sharing more… I discovered how badly off she really was. She started talking about missing Maureen, which would be natural enough… but she didn't mean her baby. She meant her imaginary sister. She talked about how horrible it was to watch her drive off the road. How Maureen's teacher surely would have changed his mind and helped 'Maureen' raise the child if only she'd been able to get to him that night. I had to remind myself, she wasn't just pretending, it wasn't a conscious process. But I didn't know what to do. Confronting her felt too dangerous; not confronting her felt complicit. But now, thirty years later, she still hasn't healed."

I wonder what my own mother would have done? She always had the right answer for everything. But maybe in some situations, there just isn't a right answer?

"It still seems incredible," I say. "That Shannon could somehow just forget almost everything that really happened during so many months."

"Doesn't it? Her psychiatrist told me that it's not common, but repression on such a grand scale does happen sometimes. He actually seemed pleased, to have come across such an interesting clinical case. He said the brain injury not long before giving birth, her history of emotional difficulties, the traumatic labor, her vivid imagination—I suppose they all contributed. And it's true: Shannon has always been a master at conjuring up alternative realities."

"Like now. With her cat."

Nora nods slowly.

"And actually," she says, "I don't think she's forgotten what happened to her, so much as transposed her memories. Like changing the key a song is played in. The melody is still the same, but the notes are all different. Having sex with her teacher? Yes she remembers that, but thinks it's because Maureen told her all about it. Getting drunk and driving the car off the road? She remembers, but sees herself as just the passenger. The pain of giving birth? Yes, that was excruciating, but it must have been the aftermath of the car accident. Her grief over the loss of her baby? She was mourning her sister Maureen."

Nora goes quiet. Looks at the frittata on her plate, cuts off a bite. Pokes at it with her fork, contemplates it, as though wondering how it got there.

"Did you eventually tell her though?" I ask. "That the baby didn't die? And that Maureen was imaginary?"

"Oh yes, so many times! If only I hadn't waited all those months to start the conversation. Because when I finally did, she refused to believe me. Her delusions were too entrenched. If I were right, that would turn her world upside down. And over the years, each time I'd broach the subject, no matter how carefully, she'd refuse to have anything to do with me. So I stopped trying. Ages ago. But she's still so wary. We trade brief phone calls over the holidays, talk about trivial things, that's all she'll allow me. Honestly, I'm not sure if any of her doctors ever tried very hard to challenge her version of reality. They'd just 'build rapport' and give her support to get through her days. I suppose she's more functional, less likely to cause trouble, just living with her delusion."

We both go quiet for a moment. I can hear Luisa in the kitchen, water running, pots and pans clanking in the sink.

"And so what happened to the teacher?" I ask.

I'm hoping he got locked up for statutory rape and served a very long and brutal sentence.

Another long silence.

"Nothing," she says. Her voice is icy.

"Well, we told the principal, who quietly dismissed him. And we went down to the police station, talked to an officer who was very sympathetic. But when we explained that Shannon was not only still in love with the man, but no longer even thought she'd ever had sex with him… well, it was clear we'd get nowhere."

"So he got away with it."

She nods.

"I hope karma gets him at least," I say.

"Well, karma is taking its sweet time," she says. "After he got fired he started writing. Became quite a successful author, from what I understand."

There's nothing I can really say, I just hope she can feel my empathy. I finish my orange juice. The town car she hired to take me to the airport is coming to pick me up soon.

"Allison," she says, "did Shannon ever tell you how much your friendship meant to her?"

Nora's question takes me by surprise.

"Maybe not in so many words," I say.

"Well, in my mind, you saved her life. The suicidal ideation—that all stopped when you came along. She needed a real friend, not an imaginary one. In your own quiet way, you steered her in the right direction. I'm not sure anyone else could have navigated her contradictions with such grace, such generosity. I'm so glad it's you again, who's here for her now."

I feel so moved—what a kind thing for Nora to say! But could it possibly be true? I always thought it was Shannon who saved me, not the other way around.

"I'll do my best," I say.

But that sounds so inadequate. I want to promise her more than that.

"That's all any of us can ever do, Allison: our best. Thank you."

CHAPTER NINETEEN

ALLISON

A flight from Logan to Provincetown isn't cheap, so I don't usually splurge during the summer when the ferry's still running. But Nora's paying, and it feels like a treat. Plus, it's my last window of freedom before I have to try to figure out how to deal with Shannon. What can I say to her that won't make everything worse? I'm allowing myself until we touch down to put it out of my mind and just enjoy the ride.

The other passengers all look grim. It's windy today. So many people find the tiny plane terrifying. It shimmies and bounces and swerves and dips way more than a regular plane. The walls seem so thin, and the instrument panel looks somehow old-fashioned. The pilot isn't in a sealed-off cockpit, he's sitting right there as you watch him crank open his window like it's an old Chevy, then poke his head out to check for traffic on the runway. You can smell if he's wearing too much aftershave.

A flight on a bigger plane is like sitting in a movie theater for the most boring movie ever. This flight is an *adventure*.

It's only about twenty-five minutes long, though. We've barely taken off, pitched around a little, soared upward through a cloud bank, and made a rather steep and thrilling descent, before we're already tilting and tipping our way toward the runway. The woman next to me is gripping her armrest, her eyes squeezed closed. When the wheels slam down and the plane finally slows, she opens her eyes and looks like she's about to burst into tears—whether from terror or relief I'm not sure. I feel bad for her.

I have no idea why flying doesn't bother me. Going to a party where I don't know any of the guests? Far more frightening than the very small possibility of a sudden fiery death in a small airplane.

We're all wired differently, I guess.

I follow my fellow passengers into the tiny and adorable Provincetown Airport. It features a collection of snow globes from around the world, and a sign warning passengers not to travel with poppers.

Has anyone actually done poppers since the '80s?

Fortunately, when Bobby and I traded texts during my layover in Boston, Shannon was calming down a little, getting tired. He was hoping she might be able to get some sleep.

A young woman, slim, with dark reddish-brown hair, catches my eye, approaches.

"Allison? I'm Wylie," she says, "a friend of Shannon's."

I'm pretty sure she's the writer who's been helping Shannon with her comic book. I got the impression they'd hit it off.

"Your neighbor Bobby sent me over to meet you. I was worried about Shannon, went over to see her earlier. But she wasn't in a good place for a conversation. You already heard, right, that she's, uh…"

"Kinda losing it? Yeah. I was down in Florida, talking to her mother."

"I didn't go into It all with Bobby," Wylie says. "I think neither of us knew what was okay to say. But I was with her yesterday. There's a lot you should probably know before you talk to her."

We thread our way through several chatty congregations of travelers, excited new arrivals being greeted by their hosts, and head out into the parking lot.

"Her history, it's way more complicated than I realized," I say.

"No kidding," Wylie agrees.

"You want to go first?" I ask.

Wylie motions toward the left end of the parking lot and we start walking.

"Sure," she says. "It's a long story, but I'll cut to the chase. I'm Shannon's daughter. Only she doesn't know that yet."

I'm aware of the rumbling scrape of the wheels of my suitcase against the pavement so at first I'm not sure that I've heard her correctly.

"*You're* Shannon's daughter?"

"Wait. You knew she had a daughter?"

"No! Not until a few hours ago. But how could it be you?"

We both just stop walking, as though the situation would make more sense if we could just stay motionless long enough to absorb it.

"I was going to tell her yesterday," Wylie says. "We went to Herring Cove. But she was acting pretty strange. She's clearly not well. But I didn't realize that at first, and I told her about my background. I mentioned the hospital I was born in. So maybe that triggered some bad memories for her? But she doesn't even seem to realize she was ever pregnant! She thinks it was her sister, Maureen. How is that even possible?"

"God only knows. But I can tell you a little more about it, at least from her mother's perspective," I say.

We start walking again, and I give Wylie a quick summary of everything I just learned from Shannon's mother. Wylie's car is at the far end of the lot, a beat-up compact, but the interior is spotless and it smells like a spa. When we get in she rolls down the windows, but doesn't start the engine. The drive to my house takes only a few minutes, and there's so much to share before we come face to face with Shannon again.

"You're sure about being her daughter?" I ask. "It seems like such a crazy coincidence!"

"Well, we'd both done the same thing, right? Stalk Grant Pritchard? Looking for answers, maybe for some sort of payback. The only reason she was in my class was because she followed him here."

"I'm sorry," I say. I'm completely lost. "Grant Pritchard?"

It takes me a minute to make sense of it.

"So was he the high school teacher who got Shannon pregnant?" I ask. "And he's here? In Provincetown?"

"Yeah, he came here for the writer's conference, and to spend the summer working on his next novel," she says. "That's why Shannon signed up for my class."

So that's the real reason she came to Provincetown?

And the name is sounding more familiar. I'm remembering a conversation during the fourth of July party, something about a predatory writer. But Shannon didn't seem to know anything about him, like she'd never heard of him.

More pretending. With each revelation I feel more and more gullible.

"I've hung around because Grant helps me out financially," Wylie explains. "But he's never acknowledged publicly that he's my father. He pays me off instead."

She says it with contempt. Then shakes her head.

"I'd always fantasized that someday my mother might come looking for me. And then at the opening reception, I see Shannon standing there, just staring at me. Something about her intensity. We've both got some red in our hair, even if mine is dark and hers is much lighter. It made me wonder. Especially when I found out she'd signed up for my class, but had never even read a graphic novel before. So why was she here? And she always seemed, I don't know…very *aware* of me, the same way I was aware of her. Like there was this connection."

My phone vibrates in my pocket. But Wylie hasn't heard it, and I want to let her finish.

"Then one day, Shannon forgot her purse in the classroom. And I realized that was my chance. So I dug some hair out of her hairbrush before she came back to get it. Sent twelve strands to a lab in Canada, and they just confirmed it last week. She's my biological mother all right."

"That's so… so…" But I don't even know how to finish my sentence, so I just shake my head.

"But Shannon wasn't looking for me after all, was she? She was looking for Grant."

Her face: it's so bereft.

"Yeah, but Wylie, if she'd known you were out there, alive—she would have searched everywhere for you!"

Wylie doesn't look convinced. But I feel a hundred percent certain of it.

I take out my phone: it's a text from Bobby.

"Things heating up again, landed yet? Pls haul ass!"

Wylie sees my face and starts the engine even before I tell her what the message said.

* * *

As we pull up, I can see Chloe's car is here. Just the sight of the green Outback gets me a little twisted. Will I at least have a chance to talk to her?

I've got two overwhelming emergencies to deal with at the same time, and I don't feel level-headed enough to cope with either.

I'm in love with Chloe. I have to try to get her back.

And Shannon needs me. She's my oldest friend, and she's in danger, and I'd feel devastated if anything terrible were to happen to her.

Wylie and I get out of the car and head for the cottage.

"Over here," says Bobby. He's standing in front of my house. "She's not in there. She's up here."

Christ. Sure enough, she is. On the roof.

We walk over to meet Bobby.

"I hope it's okay," he says quietly. "I called Chloe. She knows about hospital admissions, psych beds, all that sort of stuff. She's inside, making some calls. She thought she'd stay out of sight; didn't want to trigger Shannon. She helped me move the cat in there too. Apparently he's still yelling at Shannon, giving her really shitty advice."

My roof is two stories high. At least Shannon's not trying to balance on the steeply pitched section. She's wearing a pair of pink pajamas and bunny slippers and her gray fedora. She's perched right on the edge, dangling her feet.

"I was so careful about everything," says Bobby. "I took away all the knives and scissors, and also shoelaces, belts, her bathrobe tie. But then I left the room for two minutes to use the bathroom; I thought she was still asleep. I come out and she's gone."

"Hey Shannon," I shout. "I'm coming up, okay?"

"Suit yourself! The view's not actually that great."

"Please just wait for me, okay? It may take me a minute to get up there."

"Ladder's over on the side," she says. "Be careful, Alley Cat."

I head for the ladder, then I can hear a text come in.

From Chloe, finally. With the name of a private hospital she says is pretty good, one that has a couple of psychiatric beds open. I'm sure it's expensive, but I'm also sure Nora would happily pay for it.

But there's nothing personal in her message.

"Thanks," I text back. "Hoping we can talk at some point?"

"At some point," she texts back.

As I start up the ladder, I realize I have no idea what to say to Shannon. Wylie and I agreed that now was not a good time to share any huge revelations.

I reach the top.

"Okay if I come sit down?"

"Yeah. It's not very comfortable. But it's, like, a roof, so that makes sense."

"You're right," I say, sitting next to her. "It's too hard and a little too tilty."

"And I can still hear him, even up here."

"Niccolo, you mean?"

She nods. "He's mad at me."

"That must suck. I mean you guys are so close."

"Right? But now he's getting so bossy."

"He's trying to boss you around? Like get you to do things you don't want to do?"

"Well, not really. I mean, I *want* to do them. But like, not right away. Not until I'm totally ready. But he wants me to hurry up."

That doesn't sound good.

"Are they things that might be a little dangerous? Or like, that might be hard to take back again?"

Shannon turns to me, narrows her eyes.

"I do not plan to harm myself or others." Her voice is robotic. "So I cannot be involuntarily confined."

"Sure, I know that," I say.

I guess she knows the drill. You can't force someone into treatment unless there's imminent danger of serious harm. Is there? Quite possibly. But calling 911, having people in uniforms haul her off against her will—how would she ever trust any of us again? That would be the worst outcome possible.

Okay. Second worst.

"The thing is, Niccolo—well, he's so smart, he almost seems human!" I say. "But he's not, right?"

She doesn't respond. Have I offended her?

"Even really intelligent animals like Niccolo don't always understand the human world. They eat things that aren't good for them; they run out in front of cars. That's why you have to take care of them. So even if Niccolo is super certain he knows what you should do, maybe it's better if you make your own decisions? I mean, you're *Shannon*! You don't let anyone boss you around, right?"

She smiles a little, that's good.

"But he's so insistent. All the time now. I can't tune him out."

"I can't imagine. That would make me crazy too. You think maybe if you adjusted your medications a little, he might not be so loud, so bossy?"

"I can't go back on meds. I just can't. I'll lose him! I need my baby boy."

She looks so hopeless.

"Well, maybe they could just turn the volume down a little? So you could have quieter conversations. And sometimes some peace and quiet just to think?"

I have no idea how psychiatric meds work, if that's even possible.

"Like you said," I continue, "you're not a danger to yourself or others. What if you spent a few days somewhere calmer, with people who understand how to quiet down loud voices, just to give yourself a chance to chill a little? We found a place; it's supposed to actually be pretty nice. I talked to Wylie; she'd be happy to take care of Niccolo for you. You'd be going there voluntarily, right? So then you could leave again if you didn't like it."

"I don't know," she says. "I'd have to think about it."

"So hey," I say. "Any chance we could come down off the roof now and think about it down there? Being up here creeps me out a little."

She takes a deep breath, rises slowly to her feet.

"Okay, Alley Cat. Let's get you back down, safe and sound."

* * *

It's after midnight when I finally get back home. I'm exhausted, and at the same time, pretty wired. But Shannon is okay! At least for now.

She was even willing to let her mother fly in from Florida tomorrow morning to be there for her. Mission accomplished.

But why is Chloe's Outback still there in my driveway?

We did trade a few messages while I was in the lobby of the treatment center. I texted to say we'd arrived; she asked how everything was going. I let her know that the place seemed good. It did, actually, from what I could see. The building was reassuringly clean and tranquil, and the staff members seemed warm and smart. I didn't catch any *One Flew Over the Cuckoo's Nest* vibes.

I told Chloe that Shannon had been calm in the car, and cooperative. It was so sad, though. She kept saying, "I'm so sorry, Niccolo, I just can't anymore," and sometimes she'd cry. It made me feel sad too. But I didn't go into all that with Chloe. Nor did I ask her one more time if we could talk, or offer her yet another apology. I decided to stop pushing so hard.

I open the door and there's Chloe, asleep on the couch.

Damn. She's curled under a throw that's not quite big enough to cover her. I want to hold her so bad.

I try to close the front door behind me quietly, but she stirs. Rises. Sits up. I watch the sleepy confusion on her face slowly shift and sharpen.

"Sorry," I say, "didn't mean to wake you up."

It occurs to me that today must have been stressful for her too.

"So I shouldn't be talking to you yet," she says. "At least not according to this relationship self-help book I'm reading. I'm supposed to wait a week. We're still a few days short."

"Wow. A week? That seems pretty harsh."

"I guess there must be a good reason for it, right?"

I feel awkward just hovering, so I sit down. But across from her, not right next to her, so she doesn't feel hemmed in.

"Well if a relationship self-help book says something like that, then you have to believe it a hundred percent, right?"

"Exactly."

"Because they're so scientific and everything."

She nods. And is that a bit of a smile?

"Like, remember that *Total Woman* thing?" she asks.

"I'm not sure I do."

"More our parents' generation. Marriage tips for women. It was always sort of a running joke between my mom and her friends. You were supposed to greet your husband at the door stark naked, wrapped in Saran Wrap, holding a martini."

I try not to picture Chloe dressed only in Saran Wrap. That's a distraction I definitely don't need right now.

"Super scientific, I can see that," I say.

"My book wasn't wrong though, about me needing time to cool off. You hit a nerve, Allison, and it freaked me out."

I want to break in, to apologize one more time. But I know I need to let her talk.

"I mean, you were right. I *did* feel uncomfortable with Shannon, and a little bit with Bobby too. It wasn't totally unjustified though—they never did warm up to me, no matter how hard I tried. And you couldn't see the things I did; you *wouldn't* see them. So I couldn't even talk about it with you."

"I'm so, so sorry about that."

I hope she can see how sincerely I mean it.

"But yeah, probably some of it was jealousy, too. Because I want to be as important to you as Shannon is! I haven't always felt like I am. And then you accused me of my worst fears about myself—being too insecure, too needy. It was because I just wanted to be the most important thing for you. Like you are for me."

"And you are for me too! I'm so sorry I let you think that you weren't."

She smiles, but weakly.

"But am I, really?" she asks.

Does she not believe me?

"Of course you are!"

Saying it loudly doesn't seem to help it penetrate. She still looks skeptical.

"I'm not like Shannon," she says. "Or your ex. Courtney. You seem drawn to people who carve their way through life, sometimes oblivious to those around them, but they're always moving forward. They've got so much confidence! And so you follow along, smoothing things over, making things work. You're really good at it. And maybe it seems easier than making your own decisions, taking more responsibility, risking that you might screw things up sometimes?"

Should I be offended? But I'm not. Because she's not wrong.

"You're a Marcy," she says, "and you're looking for your Peppermint Patty."

I have to laugh a little at the comparison.

"You're Sancho looking for your Don Quixote. You're Robin and you want your Batman. You're Ethel looking for Lucy. You're Dr. Watson and you want a Sherlock."

I can see she's spent a *lot* of time thinking about this.

"But the thing is, Allison, when it comes to relationships, I've always been a Marcy too! I'm Robin, not Batman. I think maybe at first you didn't get that. And so, two sidekicks together? With no one in charge of calling all the shots? That may not be what you're really after. Deep down."

I move over right next to where she's sitting, take her hand.

"I think two Marcys together would be amazing."

It occurs to me that my parents: they were both sidekicks. Partners. Equals. And they couldn't have been happier together.

Chloe curls into me and I put my arm around her shoulders, warm and precious. I just want to dissolve right into her.

"So there's something else I need to tell you."

I ease my arm off, shift so I can see her face better. My heart is speeding up. Because I can sense it in the seriousness of her tone, and I don't know if I can bear to hear it. She's going to tell me it's too late. She's already found someone else.

"There's a job opening coming up, and it's mine if I want it. A regional VP is retiring at the end of the year."

"Well, that's great!"

"It's in San Diego."

"But that's in California!"

She smiles. "Last I heard."

She reaches over then, gently runs a hand through my hair, electrifying my scalp.

"Don't worry. I have no problem turning it down. If we're really a thing, like together together? I'd rather be with the perfect person than in the perfect job. And I have three weeks to decide."

I exhale with relief.

"But before I let that chance go, I really need to believe in us a little more. It's been a rough ride lately. Does that make sense?"

"It totally does. But Chloe, just so you know: I'm all in."

Because I believe in us enough for the both of us. And I'm not going to let her down.

* * *

I'm in the kitchen in Chloe's condo, just off a slightly alarming phone call. I find her where I left her half an hour ago, in the tiny windowless second bedroom, pedaling away on her exercise bike.

"Today?" Chloe says, incredulous, after I explain that Shannon's coming back in a few hours.

Shannon's program was supposed to take a week. It's been only three days.

"The doctors didn't want her to leave yet," I explain, "but she said she's feeling a lot better. They're already on the way back to Ptown. I told Nora she could stay at my place. And I should probably let Wylie know what's going on too."

Chloe gets off the bike, sweaty and sexy, but I need to focus.

"I hope they at least stabilized her," she says. "How can I help? Should I be there with you? Not be there?"

"I'd love it if you were there with me," I say.

"But would Shannon love it?"

I wonder.

"How about I go over with you," she says, "but I'll do what I did last time. I'll steer clear of the cottage and let you get her situated. I'll hunker down in your office, and I can be available whenever you need me."

Because that's Chloe.

* * *

In some ways Wylie is so different from Shannon: her delicate build, the way she seems so cautious and reserved. But now I can see the resemblance. Her expressive blue eyes, the shape of her face. Especially when she smiles: I see a younger version of Shannon right there, smiling at me too.

We're standing in the cottage, and Wylie puts the carrier on the floor. I crouch down and look in at Niccolo through the door.

He hisses at me.

"He's probably a little on edge from the car ride," Wylie explains. "And I bet he's impatient to get out of his carrier. Okay if I open the door?"

"Although…"

And it's not just because it looks like he wants to shred me to bits.

"I'm wondering if maybe we should take him back to my house for now, in case he upsets Shannon when she comes in? The last time they were together, it didn't go so well."

237

She considers.

"But I think Shannon would be even more upset if he's not here waiting for her. I mean, logically, if we tell her we took him away, it's not his fault. But emotionally? It could seem to Shannon like he's mad at her."

Now I wonder if she's right? On the drive to the hospital, one of Shannon's biggest fears was that the cat would feel betrayed if she couldn't talk with him anymore.

Both options seem problematic.

"I guess we give it a shot then?"

I step back a few feet as Wylie opens the door. Niccolo sticks his head out, glances around, and strolls out. He looks at me briefly and I tense up, but he looks away again. He walks over to Wylie, rubs against her legs, sniffs around at the furniture a little, and then settles into a sunny patch on the living room rug.

"So," says Wylie. "Next big decision. What do we say to Shannon? Do we go ahead and tell her the truth?"

"You mean the whole thing? Today? No. I mean, how can we?"

"But how can we *not?*"

Now I'm seeing even more of Shannon in Wylie's face. Is it the set of her jaw? Is there something she's doing with her eyebrows? Whatever it is, Shannon does it too, especially when she's feeling stubborn.

I hadn't pictured Wylie even being here when Shannon got back. Now suddenly this new person, a woman I'd thought of as a peripheral character in the drama of Shannon and Her Problems, turns out to be central. She's her daughter! But as much as I didn't want the responsibility of keeping Shannon out of crisis, I also don't want Wylie to just waltz in and blow everything to pieces.

"Right now, Shannon's so fragile," I say. "It would be too dangerous, right? Triggering those memories of Pritchard's abuse, of giving birth, of having to give you away? Telling her Maureen never existed? The psychiatrists were always warning Nora that she couldn't handle all that."

I can see from her face that Wylie's not having any of it.

"But the situation is so different now. The daughter she lost—I'll be standing right in front of her! Sure, she'll lose 'Maureen.' But she gets me instead, and we already have a real connection. You're saying I shouldn't even tell her who I am to her?"

"I know. Jesus. I can't even imagine how hard that would be. And I'm not saying never. But maybe not right this minute? She's just recovering from having a total meltdown. I worry that if you dump this on her, she might land right back in crisis. She could lash out at you, at me, at her mother, at anyone who's threatening her reality. Like she's done before. And she might not be willing to go get help, the next time."

"Of course I worry about that," says Wylie. "But we can be there for her, help her through it. Everyone's been tiptoeing around the truth all her life, and where has it gotten her?"

We've reached an impasse.

But I realize that if Wylie wants to tell her, I have no way of stopping her. She's been waiting all her life to find her biological mother, and very shortly she'll be right here in this room, during a brief window before she heads back home in a few days. Wylie will be hugely tempted to just blurt it out.

I just wish there was a way to hold off for a bit, to do it more incrementally. But how do you divide something like that in half, make it easier to adjust to? What is "here's your long-lost daughter, your whole life has been one big delusion," divided by two? I consider and reject a few scenarios. It seems impossible.

And then something occurs to me.

"So Wylie," I say after thinking it through a bit. "I have an idea. It's not perfect, and we'd have to run it by Nora, but if you don't mind hearing me out…"

"I'm all ears," she says.

Chapter Twenty

SHANNON

"We're here, Shannon," says my mother.

I must have dozed off. The car ride made me so sleepy.

When I get out, it takes a moment for my body to adjust. Gravity has gotten quite a bit stronger since the last time I had to stand up in it.

My mom knocks on the door to the cottage, which seems silly since it's where I've been living all summer, it's my house. But it turns out Allison and Wylie are there waiting for me.

And there's Niccolo!

He runs to meet me and I pick him up, drinking in his musky Niccolo-smell.

"I've missed you so much!" I tell him.

He rubs his face against mine, over and over, he's purring and kneading his paws against my collarbone. He missed me too.

"Niccolo, Niccolo, Niccolo, my beautiful boy."

We cuddle and I hold him, swaying gently back and forth.

My mother and Allison and Wylie are all talking together, but it's not normal chitchat. They're being furtive, so quiet I can't hear their words. And they keep glancing to see if I'm listening, so I make a point to look like I'm not paying any attention.

I get it. They're worried about me. But still, it grates.

I turn my attention back to Niccolo, pull him a little farther away from my face so I can make eye contact.

"Are you talking to me, Niccolo? If you are, I can't hear you. I'm so, so sorry."

I feel a few tears slip down my face. I pull him close again and try just to concentrate on how good it feels to be with him again.

I get tired of standing, so I sink down into the couch, moving Niccolo from my arms down to my lap. The weight of him grounds me. And after a few nights in a sterile institution, however upscale, the silky feeling of his fur is a luxury. I've missed the familiar fabric of everyday life, of being here with him, of home.

Home? But no. It's better than a psychiatric hospital, but the cottage isn't my home.

Though I have to congratulate myself, the remodel came together so well. The colors and textures, the warm woods, the creative homespun touches. Allison's Airbnb guests will love it. Although the jungle mural—perhaps that's just a bit *too* creative? I realize the blood dripping from the freshly killed gazelle, that might not be a crowd-pleaser.

I'll paint the whole thing over before I leave.

I feel so much calmer now than when I painted it. Which will probably get boring soon. But right now, it feels restful. Life isn't rushing at me so intensely, exploding with so many decisions to make, so many colors and sounds coming at me. And I don't have to explode right back, spewing my own colors and sounds, reacting with quick decisions, impulsive actions, heightened emotions.

Although there's one decision I do need to make quickly: tomorrow is the Carnival parade. Everything is ready. If I still want to do it, I just need to "go run a quick errand," punch the door code into Pritchard's empty condo and swap out the pills.

And he'll be dead. Out of my life forever. I'll finally be at peace.

I look over at Wylie, Allison, and my mother all standing there together.

"Totally backed up for miles," I hear my mother say.

Allison nods, commiserating. "Always a nightmare this time of year."

Now that they can see I'm paying attention, they've moved to the traffic on Highway 6.

It's so bizarre to see the three of them together at the same time. Like one of those dreams where your high school prom date and Edgar Allan Poe and Cher all show up at your house for dinner, and you just have to roll with it and set the table.

"Are you tired?" asks my mother. "Would you like to take another nap?"

"No, I'm fine. It's good to see everyone."

I do appreciate that they all rallied, cared about me enough to keep me from completely going off the deep end.

My mother smiles at me, and her face crinkles so much more than it used to. A lot of years have gone by. We're still uneasy with each other, but I don't seem to be feeling the frustration, even rage, that she used to trigger. Maybe because she's been on her best behavior—not interfering, not getting annoyed with me, not even offering advice. Just acting all empathetic and opening up her wallet in a very helpful way.

Could also be because I'm dosed to the gills with tranquilizers.

"I'm just going to feed Niccolo," I tell them. It's not mealtime, but I want him to know I'm thinking of him. "And sort out his litter box. Can I get you guys something to drink? Not much on offer though, sorry. Might be some seltzer and beer in the fridge?"

"We'll forage if we need anything," says Wylie.

"Be right back," I say.

I go back into the utility closet. His litter box is poop-free; of course Wylie cleaned it before bringing it back. But the real reason I'm in here is to see if my toolbox has been opened. It's the oversized kind contractors use, my "treasure chest." Before I left for the hospital, I made sure everything was still in there, then put a bit of caulk on an inconspicuous part of the seam in the back.

I check: the caulk is smooth, no cracks. No one's looked inside.

Back in the kitchen, I put some food in Niccolo's bowl. He hesitates, looks up at me.

"Not hungry?" I ask. "Or do you want another kind?"

He continues to stare at me, but there's no way for me to know anymore what his answer is.

I sit with my mother and Allison on the couch, Wylie is in the armchair, and we sip our seltzer waters. We talk about the weather; it looks good for Carnival tomorrow. They compliment me on the cottage renovation, although they seem to avoid looking anywhere near the mural.

But I know what they really want to hear about: how my hospital stay went. And have I stopped being crazy now? I wait for the next pause in the conversation.

"So the place wasn't so bad. A lot nicer than the other psych units I was in. Decent food, not like a hospital cafeteria. I had my own room, a view of some trees out in the back. Soft sheets on the bed, fancy soaps and shampoo."

It had to be super expensive.

I look over at my mom. "Thank you."

"You were brave to go," she says. "I'm glad it wasn't too horrible."

I tell them about Jamal, my individual counselor. He looked a lot like LeBron James, and he wore aftershave that smelled like pine trees. Very chill, down to earth. I liked him.

"He wasn't judgy at all. Totally understood why I'd go off my meds, if I was feeling so dead inside. He thought my shrink could have done a much better job managing that with me."

He gave me a couple of referrals before I left, so I'm hoping I can find someone who can do a better job.

"We also had group therapy every day," I say. But I don't want to paint too full a picture. I leave out the raw stuff that comes when people in extreme states of disturbance sit in a circle and take turns retching up their pain, their nightmares.

"Anyway, it's all good. The tranqs kicked in already, they started me on the fast-acting kind. So things got a lot less intense. The rest of the meds will take longer to sort themselves out, but already I feel a lot better. But enough about me!" I say. "How's your graphic novel coming along, Wylie?"

She cocks her head, like she's not crazy about the change of subject, or being the focus of attention. But I'm tired of being in the spotlight. Her turn.

"A little frustrating, honestly," she says.

I ask a couple of follow-up questions, and everyone eventually shifts into more of a normal social-gathering mode. We're just four women talking about random shit: HBO series and Ukraine and Gaza and assault weapons and the insidious rise of fascism, trying to pretend everything isn't super awkward.

But then I see the three of them do that thing again. Trading quick looks. What were we just talking about, MAGA? Abortion? The Supreme Court?

And I feel like I can't stand it anymore.

"Okay," I say. "Out with it."

They trade looks again.

"Out with what?" says Wylie.

But it's barely a question. Her voice is level: she's not feigning innocence, pretending there's nothing going on. It's more like she's curious what I think it might be.

"You have to tell me whatever it is you're hiding. I can't deal with this conspiracy you guys have going."

I look at them and feel suddenly very emotional. The three of them, as different as they are, are super important to me. Which makes this feeling of being on the outside even worse. I can't let them be that important, not if I can't trust them.

"I'm serious," I say. "Tell me. Or you know what? I need you all to leave. You did your jobs, I'm very grateful. But I'm fine now. I just can't be around this kind of energy."

Allison looks to my mother, then to Wylie—like she's about to say something. But she doesn't.

Finally, it's my mother who starts off.

"It's actually good news. But it's about something difficult. It could bring up some bad memories. We were going to wait until you were feeling more settled."

Niccolo walks across the room, up from another nap. Jumps up and snuggles next to me, like he can feel the tension in the room and knows I could use some support. I let my hand linger on his fur a moment, then take a swallow of seltzer water.

"Mom," I say, "if there were ever a time to tell me something difficult, it's now. I'm already up to my eyeballs in tranquilizers."

A slight smile, a deep breath. "Okay then."

She drinks a swallow of her own water, sets the glass down on the coaster so slowly and carefully you'd think it contained explosives that would blow the place apart. The longer she takes, the more impatient I feel.

"Maureen—she didn't actually get killed in a car crash. She had her baby after all. A baby girl."

What? Is she tripping?

"That's not possible."

Even through all the meds I feel my heart start to beat faster.

"Because I remember…"

I pause to search for memories of that time that I'm sure must be there, but they're elusive. Probably because I've always tried to avoid thinking about them. I try to remember her funeral, but what I come up with is a funeral scene from a TV show or an old movie I saw, rain falling, mourners in black crowded under umbrellas, and I'm looking at it like I'm floating above, not down on the ground with everyone else. I do remember weeping in my bedroom, sick with grief, but I can't remember who told me about it, was I still in the hospital? I'm even having trouble remembering our bedroom now, let alone what we did with all of her clothes, her schoolbooks.

"She's alive?"

"Your grandmother told you a lie."

So she was the one who gave me the news. That seems familiar now; I think I remember her voice quivering when she told me Maureen hadn't survived.

"She didn't do it to be mean," my mother explains. "It was the opposite. She thought losing someone forever would actually be easier than knowing they were still out there somewhere, but you'd likely never see them again."

I know people do this to kids. I had a roommate with a supposedly "dead" father who found out he'd actually just skipped town. But I can't believe my grandmother could be so wrongheaded.

"So then what happened to Maureen? She ran away? Where is she now?"

"Honestly," my mother says, "I think the only person who could ever find Maureen—that would be you, Shannon. You would know better than anyone where to look. But we did find out where her baby girl ended up."

"I have a little niece?"

"She's already thirty years old," says my mom. "But she says she'd like to get to know you, if you were willing."

"She would?"

I like this idea a lot.

"And maybe she could help me find Maureen."

"Maybe she could," says my mother.

"But how long have you known? Why didn't you tell me?"

"We just found out who the baby was. But I've always known the truth about Maureen. I tried to tell you a couple times before, but at the wrong times, in the wrong way, and it always ended badly."

I can't remember our exact conversations, but I do remember the feeling of betrayal, of her denying my reality. I just assumed she couldn't face the truth.

My mom is blinking back tears, and I've never seen her cry before. My mother is a rock, rocks don't weep. I'm not actually sure I want to see it. I look away.

And now Wylie is full-on crying too.

Wylie.

Oh my God.

Wylie!

She was telling me some wild tale at the beach that Pritchard was really her father, and I've been assuming that was all part of the hallucinatory state I was in. Even the seagulls were talking to me that day. But maybe that part wasn't a hallucination?

So Maureen had a baby girl by Grant Pritchard, and that baby is Wylie?

* * *

When Allison calls, I'm just back from a short walk on the beach. I needed to feel the sea breeze. Though my body feels tired, my mind is still scrambling. I'm trying to reassemble a new picture that makes sense, from pieces that have drastically changed their shapes.

"Not quite yet, just give me fifteen minutes to get cleaned up. That's really nice of you guys. And tell Chloe she's welcome too."

"Welcome" is an exaggeration, but I'm wondering if Chloe and Allison are back together again. I can see Chloe's car from my window, so I'm going to play nice.

I shooed everyone out a couple of hours ago. I needed a breather and I figured they did too. But this time they're bringing food, like a bunch of church ladies bearing casseroles after a funeral. My mom hasn't left yet like I thought she would; she's spending the night in Allison's guest room. Everyone's keeping watch. Worrying about me.

The warm water from the shower cleans my body but it can't wash away the constant ping-ponging in my head.

Maureen. Maureen! Where has she been? What really happened? Why has she not tried to find me?

Wylie. Who will she be to me now? Will we have a relationship?

Grant Pritchard. Preying on young women and underaged girls, never paying a price.

Can I really kill Wylie's father, even if she may detest him herself?

Is my plan as foolproof as I think? Do I want to risk going to jail… or worse?

Kill the bastard? Or let him go unpunished?

He deserves to die, and I'm the one who can make that happen. I've come so far, everything is in place, and there will probably never be another opportunity.

I look over at Niccolo, lying on my bed, silently cleaning his tail. I can't ask him anymore. It feels so lonely.

But I know exactly what Niccolo would say.

By the time I open the door for Allison, Chloe, Wylie, and my mother, I'm still not sure what I want to do.

They've brought way too much food. Some of it, like the chicken curry and the baked ziti, are deliciously fragrant. After so many weeks of barely eating, I feel my hunger returning like a giant alligator charging out of a swamp.

Bobby isn't here yet; he wasn't sure what time he could get free. He said to start without him, so that's what we've decided to do.

We spread everything out on the kitchen counter, buffet style.

Allison gets plates from the cabinet, Chloe gets out glasses for beverages, and Wylie opens drawers, looking for silverware.

"I don't see any knives," she says.

"No knives?" I start opening drawers and cabinets too. "Did you guys seriously think I was going to kill myself? Is that why there's nothing sharp in here?"

"I think Bobby was just being on the safe side," says Allison.

"I can just go get some from Allison's kitchen," says Chloe.

This is too funny. I start laughing.

"Are you okay?" asks my mother.

I'm laughing quite hard now, out of proportion to the joke that only I get. I finally compose myself.

"I'll be right back," I say. "Chloe, you may want to hold off on the knife run. You'll appreciate this too."

As I walk to the utility closet, I realize I'm making a decision. Spontaneously, with my body, not with my head. All that thinking, weighing, I'm sure it's factoring in there somewhere, but I don't have access to it.

I come back with my toolbox, put it on the dining room table.

The others come in from the kitchen.

I open up the toolbox, slide the top tray aside, and from below take out the forged suicide note and the bottle of Testo Blast and put them on the table.

Then my cardboard box from Home Depot with a picture of a drill on it. But it's not a drill. I open up the box and put my Glock on the table.

"Jesus!" says Wylie.

"Shannon, oh my God!" says Allison.

"You have a gun," says my mother, a simple declarative statement. She's known me the longest, so she's much harder to shock.

"If I had wanted to kill myself," I say, "I would not have needed to use a butter knife."

Wylie picks up the piece of paper. "May I?"

She reads it to herself. I watch her face as she starts to understand what she's reading.

"Grant Pritchard's suicide note," I explain to the others.

"I would have thought it was real," says Wylie. "It looks exactly like his handwriting. Sounds like his voice. And that bottle—those are his supplements. He gulps down a bunch of them, twice a day."

"Well, each pill at the top of *this* bottle is laced with enough fentanyl to kill a buffalo," I explain.

They all look so shocked. But I can't help wondering if they're also a little impressed. It was a solid plan.

"And the gun is just my gun. I like to have it around. You never know."

Allison is still staring mutely at the Glock with repulsed fascination, like I just took a big shit in the middle of the table.

"I'm hoping you have a license for that? Is it at least registered?" my mother asks.

I shake my head. Back in my twenties I wasn't big on the formalities.

I wait for my mother to admonish me, at least remind me that I'm risking fines, maybe jail. But no. She just looks concerned, keeping her thoughts to herself.

There's a knock at the door. In walks Bobby, holding a plate with a big pink cake on it.

"So what did I miss?" he asks. Then his gaze falls to the tabletop.

"Not much," I say. "It's just that I've recently decided to abandon a pretty clever plan to murder someone, make it look like suicide."

"My goodness. You *are* full of surprises, Shannon."

But he looks a little shaky as he goes to set down the cake with the rest of the food.

"So… what changed your mind?" asks Wylie.

I don't honestly know, since it wasn't a conscious decision.

I look at her, Maureen's daughter. Here in this room, a living, breathing, real person.

Maybe finding you?

I look at my mother. Not being quite the cold, impenetrable mannequin I'd remembered, but a vulnerable older woman, trying awkwardly but sincerely to connect.

And Allison. Of course Allison. Always loyal, so patient, talking sense to me, ready to be there whenever I need her, never mind how messy or inconvenient it might be for her.

And Bobby. Who gets me. Who understands my sarcasm, my darkness, my propensity for criming. And what it is to make your own jagged path around the edges of "normal."

I look at Chloe. And… well, she's still Chloe. But four out of five ain't bad.

If my plan had failed and I'd gone to jail? I'd have lost all of them. And my Niccolo. He's sleeping on the couch now, missing all the drama because I can't share it with him anymore.

"Hard to explain," I say finally. "I just decided not to. Probably the meds."

There's a long silence. I guess no one knows what to say.

"I was going to swap out the pill bottles tomorrow. I knew he'd be gone during Carnival, and Wylie has chauffeur duty so she wouldn't hear anything when I went in."

"Tomorrow," says my mother, shaking her head.

I can see from their faces they're thinking what a close call this was.

"I knew he'd be out of town, and I know his door code. Not exactly hard to remember, it's 1234. And with a suicide note in his handwriting? I totally would have gotten away with it."

"Well, it's a good thing you changed your mind," says Wylie.

"I guess. I still honestly have mixed feelings about it. Someday he needs to get what's coming to him."

"But I meant, *tomorrow*. Because his meeting in LA got canceled," she says. "He's flying back tonight. So he could have been sitting right there in his living room when you walked through the door."

"Tonight?"

"Decided to take Cape Air. I told him to get his own goddamn ride in from the airport this time."

Jesus. That was close!

I imagine punching in the door code and walking in the door. Seeing him sitting there, staring at me with those cold deadly eyes. I don't want to think what could have happened next.

So. Maybe my plan wasn't quite as brilliant as I thought. But how was I supposed to know he'd cancel his trip?

Later, after dinner, I'm at the sink finishing up the dishes. Everyone has left but Bobby, who's been busy putting leftover food into Tupperware.

I'm so tired. But feeling at peace with my decision. I still think Pritchard deserves some sort of punishment. But maybe fate didn't want me to be the one to administer it?

Bobby joins me with a dish towel, drying as I wash. He seems a bit subdued.

"So, Shannon," he says. "What were you thinking would happen exactly, if your crazy plan to kill Pritchard had actually succeeded?"

The plan wasn't flawless, clearly, but I don't know that it was "crazy." If the L.A. meeting hadn't been canceled, and I hadn't changed my mind, I think it actually would have worked.

"Well, Pritchard would be dead. And he'd never put his hands on another young girl or woman again! That was the idea."

He puts the plate down on the counter, then turns to look at me.

"And so when Pritchard's dead body got discovered, poisoned by an overdose of fentanyl—you didn't think anyone would wonder where it came from?"

His voice is measured, not loud, but I can hear an edge.

"Well, there was a suicide note."

I turn back to the sink, dunk a wine glass in soapy water. My hands are shaking.

"And so? What difference does that make? Murder or suicide, either way it wasn't Pritchard's prescription. You didn't think there might be questions? Investigations? Arrests?"

No. I didn't.

I didn't consider it at all. All I was thinking was that Pritchard would be dead, and *I'd* be long gone—a tourist with no obvious ties to the dead man. An unlikely suspect even if the police did figure out it was murder.

But Bobby would still be here in Provincetown, wouldn't he? Where countless people know he's a drug dealer.

"I know you weren't entirely well," he says, "especially lately. But you seemed pretty 'with it' weeks and weeks ago, when you talked me into getting you a drug I've always steered clear of. Because I believed what you told me. And I thought, well yes: a dying cancer patient, doesn't she deserve relief from her excruciating pain?"

I turn back to the sink.

"I mean, Jesus Christ, Shannon."

I rinse the soapy wine glass under the tap, first the inside, then the outside, then the inside again. There's just too much soap; I can't get all the bubbles to go away. I keep turning it at different angles, I'm using way too much water, but there are still bubbles.

"I… I didn't think."

"No. You didn't think."

I turn to hand him the wine glass to dry, but it slips. Shatters on the floor. Glass shards everywhere.

As I pick up the bigger pieces, Bobby gets a broom and a dustpan. After we clean up, he puts his hands on my shoulders and steers me to the couch.

We just sit there a long minute or two.

"So," he says eventually, "I'd be a lot more furious with you right now if I hadn't done the same kind of selfish shit myself a few times. Thinking the world revolved around me and what I wanted; stupidly putting other people at risk, people I cared about. I guess the trick is to learn from it, right?"

I nod. I can't quite make my mouth say words yet. I'm so horrified, thinking what could have happened to Bobby if I'd gone through with it.

Finally I eke out an "I'm sorry." But it sounds weak and wispy; my breath is so shallow.

I just keep sitting there, frozen. Bobby looks equally stiff. He stares straight ahead. Just breathing. I keep wanting to say more, but the words aren't coming.

Finally he stands up.

"We're good," he says. And, incredibly, there's a lightness to his voice. He sounds like Bobby again.

"Now don't forget: we've got Carnival tomorrow. You need your beauty sleep."

A few tears are slipping down my face.

"See you then?" he asks.

"Wouldn't miss it," I say, my voice a bit croaky.

He puts a hand on my shoulder before he leaves with a gentleness I totally do not deserve.

* * *

Festive energy surges all along Commercial Street, even if the official parade doesn't start for an hour. It's a king tide spilling over seawalls and sandbags, drowning us in high spirits. Even my tranquilizers can't dampen a giddy sense of excitement. A perfect way to end my stay in Provincetown.

So many of the people who crowd the streets are wearing costumes, it feels like the parade is already here. Do we even need another one?

Yes, I think we do. I've been promised elaborate floats, funky home-spun drill teams, enormous speakers blasting dance tunes that force you to shimmy whether you want to or not. Tons of scantily clad men and women, and plastic Mardi Gras beads flying everywhere, which Bobby swears I will find myself fighting to the death for, even if I have no possible use for them.

Four Crayola Crayons stop abruptly right in front of us, and I almost run into Purple. And for the umpteenth time we decide to take a group photo. My mother asked Bobby to send her plenty of pictures; she had to head back to Florida this morning. Her best friend's husband just had a heart attack.

So we all crowd together with the crayons and smile, and I'm trying to look happy but not too crazy-happy, offering my mother an image of a normal, stable daughter, one that she can finally stop worrying about. At least for now.

It's strange: I actually find myself a little sorry that she's not here with us.

Gotta be the meds.

This year's Carnival theme has to do with toys, and our last-minute outfits were scavenged from Bobby's basement. He collects cast-off costumes from friends and clients, those who'd never think of wearing the same thing twice to a parade or theme party. Two whole racks of them down in his basement, like he's the wardrobe mistress backstage at the Rockettes.

"You're Barbies!" calls out Raggedy Andy, who is also the cashier at the liquor store where I buy my wine.

We are! Bobby had plenty of drag, pink accessories, and '80s outfits. So Chloe is Superstar Barbie, Wylie is Malibu Barbie, and I am, obviously, Weird Barbie. My Rod Stewart wig just needed a touch of pink and a couple of inches off it.

"And look at the Beanie Babies," Raggedy Ann says to the rest of our group. Bobby had a lion, tiger, and giraffe left over from the jungle-themed Carnival years ago. All the outfits needed was a big red heart tag with "TY" inscribed on them to turn Bobby, Allison, and Dyke March into adorable collectibles.

Olivia. Wylie's girlfriend has a name, and it's Olivia. Not Dyke March.

Allison has been glued to Chloe's side all day, so that answers that question. While I still think Allison could do better, I'm glad I wasn't responsible for breaking them up.

Watching two couples still mooning over each other, I feel nostalgic for the early days with Brian. He'd sometimes take my hand for no particular reason, and his grasp felt so comforting. His hands were so much bigger than mine, warmer and stronger too.

Could I ever see myself trying to get back with him again?

No, I don't think so. The Shannon he wants is not the Shannon I am. We're both better off moving on.

And where will my life move next?

Will Wylie be part of it?

Funny, I felt so compelled to come to Provincetown, and I assumed it was to get revenge. But I guess the universe sent me here for an entirely different reason?

I watch Wylie doing simple things, walking and waving to other Barbies, slipping an arm around Olivia's waist, all with new eyes.

She's Maureen's daughter! I just hope this isn't the last time I ever see her.

But I don't have to think about any of that yet. Today I'm just going to enjoy the festivities. Cheer on the parade floats. And then, in a few days, put Niccolo—my ordinary, nonspeaking cat—into his carrier, and take him home. Where he'll still love and comfort me, even if I can't understand what he says.

I'll get settled again. Maybe Emily would want to stay on as a roommate? I like her energy. I'll get back to my jackets and jeans. Find a new part-time job and a better therapist. Water the plants. Fill up the bird feeders. Pull the weeds, trim back the perennials, put in new plantings. And wait to see what might blossom.

* * *

We're not the only table of people in the restaurant still wearing costumes, and it's starting to seem normal to see Allison in giraffe horns and perky ears, and Wylie in a swimsuit, beach towel wrapped around her waist.

"More coffee?" asks our ponytailed waiter, his voice mellow and undemanding. As though he doesn't care that it's one of the busiest nights of the year and there's a long line of people waiting for our table. Might we still want to linger?

"No I'm good," I say.

And I realize it's true, I *am* good. What a day! The parade was as raucous and clever as I'd hoped. I've been trying to slow down, and consciously savor Provincetown's unique vibe. The way you do with a delicious dish in a foreign country, knowing you'll soon be home again, where you'll never find exactly the right ingredients to replicate it.

Before she flew off, my mother got us an early dinner reservation at this swanky restaurant, her treat. An apology for leaving so abruptly— not that helping out a friend in need should be anything to apologize for. While I was in the shower this morning, she slipped in with a kind note of apology and encouragement, in an envelope that also held ten crisp hundred-dollar bills. "To help you and your friends celebrate Carnival."

When we get outside, Commercial Street is still full of revelers, and the six of us slowly saunter our way back home.

Bobby joins me, walks beside me quietly for a bit. I realize I've been a little afraid of him today, not exactly avoiding him, but taking a step back. Wondering if he can forgive me.

"I can't tell you how sorry I am. I still can't believe I was such an idiot about the fentanyl," I tell him.

"Some serious advice?"

I nod.

"Where's the flair in fentanyl, Shannon? Barely a headline! Go big or go home, they always say. So next time, why not sneak onto his fishing charter, chop him up with a hatchet, then feed him to the sharks? Or maybe use a bow and arrow? A vat of boiling oil? No, I got it. Lure him to the top of the Pilgrim Monument and push him right off!"

I laugh. "I promise, if there's ever a next time, you'll have nothing to do with it."

"Well, hold on. If you go the Monument route… you could give me a little advance warning. I do an amazing karaoke version of 'It's Raining Men'."

It takes me a second.

"Oh my God, Bobby. I'm *so* gonna miss you."

"Well, you'll be back. Right?"

"Of course!"

And I realize: yes, I will. And not for Pritchard. Provincetown is a place that gets to you. And there are people here I'll really miss.

As we get further along, Bobby drifts over to talk to Wylie—he's told me how curious he is to find out all about my new niece. And I see that Allison has finally detached herself from Chloe. Who is now talking with Olivia, who apparently plays clarinet. From what I can hear, the two of them are having a spirited discussion about chamber music, God help them.

"Alley Cat!" I say as I fall into step with her.

"Shannon!"

She smiles, but it's a careful, tentative smile.

"That sounds wrong though, doesn't it?" I ask her.

"What sounds wrong?"

"Alley Cat and Shannon. I should have a nickname too. You never gave me a nickname."

"Hmm… Baldy?"

I laugh. "Okay, maybe not."

We walk for a bit.

"You doing okay?" she asks.

"For now, yeah. That's what I'm going to focus on."

"Good plan."

There's so much I should say to her—to thank her, to apologize, to explain. But somehow it feels better just to keep walking along together. I pretend she's Niccolo, and I send all of that to her, silently, straight to her mind.

Our time together is coming to an end. Soon I'll be back where I belong, deep in the woods, and she'll be out here at the very tip of Cape Cod, the end of the world.

"We're going to stay in touch now, right?" I hear a slight pleading sound to my voice, which surprises me.

"Of course!" she says.

I hope we both actually mean it?

When we reach the turn for Allison's house, we all stop for a moment—it's time for the group to split off in two different directions. But since Olivia is heading back to Boston tonight, she and Chloe are trading contact information.

"You're leaving soon, right?" Wylie asks me. "Want to walk us home?"

I nod. I've been wondering how Wylie would want to leave things, but I've been hesitant to bring anything up.

"You two go on ahead," Olivia says, still chatting with Chloe. "I'll catch up later."

I don't know whether it's to give us a chance to talk, or to schedule some horrific future violin and clarinet jam session, but either way I appreciate some alone time with Wylie.

She takes my arm for a moment as we walk. The soft pressure feels absurdly precious.

"So how are you doing?" she asks.

It's what everyone wants to know.

"Hanging in there."

"Any word from Niccolo yet?"

"No. Nothing."

Only Wylie would understand the desolation in my voice.

"You'll get him back. Maybe not as strong as before. But he'll be back."

"I don't see how. Not if I stay on my meds."

"Trust me," she says. "Hypnosis. Maybe a little microdosing once you're stable? I'll show you."

"But would it really be Niccolo? Or just my imagination?"

She doesn't answer for a few moments. Then says, "It was really him before though, right?"

I nod. Because it was. I know most people would think I'm crazy for believing it, but I do.

"Who knows where he comes from," she says. "Are you real? Am I? Is everything as it appears? There's so much we don't know. Reality… we're always so confident we know what it is. But it's a much trickier concept than we give it credit for."

Wylie's right. Everyone has their own "reality," and so many of those realities are contradictory. Is there an ultimate reality? Who decides which one it is?

I can only know my own reality. And in it, there is a Niccolo who speaks to me. I just need to figure out how to find him again.

As we approach Wylie's building, at first I think the colored lights have something to do with Carnival.

But no. Police cars. An ambulance. A fire truck. Yellow tape. A small crowd of curious neighbors.

Wylie recognizes a chunky bearded man, one of the neighbors. She asks him what's going on.

"It's that tall guy, the writer. Rents that unit up there?"

"I know who you mean," says Wylie.

"Unbelievable," he says. "I just saw him this morning, taking out the recycling. So I overheard one of the cops. A UPS guy shows up with a package, needs a signature, looks in the window and… well. Holy mother of God. He called 911, but like, the guy's head was practically blown off. Not much they can do, right?"

He looks over at the ambulance.

Then he looks at us again. "Oh shit, sorry. I hope he wasn't a friend?"

I shake my head.

"No, not at all," says Wylie, her voice level.

I take her hand, which is trembling, and we walk to the other side of the street, away from the crowd.

"Are you okay?" I ask. "Do you want me to stay with you a while?"

"No, I'm good."

I can tell from her face: that's not entirely true.

She squeezes my hand before she releases it.

"But Shannon—call me sometime, okay?"

I nod. I sure will.

Then I give her a sudden big hug, which I can tell startles her, but she manages to return it before I go running back home to the cottage.

I'm out of breath when I get back. Running, walking, running again, the whole way home. Charged up with exhilaration, unreality.

So Grant Pritchard is no longer among the living. Very, very, dead from the sound of it.

The first thing I do when I walk through the door is pick up Niccolo. Look at his sweet face.

"He's gone, baby. The bad man is gone. Maybe you were right—maybe I'll be free now?"

He looks right into my eyes. Then meows. A reassuring "yes."

Niccolo watches me closely as I prepare his dinner and set down his bowl. Then eats noisily, chomping and lapping in a way that definitely strikes me as celebratory.

I should go over soon to tell Allison and Bobby what happened. But first I take off my costume, wipe off the Barbie make-up, and get in the shower. Scrubbed clean and refreshed, that's how I want to feel.

But as I lather up, I can't help but think how strange the timing is. A scary thought keeps trying to intrude and I finally confront it:

Could I have done it? Killed Pritchard myself, in some sort of fugue state? I wanted it so badly, and then, poof! It just happens?

But no, I've been surrounded by friends the entire day. I can summon up memories, vibrant moments from first thing this morning until right this minute. None of those troublesome gaps I have when it comes to my younger days.

It wasn't me.

I towel off and put on a pair of yoga pants and my favorite comfy shirt, in a calming shade of faded aqua. It's loose-fitting, in a soft cotton. I want gentle clothes tonight, nothing that binds or chafes.

I go on my phone, check the Provincetown Community Facebook page. Sure enough, word has already gotten out.

There's a general consensus that Pritchard has pissed off a lot of people. Someone heard that he'd failed to pay a prostitute down from Falmouth, and wondered whether her "employer" had shown up to collect the debt. Another guy floats a theory about gambling losses. A cocktail waitress thinks he probably got shitfaced the way he always does and accidentally blew his own head off.

I can't put it off any longer.

I go into the utility closet, take a deep breath, then open my toolbox.

The fentanyl pills, the Glock, and the suicide note are all missing. Jesus Christ.

Could I have left the door unlocked? Probably not, though I've gotten out of the habit of paying much attention. But even then: the only people who knew what I had in that toolbox were all at Carnival with me.

Except for one.

I remember a story my mother told me when I was eleven or twelve. She'd been sent to some incredibly dangerous country, I don't remember which, back in the late seventies. And a man she'd met, a diplomat I think, was surprised they'd sent a female reporter. He was worried about her safety. So he got her a gun and taught her to shoot it. Then he was more than a little miffed when it turned out she was a much better shot than he was! My mother liked to tell me stories like that, where the moral was: women can be just as good as men at anything they put their minds to.

But that was fifty years ago. Would she still have the skill, the confidence, to take my Glock and set off to shoot Pritchard with it?

She did know the door code, because I said it out loud. I was bragging to everyone about my clever plan. And she knew the gun was unregistered. Untraceable. During a noisy parade with sound systems blasting and bands playing—that would be a good time to shoot someone, but still. So risky!

And why? My mother is rich, respected, powerful. She has so much to lose.

It could be she just wanted to confront him, the way I always thought I would. Took the gun as back-up, in case he got violent. And maybe he did.

Or was it my own stubbornness that drove her to do it? Because I never reassured her. Never swore I wouldn't try it again. It meant too much to me, to leave that possibility open. Would she risk her own freedom, possibly her own life, to spare my future?

If it *was* her: I sure hope no one saw her going in or out. Although older women, we're often invisible. We can come and go and no one sees us.

Was she smart enough to wipe off her fingerprints and leave the gun in his hands, with the suicide note nearby? Did she shoot him from a plausible angle?

She's clever though, and cooler under pressure than I am. It occurs to me that she gave me a perfect alibi for the entire day, complete with pictures along the parade route and dinner reservations, just in case my previous stalking of Pritchard ever came to light.

I go get the note my mother left this morning and read it again. I skip the parts about the dinner reservations, the apology for leaving abruptly, the thank-you's she wants me to pass on to Allison and everyone else. I go straight to the third paragraph.

So many wasted years, my fierce, precious daughter. I'm sorry I never understood how to talk to you, how to tell you how I felt. I'm so proud of you. Keep being brave and original and creative. And keep challenging yourself! I think you'll find your truth, sooner rather than later, and your life will open up in ways you never imagined.

I only wish I had been there for you earlier, to look out for you better, to know what you needed. I failed you back then. I'll try my best to make it up to you now, though.

With much love, your mother.

Maybe I'm getting ahead of myself. Perhaps she just took the gun and the note and the pills away from me, in case I changed my mind about trying it myself. Maybe she didn't use them. And it's just a coincidence that Pritchard died by a gunshot the very same day.

In any event, I won't tell a soul about the missing gun. If somehow I'm ever asked, I threw it in the trash dumpster off Snail Road. Where anybody walking by could have picked it up.

I remember once, many years ago, my mother visited me in prison. It was an awkward visit; the conversation kept running aground. I don't think I ever told her how much I appreciated that she'd come. That she was there for me.

I'm just really hoping I never have to return the favor.

CHAPTER TWENTY-ONE

ALLISON

Chloe wanders into the kitchen, looking restless. She must have finished up the last of her work emails. I'm the same way: I hate those stray wedges of time between things—too small to be useful, too big to just stare out into space.

"Only about five more minutes," I tell her, though it's probably ten. I don't want her wading back into work, getting productive again.

"Sure smells good," she says.

She opens the refrigerator, fishes out a Coke Zero. Leans against the counter.

I take out the lasagna to let it cool. Then I split the French rolls, dollop probably way too much butter inside—though is there really such a thing? —and put them in a pan to heat up in the oven.

"Wanna open the wine for me? Corkscrew's in the middle drawer."

"Sure," she says.

Lasagna is still the only dish I know how to make. And yeah, the salad comes in a kit, which even included a little package of dressing— but at least it's green, so in my mind it counts as grown-up food. The French rolls are the good kind from the bakery section, not the bread aisle. I even bought a 12-pack of mini-cupcakes for dessert, in lurid neon colors, because I heard them calling to me, in chirpy little voices: "Hey we're so *fun*!" Plus I picked up a bottle of Chloe's favorite pinot noir.

She was surprised, of course. And appreciative. But maybe a little suspicious. It's true: I do have an agenda for tonight.

The deadline for Chloe to decide what she wants to do about the job offer is coming up soon. But I've been too scared to ask her what she's been thinking: I've worried I'll sound too clingy. Or that I'll overcompensate and act too nonchalant. So instead, I just keep hoping she sees how well everything is going between us. I want it to feel as blindingly obvious to her that we belong together as it is to me.

But I woke up feeling braver this morning. A lot braver. Maybe it was the dream I had right before I woke up? Though it had nothing to do with Chloe.

I was back on top of the huge sand dune I'd hiked up with Shannon. But I was alone this time. It was steeper than the real dune was, nightmare steep, like a hundred stories high. I started slowly walking down. And then, like I did before, going for it: bounding and bouncing, faster and faster, until pretty soon my feet weren't even hitting the sand because I was flying. And I was like, "oh yeah, right! How come I always forget I know how to fly?"

It was just a dream, but it put me in a strange mood. Lots of ruminating today, getting a bit philosophical, thinking positive, giving myself pep-talks. So. No more waiting and hoping. I want to know what the future holds, and I'd really like to find out tonight.

Can we be two Marcies together?

Chloe pours us each a glass of wine, brings me mine.

I'm so anxious to find out. But I'm saving the big State of the Relationship Address for dinnertime, when we're sitting down, not distracted.

"So Nora called today," I tell her.

It's strange that Nora and I keep in touch now. Fortunately, she and Shannon are talking a bit. But since Shannon and I have been doing Zoom calls a couple times a week, I get a much better picture of how things are going. It's a delicate balance—respecting Shannon's privacy about the details, but keeping Nora posted in case another crisis might be looming.

Nora's been so sweet to me; she gave me way too much credit for getting Shannon off the roof and into treatment. I told her more than once: it was Shannon's decision; I didn't really do anything at all! But she said: well, maybe it wasn't so much what I *did*, but who I am.

I'm not sure I get it. But I'm glad she thinks I was helpful.

"I guess she and Wylie are still doing the same back-and-forth about telling Shannon everything. Nora's hoping Shannon can figure it out on her own, with her therapist. Start recovering her own memories; letting go of her delusions. While Wylie's not sure she's ever going to get there. She wants her to know the truth, the sooner the better. But at least they agree that if she can't get there by herself, they'll tell her together."

"And how's Shannon doing? Is she keeping herself out of trouble?"

"Yeah, so far! She seems to be staying on her new meds—she's relaxed, not so speedy. And she likes the new therapist. But she's still hoping to find Maureen, somewhere out there in the real world. She doesn't get it, that *she's* Maureen. I mean, I can understand why Wylie feels impatient. What if it takes her years and years? Maybe there's some way they can slip her some hints; drop some breadcrumbs for her to follow."

Though I can't quite think how.

"Well if they do have to spring it on her," says Chloe, "I just hope Shannon can handle it, and doesn't totally decompensate."

I love when she uses her hospital words, even if I'm not always sure exactly what they mean.

I take a sip of wine; dump the plastic bag full of greens into the old wooden salad bowl that's been here forever, probably brought over on the Mayflower. I squish the dressing out of its little plastic sleeve and toss everything together. Easy peasy.

"Do I smell something burning?" asks Chloe.

"Oh shit! The French rolls!"

"Just means more room for cupcakes," she says.

* * *

"So. A regional vice president. That sounds like a promotion."

We're done with the lasagna and salad, down to cupcakes and decaf.

She takes a deep breath. "I guess. But titles aren't that important."

"If you took it, do you know who you'd be reporting to?"

"Yeah, Chuck Grossman. I worked with him before; we get along pretty well. That's why he thought of me when he heard Linda was retiring."

"Is California somewhere you'd ever thought you might want to live?"

Chloe fidgets, is suddenly busy brushing cupcake crumbs off the table and into her napkin.

"Only in the way everyone does sometimes, you know. In the middle of winter when you've just spent an hour shoveling out your walkway and the weather guy says there's going to be three more inches coming in overnight."

I hear my own nerves, too, in my voice, as I continue making myself ask her questions, questions I probably should have brought up as soon as she mentioned the job offer.

And I keep hearing her say—not in so many words, and very reluctantly—that if it were just about the job, and not about us, she wouldn't hesitate a second in taking it.

But it *is* also about us.

"Have you done any research on neighborhoods in San Diego?" I ask. "Are there some nice ones?"

"Allison. I don't get it. What's going on?"

She sounds a bit exasperated.

"It's just, it's a big decision. I want to know more about it all, the pros and cons."

"But the way you're asking, it almost seems like you *want* me to take the job. But I told you before, I'd rather be with the perfect person than have the perfect job."

And so here it is.

"And so what do you think? Is that me?"

She reaches over, takes my hand.

"Of course! You're the perfect person. And I've already decided that next time I talk to Paul, I'm going to turn down the job. But I should have told you sooner, not left you hanging."

I sigh with relief. I guess she believes in us after all.

"Well, you're the perfect person for me too. I just love you so much."

I squeeze her hand.

But I'm only halfway there.

"And because I love you, I think you should go ahead and take that job in San Diego. It's your dream job, and I'm the only thing that's holding you back."

She looks at me, shocked. Uncomprehending.

And if I had more flair for drama, I'd let it float out there just a while longer. But I can't stand it myself for longer than a couple seconds.

"And I should go with you. If that's okay. San Diego seems like it could be a pretty cool place for us to live."

Chloe is still just looking at me, still not speaking.

For way too long, actually. Did I miscalculate? Words please, Chloe!

"You would do that?" she asks finally, her face so sweetly amazed I just want to cover it with kisses. "God, can you imagine? A million little happy pictures come into my mind, like an Instagram feed full of you and me and sunsets on the beach and palm trees and street tacos. But you can't just up and do that, can you? Leave New England? Provincetown? This house? All those memories?"

"I'll still have the memories," I say.

But Chloe's right; it will be hard to say goodbye to it all. Even the dining room table we're sitting at—so heavy and old-fashioned, and now that I'm really *seeing* it, pretty ugly. But it's where we ate so many family dinners, played Scrabble and Monopoly and Go Fish.

"I guess ever since I lost my mom, all I've done is look backwards. Missing the years when she was still here. I mean, sure, it will be a transition. Getting used to a new city, meeting new people. Probably finding a new job—I don't know if I'll be allowed to keep working *that* remotely. But I can do all that, if I really want to. And I really want to."

Chloe cocks her head, looks at me like, 'who *is* this person?'

"I have some savings," I say, "and this house is worth a fair amount now I think, especially if I get it fixed up a bit. I'll have plenty to tide me over."

"You'd really sell it?"

My comfy dumpy house. Spilling over with memories of my family, the ups and downs, the stormy days and the sunny ones, all that love and laughter.

But having the house hasn't made me happy. Chloe, right here in front of me, wearing a little smear of tomato sauce above her upper lip—she's the one who makes me happy.

"Yep. I'd really sell it."

I lean in and kiss the tomato sauce away.

I look around again, and my eyes fall on the picture of my mom and my dad on the sideboard, one I took of them myself at a Red Sox game long ago. They're both on their feet cheering, arms outstretched, fists clenched, faces lit with joy after a big home run.

I'm definitely taking it with me.

CHAPTER TWENTY-TWO

ALMOST A YEAR LATER

SHANNON

I'm just back from a long walk in the woods. The leaves haven't started turning yet, but I can tell they're seriously thinking about it. The gentle early September morning was too inviting; I hiked much farther than I'd meant to. I feel well-spent and ready for a rest.

It feels so good to be back in my magical forest. There's nowhere else that feels quite the same. Maybe something to do with the smell—a very particular combination of shrubs and trees and earth. Or the play of light in the branches overhead, or the nooks and burrows and fallen tree trunks that could hide something wild and thrilling.

For me, this is home, where I belong. It was so sweet of Allison to offer me the remodeling job in Provincetown, but it just didn't feel right. Hard to believe she sold the place so quickly, and is busy making a new life in California. With boring Chloe, who is apparently her soulmate. Go figure. But I talk to her almost every week, and she seems to be happy. Good for her.

I enter the kitchen to the piercing shriek of the tea kettle, but Emily is quick to grab it off the stove. When she pours it into her cup, it's all flowers and tropical fruit at first. But sure enough there's a stink creeping in too, like tar, or burnt cheese. Emily is a big believer in detoxification. There must be twenty different cartons and canisters in the cupboard.

"What time's the call with your shrink?" she asks. "I've been wanting to wash the car, maybe I'll time it so I can be out of your hair."

"In half an hour. But I can just close the door, you don't have to leave."

"No worries!" she says, "I need the fresh air. Plus you know me, I'd be too tempted to listen in. She must love you as a client. Just the right amount of weird to be interesting, but like, not nearly weird enough to be annoying."

"Um. Thanks?"

I like having her here. Emily's just the right balance between companionable and independent. She does more than her fair share of the chores, too.

Do I miss Brian? Sure, sometimes. Funny though: not nearly as often as I would have thought.

But I do miss sex. And there's something about masculine energy—rough and scruffy, blunt and uncomplicated. I may not want to live alongside it 24/7, but I haven't given up on it entirely.

There's a new bartender at the Broken Bucket, Matthew. Kind. Low key. Sad eyes. There's a story there, I'm guessing. He used to be a DJ for a jazz station, so he has an incredibly sexy voice. I'm still in no place for anything serious at the moment, but we've been semi-flirting. When I get my head screwed on straight again...who knows?

"So, I'm off," says Emily. "Enjoy your chat with Dr. Melfi."

"Will do!"

Her name is actually Dr. Tomaso. But I call her Dr. Melfi because she looks and sounds a bit like Tony Soprano's therapist. And I like to think I'm still at least a little bit gangster.

I first started seeing her because of all the nightmares.

"They'll get worse," she told me, "before they get better."

"Seriously?" I said.

But still, I keep showing up. Spilling my guts.

As I leave the kitchen I can hear the *squee-bonk, squee-bonk* of Niccolo butting his head tentatively against his cat door, trying to work up the nerve to push all the way through and come inside. He's had it for months now, but it still spooks him.

He loves to watch the squirrels and birds from the deck railing, and sometimes he'll wander maybe fifteen feet into the yard. Turns out he's not so much the intrepid explorer as the trepidatious mama's boy. So I'm feeling a little more comfortable about giving this a go. Could he encounter a wild animal? Catch feline leukemia? Decide to make a run for it?

There's always that chance, and it scares me. But he wanted his freedom so badly. And with freedom, comes risk.

* * *

I'm always ready at my computer right on time. My mother's forking over a fortune for my appointments, so I'm not messing around.

Dr. Tomaso's blouse is forest green today; she has ten that she rotates. I've counted.

"So my mom called a few days ago," I say, after some preliminaries. "She and my niece, Wylie, they want to come for a visit. Mid-November. She wanted to give me fair warning."

"Really," Tomaso says, and falls into her usual encouraging silence.

I prefer it to my last therapist's saccharine: "*And how does that make you feel?*" I like the way Tomaso can hold her silences comfortably, endlessly, for however long it takes, the whole time managing to look thoughtful and curious. Years of practice, I guess.

"So, part of me is really excited. But I'm also pretty nervous."

She knows how strange I've been finding it, communicating again with my mother after so many years of silence.

"I can imagine you'd feel some mixed emotions."

My mother was so unexpectedly *there* for me when I spiraled into chaos, landed myself in the hospital. Compassion, empathy, warmth—who knew all that was hiding under her imperturbable surface? Was she human all this time, or did she just age into it?

But it was what she did afterwards that I still can't quite believe. The medical examiner may have found Pritchard's death "consistent with suicide," but I'm pretty damn sure it wasn't. My mother hasn't confirmed it outright, but she hasn't denied it either. I haven't asked directly. We've had a few coded conversations, like mafia dons, skipping over loaded words, stepping sideways, leaving so much unsaid. But I can read between the lines.

It all makes me want to understand her better. Find out who the hell Nora Callaghan actually is. Is it too late?

And then there's Wylie. So original, so exceptional.

We trade emails, and have video chats more often than I would have thought, especially for someone young, with her own life. But I can tell she's still being cautious. Not letting me in too far yet. And why should she? But I'm remembering back to that day on the beach, when she seemed so intense, ready to go deeper, to tell me all her secrets. I just wish I hadn't been too fucked-up to take advantage of it.

"So" says Tomaso. "You feel excited, but nervous. How about let's start with 'nervous?'"

Because of course. She's a therapist.

I can feel it even now though, thrumming just under the surface.

"It's just that my mom seemed a little cagey. Didn't really explain why they both wanted to drive all the way out here, together. And the timing's weird. Too late for the leaves, but not quite the holidays. I think there's something they want to tell me."

"Ah," says Tomaso.

"And I bet it's got something to do with Maureen. They want to break it to me carefully, so I don't end up in the loony bin again. Maybe Wylie got another match with her DNA? I'm guessing whatever they found isn't good, or they'd just tell me over the phone."

"Something not good," Tomaso echoes.

"Like they found Maureen, and she doesn't want to talk to me. Or even worse. They found out she's already dead."

The word hangs in the air. Dead. My worst fear.

"What comes up for you when you imagine that? Losing Maureen, all over again?"

Tomaso's face is still the picture of patient attentiveness, but she slowly leans back into her chair, picks up her water glass and has a sip. A signal that I should sit with it for a while, not rush to answer.

Maureen. Such an inspiration in my childhood, yet ultimately so easily broken.

It's odd though: whenever Tomaso asks me to talk about her, I always struggle to remember any specifics. The car accident really did a number on my childhood memories. I can find adjectives to describe her, I can sketch her outlines, but I can't call up the details to shade them in. Emotions and impressions, sure—but visuals are so elusive.

"I guess Maureen was everything I always wanted to be," I say finally. "Smarter, prettier. So graceful. And she could talk to anyone, so charming and hilarious. Outgoing, but never 'too much,' you know?"

"Hmm."

No doubt Tomaso is bookmarking that "too much" for later. Noting the unsaid *like I was*.

"But something's been bothering me. A girl like Maureen, who had so much going for her—I can't get my mind around it. How did she just let a man like that destroy her?"

I've spent so much time mourning the loss of my "perfect" sister. Yet now I'm just starting to realize how much disappointment, even anger, I feel. Pritchard was a predator, sure. But Maureen was all too willing to be his prey.

"You told me she was what, fourteen years old when it started? What do you think? How do you imagine she might have 'let' him destroy her?"

I see where she's going with this. She wants me to absolve Maureen, let her off the hook. But I'm not sure I want to.

"I mean, I guess to Maureen, Grant Pritchard was like a prince in a fairy tale, nothing at all like the bonehead high school boys in her class. So I can see why she might have been attracted to him initially."

But how could she lose herself so completely under his spell?

"And then?"

I sit with it for a bit. Watching her stay with him when it was clearly destroying her… that's the part that haunts me. Why didn't I beg her to stop, or threaten to expose the man abusing her? I try to remember our conversations.

"I think… I think what really hooked her, what she couldn't stop talking about? It was how different he was when they were alone, just the two of them."

I've run through it in my mind so many times, it almost feels like I was there.

"Gentle. Vulnerable. Unsure of himself. He told her he was falling in love with her."

I'd forgotten that part. The way he'd smile so shyly, hold her so tenderly, kiss the top of her head. Confessing how scared he was. Telling her how powerless he was to resist his feelings for her.

"And Maureen, well, she totally fell for it."

"She believed him you mean," Tomaso says.

"But that was so naïve of her! He appealed to her vanity. Made her feel beautiful, special, powerful."

I can hear the contempt in my voice. And I know I'm being harsh. But how could she delude herself like that? How could she think he ever wanted anything other than sex, that he could actually feel love for her?

"But once he gets his hooks in, she's totally infatuated with him. She can't imagine life without him. She starts believing they're going to have a happily ever after. At first she doesn't notice that he's getting more distant, making it more and more obvious that all he ever wanted was her body. Sex in the back seat of his car, blow-jobs in the utility closet. She felt dirty, disgusting. But she thought she could hold on to him if she gave him what he wanted. That it would make him love her again."

I stop; it's hard to go on. After a long silence I hear Tomaso's voice, curiously disconnected from my computer screen, almost like she's speaking from the heavens.

"So. Maureen just wanted to be loved."

I sigh.

Was it really that simple?

Maybe it was.

"I guess so. To be loved. That's all she really wanted."

I feel it welling up now, the sadness. Wet and heavy, rising until the dam bursts, and then it washes through me, spilling over, flushing everything else away.

She just wanted to be loved.

My body contracts and releases as I cry, and I let myself just keep emptying. I finally feel it slowing down and then I rest. Pull soft sheets of Kleenex from the box, mop up.

Can I forgive Maureen for offering herself up like that, with so little resistance?

She was so young. He sensed the void in her and exploited it.

"Maureen may have even *wanted* to drive off that road," I say.

I hadn't really put that together before now.

"She was trying to end her life?"

"Maybe. Yeah. I think so."

Tomaso leans back in her chair again. But I'm not wanting to play it all out in my head just now.

"So anyway," I say, "back to your original question."

She looks expectant, although I'm guessing by now she may have forgotten what her original question even was.

"So how would I feel, if it turns out Maureen's already dead?"

She nods.

"I guess it's this. When I found out my sister didn't really die, it gave me this amazing sense of hope. More hope than I've felt since I was a little girl. It would mean so much to me to see her again. Happy or sad, successful or a loser, whatever. To see that you can be damaged, nearly destroyed—but still survive."

We sit for a moment, reflecting.

"Like you, you mean," Tomaso says.

"Like me?"

I'm not sure what she's getting at. But I look at my watch and I see our time is up.

* * *

I'm down on my knees in the dirt, plunging into it with my trowel, turning the soil, uprooting dead and dying plants. Plants decompose gracefully, not like animals. Instead of a putrid stench, the smell they leave behind is earthy, comforting. Sometimes it helps settle me. I've taken to the garden to cope with the latest blow, to try to find some comfort in the cycles of nature.

I felt so uneasy after the last few therapy sessions. Recounting more memories of Maureen and Pritchard together, it struck me how intimate they felt. Personal. I could almost smell him. Feel his hand stroking my hair. Feel the weight of him on me.

I kept trying to tell myself that Maureen always told me everything. Those were just her memories, meticulously described. Not my own.

Then yesterday a package arrived from my mother. It might as well have contained a grenade. It was my high school yearbook, from the year Maureen died. I remember I'd thrown it away as soon as I looked at it, but then my mother took it back out of the trash. We'd fought. I said I didn't want those memories anymore.

I thought I'd won. But it seems she kept the yearbook anyway.

The note she enclosed was mostly about how much she was looking forward to her upcoming visit. All she said about the yearbook was that she'd recently found it in her basement. So then why didn't she just wait and bring it with her?

But I imagine she was doing the same thing I'm doing now myself: upending, uprooting, preparing the soil.

The first shock was when I discovered that there wasn't a single picture of Maureen in the whole yearbook. Did they edit her out, once she got pregnant and ran away? Was she no longer a student worth remembering?

But what shook me even more was the picture of Grant Pritchard and me, talking together at his desk. It was one of those "Dedicated teacher advising puzzled student" shots you often see in yearbooks.

As I looked at it, I started to remember the boy from the yearbook who took it. Dark-haired, bad acne, had a stammer. And then later, I remember laughing with Mr. Pritchard about it. About how ordinary and innocent the picture would seem, because it was posed, not candid, and we were so careful about our expressions. But if people only knew…

If people only knew that I was having sex with him, they would be so shocked.

I remember thinking that. And feeling so naughty, so grown up.

Did Maureen know I was sleeping with him too?

Is that why she ran away and left, why she never wanted to speak to me again? Because I'd taken what was hers?

Those memories of backseats and utility closets: they weren't Maureen's memories. They were mine. And more memories are coming up now, graphic, physical, the two of us naked and sweaty in a motel room, the coarse hair on his arms, the smell of his breath.

Nightmares, even worse than before, horrific.

There's a horrible sense of self-betrayal too. How do I trust my own memories now? I lied to myself for over thirty years, because I couldn't face the truth.

I look down. I see that in my frantic digging, I've cut a poor earthworm in half with my trowel.

And for probably the fourth time today, I start crying. For the worm, for Maureen, and for me.

* * *

It's finally Halloween, the day I've been waiting for. Niccolo sleeps next to me on the couch. The 'shrooms have started to work their magic; the boundaries of my body are getting blurrier. I'm opening up.

These last weeks have been so painful. But my suffering has been cathartic. I'm feeling ready to start loosening my grip. I want to stop clinging so hard to outrage, to grief, to guilt.

Maureen and I were so young. He took advantage. I can never forgive him. But I can forgive the two of us for believing him, for thinking he was sincere, not realizing he cared nothing for us.

The warm flickering light from the fire makes the living room feel gently alive. I can sense possibility stirring. I stroke Niccolo, feeling every single separate soft hair against my palm. It's almost time.

The alchemist enters the living room in her flowing cape. The outfit seems fitting, since Emily is the sorceress who supplies the enchanted ingredient: the humble mushroom that turns my tea into gold. She's heading off to a Halloween party soon, wearing a Victorian steampunk hat. Under her black velvet cape: a tunic banded by a broad leather belt, from which dangle mysterious vials and pouches. She wears formidable tall black boots with an abundance of buckles.

"You'll phone me if you need me?" she asks.

A mutual pledge: one of us always stays on-call when the other is tripping.

"I will. Thank you."

I sit quietly for a few moments after she leaves. Then I light the lavender candle, put in my earbuds, and stare at the flame. I start to play the recording Wylie sent me.

I'm not sorry I went back on meds. I've got a much better cocktail this time, not so suffocating. But it does mean that I need hypnosis, plus a hefty amount of psilocybin, in order to be able to talk to Niccolo.

Tomaso once warned me that people prone to dissociating should steer clear of self-hypnosis. Let alone psychedelics. But, I figure Tony Soprano didn't tell Dr. Melfi every last detail about his life either, right? It's only my fourth excursion since Provincetown. My talks with Niccolo are too important to treat casually, recreationally.

"Are you ready, Niccolo?"

I'm always ready, Shannon! I only wish we could do this more often.

Hearing his voice again, it thrills me.

"Me too, baby! But this way it's special, right?"

It certainly is, he agrees.

We stare for a moment at the flames dancing in the fireplace; they join us in celebrating our special time together.

"Are you still enjoying your cat door?" I ask him.

I love going outside, thank you for installing it! But… if you could consider removing the squeaky cover? It would be much easier to use if it were just a nice big hole.

"So that spiders and mice and rats and snakes could have the run of the house too?"

He considers.

Well that could be amusing, don't you think?

"For you, maybe. Emily and I might not find it quite as entertaining."

We fall silent again, and I hear the sound of spirits swooping and soaring outside, calling pleasantly to each other. They flirt with the trees, stirring them into movement, taking with them the leaves that are ready to let go. I hadn't realized before: that's what wind is. Souls that are no longer imprisoned in bodies, swirling through the air, creating movement, ferrying change.

There's a special reason, isn't there, Niccolo asks, *why you wanted to talk to me tonight?*

He looks at me so knowingly.

"Yes. I suppose so."

You've seemed upset lately. Even though that horrible man is gone. I was hoping that would be enough to make you happy.

"I was hoping that too! It sure helped, for a while. But I'm still having the nightmares. And my memories are so confusing. They don't add up. It's like there's something important I'm missing."

Are you sure you want to remember? asks Niccolo.

"I think so," I say.

We watch the fire for a bit, and it's becoming so three-dimensional I almost feel like soon I'll be sitting inside it, but I also think it's friendly so it wouldn't hurt me. The tea is hitting a little more strongly now.

My previous owners, they had a son. A horrible little boy.

Niccolo has never talked to me about this before. I slow my breath, preparing.

And I've allowed myself to remember that he was the reason I went to the shelter. But the details of what he did to me? I can't recall any of that anymore.

"So you made yourself forget?"

I allowed myself to forget. For me, it brought peace.

He does seem so peaceful. Content in the moment. Not so focused on the past like I am.

"But for me," I say, "not remembering—it's not bringing me peace. It's the opposite right now."

And you'd like me to help you?

I know Dr. Melfi would prefer that I'd work only through her. And her kind face on my computer screen has taken me a long way. But to go any further it's Niccolo I need.

"Yes. I think I'm ready."

Niccolo shifts his position, puts his paw on my thigh. It's very sweet.

So which nightmare do you fear the most? You could go inside it now, while I'm with you and you're safe. Dreams and memories, sometimes they wrestle around and play together, like kittens.

There are quite a few, but one is by far the most persistent and frightening.

"So I'm in the hospital. There are scary instruments on the tray. I'm looking down at the patient. Or am I looking up? Sometimes I'm the doctor. Sometimes the patient."

And where is Maureen?

"She's on the bed. When I'm the doctor. But sometimes I'm on the bed."

Looking up at the bright lights, tense faces with furrowed brows. And then I hear it again.

"The screaming—I can't stand the screaming!"

I put my hand over my ears. The 'shrooms are making the terrible sounds seem so present.

What is happening? asks Niccolo. *Why are you there?*

"The baby is coming!"

As I hear myself saying the words, I realize this is new. But it feels true. Similar to the usual dream where an arm or a leg is being cut off, but a little baby is being extracted instead.

But I wasn't there when Wylie was born, was I? Back then I thought Maureen had died, how could I have been by her side?

Whose screams are you hearing?

"What do you mean, whose screams? They must have been Maureen's screams."

Whose screams, Shannon? Listen carefully.

"But who else would be screaming?"

It's so long ago. I'm looking up at the yellow ceiling; someone is yelling, "Push, Push!" A machine is beeping, it won't stop. A nurse is gripping my hand. There isn't enough air in my lungs to expel all the horrible pain that consumes me.

"*I* was screaming?"

Did it surprise you, how loud you were screaming?

"I thought it was someone else at first, I couldn't believe those sounds were coming out of me. Because it hurt so bad. It hurt really, really bad."

I put my hand on my lower belly. But I'm okay. Nothing hurts when I prod myself. I'm only remembering the feeling from before. Like someone swinging an axe and splitting me wide open.

It's not happening now. I'm here, safe with Niccolo.

Though I'm shaking.

I think you already know where Maureen is, Shannon.

"No, I don't. They took her away!"

They let me hold her tiny body first, then they stole her from me forever.

But wait.

Maureen was my sister. She was too big to hold like that. There were two Maureens! That was the baby Maureen. But where did big Maureen go? I just want to be with her again. To know she's okay.

You can find her now, if you're ready to see her again.

"I'm ready! But I don't know where to look, that's the problem."

She's here.

"Here? In this house?"

You'll see. Just go look.

I feel my excitement rising, although it can't be true, can it? I want to leap from the couch and race through the house, but I move deliberately. The room is expanding and contracting, and I am very, very high.

I look around the living room. I crouch to see if she's under the sofa. But no Maureen.

She's not in the kitchen either.

I go upstairs into the bedroom. Check the closet, look under the bed. I still don't see her.

But then I look in the bathroom.

Above the sink. In the mirror.

There she is!

Worn, weathered. Like she's fought so many battles. Traveled thousands of miles.

She doesn't look beaten down though. More like determined. Stubborn as stone.

A smile of gentle surprise begins to soften her face, like the sun slowly easing over the horizon after a long winter night.

So much awaits.

ACKNOWLEDGMENTS

I'd like to thank the many generous people who helped me with this novel, whether by critiquing or cheerleading. And to the extent I sometimes didn't manage to follow their wise advice, they are not to blame! Some people who were especially helpful were: Kate Pechotta, Laura Graham, Tiela Chalmers, Suzanna Walters, Mindy Thompson, Louise Morris, Anne Horowitz, Sheri Southern, Karin Kroh, Lisa Wenger, Victoria Young, Debbie Zeyher, Catherine A. Moreno Gámez, Patricia Moreno Gámez, Sherri Thornhill, Michele Hawthorne, and Elena Azzoni. And of course most of all, Robin Wright.